SOLE SILENCE

I.M.Nameless

Sole Silence I.M.Nameless

Cover design: Usama Zaheen

Novel font: Times new roman 12pt
Printed and Bound in Canada
ISBN: 9798596378702

Dedicated to:

All my loved ones,
Both family and friends

One

I had the nightmare again.

I was a child. My family: me, my parents and Siara, came back from a one-month vacation in Florida. The day after we came back, we were informed that some major singer was coming to throw a huge concert. My parents were able to grab three tickets.

But then there was the problem of me.

The concert was in two hours, what would they do with their annoying four-year-old son? Well, they couldn't find a last-minute babysitter, so they figured leaving me home alone wouldn't be a problem. They set me on the sofa with snacks and flipped on some lame cartoon. It was late at night, and I didn't like the idea of being alone. When I protested, they told me they would be back in ten minutes.

I waited ten minutes.

They didn't come back.

I was alone.

I was scared.

I was four.

I panicked. I didn't know what to do, and in my innocence, I thought they had gotten lost. I pulled on my shoes and strode out into the summer night.

By pure luck I turned to the town square where the concert was being held. I was happy to hear all the sounds of people. Finally, I wasn't alone.
I unintentionally snuck into the crowd, too short to be seen by the ticket seller.
I remember seeing the biggest crowd of people I had seen in my short life.
I remember going into the crowd.
I remember seeing crazed faces screaming with laughter and joy.

I remember seeing the desperate look in everyone's eyes.
I remember looking at the stage and seeing a group of people playing instruments, one person singing.
I remember being confused and then turning around to see my mom, my dad, and my sister as part of these apparently insane people.

I remember pulling on my mom's sleeve trying to get her attention.
I remember the way she pushed me off unknowingly, not even bothering to look down.
I remember running out of the crowd and finding my way home.
I remember realizing that my family had lied to me. Feeling like an outsider.
And even now when I think about it, I can't help but ask myself why they were reaching out their hands, *so desperately,* to someone who clearly was not God.

I hated this nightmare because it had really happened. I'm seventeen now but I still remember that feeling of loneliness, of fear, pulling at my heart that had only been pumping for four years.

A memory that would never leave my mind. But in a way I was grateful for the reminder.

That incident had saved me from becoming one of them myself.

From where I was laying, I could see that the sun had already begun to set. I watched in fascination as I realized that it was only 5:00pm. It was astounding how the sun set so early in January, it wasn't just amazing; in a way it was beautiful.

Simply breathtaking.

I pulled myself out of bed and walked over to my drawer; I opened it and pulled out my camera. Apart from my laptop this camera was about the only worldly possession I loved. Its photo quality was amazing, and it was extremely expensive. I had worked an entire summer to save up enough money to buy it. I walked over to the window. Up close I could see that it was snowing lightly.

I gazed outside and stared at the white landscape in front of me. Last week there had been a storm, so every inch of ground; all the rooftops of houses, all the trees and roads were covered in a layer of shimmering snow. I pulled the window open and cold January air gently blew inside. I allowed the snow to softly brush my face as I attempted, with all my heart to capture the scenery and save it in my soul. My camera held uselessly in my hands, as I tried to accommodate myself into the peaceful scenery.

The beauty of this world was so hard to understand...

I nearly jumped six feet into the air as there was a hard knock on my bedroom door. The spell was broken. I pried myself away from the window and still shaken, wobbled to the door.

It was Siara, my older sister.

"May I help you with something?"
She rolled her eyes. "No need to be so formal, I just wanted to let you know we're headed to the movies; are you coming?"
I looked at her like she was insane.
"Do I ever come?"
She shrugged. "Your call, but we'll be back at midnight." She

turned to leave.

I was stupefied. "Midnight?! It's only five! What are you guys planning to do for seven hours? Are you guys going out for dinner too? Maybe driving to another *country*?"

She sighed and turned around to face me. "No, genius, it's the *R.T* premiere, Plus *Her Dream* is playing today."

Now it was my turn to roll my eyes "Oh, very productive way to spend seven hours of your life, staring at a—" my lecture was cut off.

"SIARA, HURRY UP OR WE'RE LEAVING WITHOUT YOU!" That was my mom.

Siara didn't skip a beat, she ran down the stairs at full speed, not even bothering to turn and say goodbye.

I had gotten used to my parents watching and listening to all the latest movies and music. Especially my mom, she acted like a teenage girl and surprisingly Siara didn't seem to mind. Most people found it strange that my parents had the same taste as an average teen, but to me it really didn't make a difference. Mainly because I myself had no clue what an average teenager would find interesting.

The door slammed shut, and the house was overtaken by silence.

I just didn't understand the concept of movies.

You watch random people pretending to live a life they are clearly not living, then, you come home and wish that you could live that fake life, and you spend all your time following the fake story of that random person pretending to be someone he or she is not.

So in your crazy desire to live a fake life, your real life gets wasted.

It took me a few moments to overcome my disgust and remember what I had been doing before the interruption. I stared down at my hand; I was still holding my camera. I didn't feel like staying in the house now that it was empty. Come to think of it I hadn't felt like staying home at all lately.

I walked over to my closet and pulled it open. A row of neatly ironed dress shirts and dress pants stared back at me. I wasn't much into wearing jeans; I had always enjoyed dressing professionally. To me dress pants and dress shirts symbolized order of mind, in other words they were a high-quality teen repellant. I couldn't name many teenagers who wanted to 'chill' with a guy that dressed so stiff.

I pulled on a random sweater and walked over to the mirror. I examined my complexion, my dark eyes and hair made my thin face look even thinner. I ran my hand through my hair in an attempt to control it; it was all over the place.

Uh oh, way too teen friendly.

I picked up some hair gel, and slicked down my hair, making sure to part it down the center. To me it didn't make much difference, but I knew I had just done something that would keep my peers a good distance away from me. One time I had gone to school without parting my hair, and people had looked at me in a completely different manner, some people even tried talking to me.

Don't want that happening again.

I finished with my hair and examined the overall effect, a grin flashing across my face. *Perfect, a stereotypical nerd* all I needed was the glasses. I knew I had a low-risk chance of meeting any person my age because most people my age were wasting away in front of a large screen that was probably destroying their lives, but still you could never be too safe. I pulled on my jacket and then my shoes. Still disgusted I left the house.

It was cold and the wind was blowing hard, nonetheless it was still a beautiful night. I had no idea where I was going, but my feet seemed to know where they were taking me.

I walked on for a while, twenty-five minutes to be exact, and then stopped. I don't know why I stopped, maybe I was tired, or maybe this is where my feet had been taking me. I looked around, the houses were behind me now and there wasn't anything near me except the town forest.

There weren't any real dangerous animals in there, but hardly anyone dared to venture near the forest out of fear, or maybe nobody had the time to take a few seconds off and appreciate nature.

Oddly, today it looked alluring to me. I was tempted to go into it.

My mind and logic said *you're crazy, get yourself out of this snow and go buy yourself a hot chocolate.* My heart said *do it.*

After standing in the cold and debating for a good five minutes I decided I would follow my heart.

I slowly walked towards the forest, unsure at first, and then as I got closer, my steps began to pick up confidence. I couldn't believe I was doing this, was I going insane? It was dark out and I was entering an empty forest. I paused outside the thick line of trees for a moment and collected myself, trying not to imagine all the creatures that could be stirring behind that veil of darkness. I braced myself and took one bold step inside. The second I walked in; everything became much darker.

I took a while to observe my surroundings. Large bare trees covered with snow encircled me in every direction. There was a rough path carved through the trees, but the snow had practically covered it all. I wondered if I was making a smart move, I braved myself to walk. The sound of my shoes crunching against the snow was piercingly loud in the dead silence of the forest. I walked straight for a while keeping track of everything around me in fear of getting lost.

The more I walked, the more difficult it became to follow the path. The trees thickened and it became darker. I didn't know what was keeping me going but I continued to walk through the maze of trees. After an age of walking, the path disappeared and in turn branched out into three routes.

My curiosity ebbed me further. I squinted and tried to see as far out as possible. All the paths were dark and covered on both sides by large bare trees. After careful comparison I decided that the path to my right was bordered with a slightly lesser concentration of trees, so it was probably the safer way to go.

I took the route and after walking for a minute more, noticed that the trees were becoming more concentrated, and it was becoming harder to see. I looked up and shuddered when I realized that the trees were so thick, I could barely see the sky. Maybe now would be a smart time to head back.
I glanced behind me; it was pitch black. I tried to ignore the urgent feeling that I was not alone, and that I was being watched. The dead silence of the forest began to feel pressing. I wasn't a person who got frightened easily but my current situation had my heart beating twice as fast as normal.

What had I been thinking? What made me come this far?

I could easily have been at home safe in my bed, but thanks to my stupidity I was here in the middle of the forest, scared half to death. Now I was too scared to go back and too scared to stand still. For a while all I could hear were my dress shoes crunching against the hard snow.

I stopped abruptly in my tracks. I had seen movement just ahead of me. On top of a giant fallen oak, I could see something shifting on top.

At first, I thought I was just seeing things, but as I got closer and peered through the darkness, my heart nearly froze.

An enormous snake stared back at me.

My first instinct was to run, but my legs refused to move. I stood there staring at the giant snake for what seemed like forever. If I ran it would only chase me, if I stood still, it would only strike me. It seemed I was doomed both ways. Finally, I took a deep breath and walked. Not backwards but towards the snake. Don't get me wrong, I wasn't charging at it or anything, I was smart enough to realize that attacking a snake of that size would likely get me killed. But I figured I would rather go to *it*

than have *it* come to me.

By the time I realized that my reasoning made absolutely no sense, I was already within arm's reach of the frightening viper.

Paralyzing fear gripped me, but I made eye contact, and it looked back at me with a gaze echoing death itself. The eyes of an ace predator. But there was something else in its eyes.

A plea for help?

The snake shifted its long body slightly and continued to stare at me. After a few long minutes of suspense, I decided to risk it. Ignoring all logic and common sense yet again, I reached out a hand until my fingertips made contact.

It felt like ice.

In the dim light, I could see that the snake was around four feet long and its skin was a light color. What was a snake doing out here in this weather? Shouldn't it be underground, somewhere warm by now?

 It would die if I left it out here.

I contemplated turning around and going home, but I couldn't.

The tree it was sitting on had fallen horizontally, and its trunk was so thick it almost came up to my shoulders. I wasn't very athletic so there was no way I could jump it, but maybe there was a way I could climb. After walking back and forth for a while I found an area on the tree that had enough branches on it. I struggled to climb up, and after much leg kicking and arm flailing, I reached the top. Once again, I wasn't very athletic, so this tiny accomplishment filled me with a sense of sheer victory.

Now to pick up the snake somehow.

All but the head of the snake remained still, it slowly turned to face me. I knelt down and reached my hand out. It glared into my eyes, I stared back, keeping my gaze as steady as possible. After a few moments, it extended its head forward. Its movements were abnormally sluggish, it was clearly on its last few breaths.

It wanted to come to me. It knew I was safe.

Without thinking, I scooped up the large ice-cold reptile, unzipped my jacket, and hugged it close to my body while zipping my jacket up again. I felt it slowly coil its long slender body around mine. Almost as if it was used to being carried this way.

Success.

I glanced down and my sense of triumph evaporated as I realized I would have to jump. Only five feet, right?
I braced myself and jumped off the trunk while holding the

snake close to my chest. It was a short drop, but I still ended up landing face first on to the snow-covered ground.

After I finished wiping off the snow and making sure the snake hadn't been crushed in the process, I looked around only to notice that the path had completely ended; I was surrounded by dense forestry. There was no way forward unless I wanted to squeeze through the clustered trees and probably end up getting lost.

Something caught my eye. There was a faint glow coming from behind a group of trees to my right.
I blinked and squinted to see better, was I hallucinating?
Intrigued, I walked forward, a smile overtaking my face as I realized how typical the scene looked:

A boy prowling in the forest finds a mysterious light, he reaches the other side only to discover that he's in a parallel dimension and he has supernatural powers, not only that but he also discovers he's a long-awaited hero, and that it is up to him to defeat the evil that has been plaguing that land for years.

I almost laughed out loud at my scenario, and immediately regretted it as the distraction made me lose balance and I tripped over a tree root. I hadn't noticed that the terrain was getting rougher.

I found myself tripping over tree roots and fallen branches, every few steps. Walking made all the more difficult because of the nearly lifeless reptile I was holding under my jacket. The only source of light was from that glow behind the trees. I finally reached the glow and realized that it was *Natural* light. Like the light you would see at the end of a cave, that meant there was a clearing ahead. I had to squeeze to get myself through, but when I got to the other side of the tree I was baffled.

No, it was not a parallel dimension.
But God was this place ever beautiful.

I took a few moments to look around, my eyes trying to absorb every ounce of detail of the scene. I was in a large open field; the area was about the size of half a football field, and every last inch of ground was covered in a thick layer of smooth, perfect snow. Directly in the center of the enclosed place was a giant tree. The tree stood all alone, with nothing but a few boulders sized rocks beside it.

Tall trees encircled the clearing, making the area look like it was bordered by a natural fence. I cautiously walked forward, not wanting to ruin the perfect snow. On the right side of the field there was a large lake, covered with a layer of shimmering ice; simply breathtaking.

No words could do justice to the way the entire scene looked. I had a feeling that the time of night had a lot to do with it. I glanced up at the sky; it was clear and open, so dark I could practically see every star in the sky. The moon wasn't out; just as I had predicted, but the stars were shining at their brightest.

I couldn't help but feel that the second I had reached this place, something special had happened. My heart felt calm, for once I forgot about my family and peers. I forgot about the fake world. I already loved this place; it was just so…real. After I felt composed enough to take my eyes off the scene, I pulled out my camera from my pocket. I held it up with one hand to take the shot, while still keeping a hand on the snake with the other; I wanted this picture to be perfect. I walked up to the lake and tried but half the lake was cut out, I walked to the left end and tried again but that made the area look too small. I ended up walking around in circles trying to find the desired angle; I wanted an angle from where I could get the entire area in one shot.

Eventually I stopped behind the large tree that was in the center. I intuitively knew I wouldn't get a shot better than this. From this area I could see the entire lake, the tree and rocks, and if I tilted the camera, I could see the sky. I fidgeted with the camera setting for a while and then took the picture. It was the best picture I had ever taken.
Satisfied, I leisurely pocketed the camera. That was one picture I was going to keep forever. I walked over and sat on one of the large rocks beside the lone tree, I felt like I could sit there until the end of time. As I drank in the scenery; an awe-inspiring feeling overpowered me. This scene was so beautiful. How was it possible that something so beautiful had existed unnoticed?

How could I let everyone I knew and cared about waste their life living so superficially, when I knew something like this was in the world? I knew it would be impossible to bring everyone I knew to this place; in fact, I didn't even want to try it. Who knew if they would even appreciate the beauty? But there was one thing I knew I could do.

I could write, and through the power of the pen bring out the essence of this paralyzing beauty. Instantly, a verse came to my mind and before I could think the words flooded out of my mouth and into the quiet night:

*"Shimmering, glowing, moonlit beauty; forgotten is the
nature of men.
Sparkling, illuminated winter beauty; revived through
paper and pen."*

I smiled, it sounded perfect. I didn't need to write it down; those words weren't going to leave my mind anytime soon.
I couldn't believe I had found such a beautiful place. It felt magical, no, it felt...*natural*.

I was in the original, the natural world of men.

I was startled by sudden shifting under my jacket.

Of course, the snake.

 I unzipped my jacket enough to see the creature clearly. Only to be surprised yet again.

Now that I could see it better, I could see the hue of its scales clearly, they were a startling golden color. I had never seen a snake this shade before. It looked marvelous, *regal even.*

Its sluggish movements reminded me that all was not well. Snakes were not meant to stay in the cold, and in all honesty, it didn't look like it would be alive much longer.

I slipped the golden wonder into a makeshift hibernaculum consisting of sweaters placed in a cardboard box. It slowly slithered into a coiled heap. Before I put the lid back on the box, it looked up at me and gradually slid its tongue in and out of its pointed mouth.

Almost as if it was saying thank you.

I glanced at the clock just in time to see the numbers shift from 11:07pm to 11:08pm. I slumped over to the end of the room and switched off the light. The *natural* feeling had followed me home. For the first time in months, I slept with a smile on my face.

Two

I spent the better half of the day searching every nook and cranny in the house for the golden wonder. It was gone.

If it wasn't for the scrapes on my body and the photos on my camera, I would have thought last night was all a dream. But it had definitely happened. Well, the trip to the forest had definitely happened at least.

The box with the sweaters in it was still there. But no snake. Now that I was in my senses — and had no idea where the snake was —I was starting to realize how crazy it all seemed.

 I felt good knowing that the snake was healthy enough to move around, but the thought of how much trouble I would get in for bringing a wild animal home was too much to bear.

After another hour of searching, I eventually gave up.

Maybe it had escaped into the winter yet again?

My heart sunk to the bottom of my stomach as another realization struck me. Was it possible I had just hallucinated the whole incident?

I needed to distract myself.

I turned on my laptop and scanned through the long list of names on the screen. After scrolling back and forth for a few seconds my fingers pressed down on the mouse; `Race14.` I flexed my fingers and began typing.

NBW: Hey.
Race14: Umm........Hi?
NBW: Guess how old I am?
Race14: Do I know you?
NBW: You will after you read my profile.
Race14: Why would I want to do that?
NBW: To answer my
question.
Race14: Why would I want
to guess your age?
NBW: Because.
Race14: Because?
NBW: Just check
Race14: Ok...

I leaned back and waited. The online community was a vast place, with millions of people inhabiting the community it was the perfect place to do what I loved doing most: Asking people to guess my age.
Weird? I couldn't care less; in fact, weird was what I wanted

if it made me different from *them*.

'Race14' was taking some time to reply so I decided it wouldn't hurt to check my profile page, just to pass some time. I had stuff on my profile that would make the average person think I was insane.

The page finished loading.

PROFILE PAGE MEMBER #3225560

Name: NBW

Likes:

Books (reading=good)
Art (colors=wow)
Photography (sceneries=awesome)
Science (Newton=smart)
Poetry (words=expressive)

Dislikes:

Romantic stories (Vampires=annoying)
Math (Einstein=evil)
Reality TV (sitcoms=pointless)
Movies (actors=ridiculously fake)
Fads (latest style=pinnacle of hilarity)

Age: Guess

I had received many comments at the bottom of my profile page replying to my *age: guess* statement. I scrolled down, 2

NEW COMMENTS. I clicked

Queen451: Wow that's one messed profile, you need a life. I'm guessing you're 8, maybe 12?

Without hesitating I deleted the comment, and moved to comment 2:

ToEdwardmySoul3456:
How DARE you??!!! Wat type of a freak are you?? You hate TV and vampires. You like reading and science. EWW you must be like 6 years old, if ure any older then ure probably crazy, freak.

This person was pledging their *soul* to someone, and *I* was the freak?

I heard a beeping sound, Race14 had replied.

Race14: You're too young to be on this site.
NBW: What are you talking about, it's a poetry community for ages 10 and up.
Race14: Exactly, aren't you seven?

I closed the chatbox, I had no need to converse with him anymore.

Did these people even read my profile? What seven-year-old would use the phrase: 'Pinnacle of hilarity?'
Apart from the occasional superficial person, I loved that site. It was an online poetry community called *Souls-ink*. Currently I had commented on seven thousand and eight poems. I had written hundreds of poems myself but only posted up a few; sixteen to be exact.

I had also asked two hundred and thirteen people in total to guess my age. The average guess had been eight and the closest guess had been twelve.

No one had even come close to seventeen.

◆◆◆◆◆◆

You can always tell if a person believes in God.

People who believe in God are always more cautious of what they do, more guilt oriented; whereas people who don't believe in God are more carefree, and their actions are based on consequence rather than morals. At least that's what I had noticed.
Just consider the famous fable: Plato's *Fable of the Gyges*. It speaks of a man who finds a ring that can make him invisible, and he uses that ring to do all forms of evil because he knows he can't be caught. The fable did make sense, but only to someone who did not believe in God. Because God

is described as a supernatural entity that can see and hear everything that happens in the heavens and on earth. And he will hold everyone accountable for their actions.
Invisibility ring or not.
That's why people who believed in God were more cautious, because they feared something other than social rejection.
When I was a child, my parents had never bothered to instill any religious values in me but somehow, I had always believed in God. Come to think of it, I wasn't sure whether my parents were Christians, Jews or Muslims, it didn't matter,
they could be any of the three, or they could be all three. The point was that they never practiced or spent any of their time doing anything related to *any* religion. They didn't even say that they didn't believe in God, so I couldn't even claim they were Atheists.
My family may not have had a clear concept of God, but the ideology that the world had been created by something far greater than chance or a series of 'scientifically justified spontaneous events' had always struck me as obvious. When you really thought about it, it seemed nearly impossible that such beauty and order could have ever been unintentional.
When I was really young, I heard an analogy that had strengthened my belief in a creator tenfold.
Consider a man who goes to an airport. He sees the mechanisms of the entire place, the way everything is so perfectly organized. He's impressed.
He moves on to the airplane and is bewildered by the amazing fact that humankind had reached the level that they can make such a heavy object fly. Curious, he looks into the mechanics of the plane and is shocked as to how advanced the mechanisms of the airplane are. Millions and Millions of

pieces all arranged perfectly.

At this point a lady comes up to him and tells him that the airplane had been created unintentionally. A big explosion had occurred, and all the pieces had just fit together to create a perfectly working plane.

The man tells her to go see a psychiatrist and still amazed he considers everything that had created this impossibly intelligent design, he concludes that it was all created by the human brain. Satisfied, he is about to board the plane until a thought strikes him.

If a brain was powerful enough to create such advanced order and intellectual design, who had created the brain?

If the idea of the plane being formed unintentionally or by chance was absurd, then how absurd was it to believe that the brain; which was billions of times more complex and organized had formed in the same manner? If it was not possible for a bunch of mechanical pieces to come together and form a plane, how possible was it that a bunch of microorganisms had just come together and formed this miraculous organ? Even with millions of years of natural selection, it was still too coincidental to be taken seriously.

It was obviously created by *Someone*, Someone far greater than man. A lot of people considered this analogy invalid because it was a comparison between living and nonliving, but when you really thought about it, it made perfect sense.

Apart from my belief in God, I also had another strong belief, and it was that one must live to learn.

That was my view; I only wish my peers would share it.

Half the school year had already passed, and I could safely conclude that I hadn't witnessed one episode in which my classmates had actually attempted to attain knowledge,

especially during Information Technology.
The IT teacher, Mr. Damon had a really strange way of teaching. He would lecture for twenty minutes, and then tell everybody to implement what they had learned, by creating something on the computer. After he assigned the work, he sat at his desk and submerged himself into his own world of marking and believe me it was nearly impossible to drag him out of that world.

Too bad for me.

It wasn't like his last fifty-five minutes for work was a bad idea; it was an innocent attempt at helping us learn— I think. But that meant the class had fifty-five minutes of free reign on the computer.
Fifty-five minutes of unsupervised internet.
My classmates utilized these last minutes to their full potential; they wasted no time in selecting the latest movie or gossip site and sat around watching and reading. If that wasn't bad enough, they had to react in such a ridiculous way. The routine was so well memorized I could probably write a screen play:

Guy A: what are we watching today?

Guy B: *Punches his hand in the air* "Real Explosions!"

All boys make a loud show of hooting and hollering. The play button is pressed, and the boys submerge themselves into the show.

Guy A: "Man did you see that! It was crazy! His head came right off!"

Guy B: *Shakes his head.* "No man, I was watching that broken thing in the background blow up."

Guy A: *Scratches his head.* "That thing? Hey wait isn't that, that children's place thingy, what's it called. Oh yeah isn't that the orphanage?"

Guy B: *Squints and leans in closer.* "Yeah, look, you can see a kids arm right where the door used to be."

Guy A: "You serious? That's disgusting—"glances *at female bystander.* "—ly cool!"

Female bystander: *Giggles with friends.* "He's so tough!"

Okay maybe that last part was a little exaggerated, but the rest was pretty accurate.

Their actions were more saddening than disturbing. Every computer class I cringed at what I heard.

Why was I even eavesdropping to begin with? Good question.

In my defense, I didn't do it on purpose. I tried to spend all fifty-five minutes working, but Mr. Damon's work was always too simple, and too short. I had learned through experience to bring a good novel with me, it was the only way I could somewhat distract myself from the voices emanating from the computers and the sad reactions produced by my peers.

Today was worse. Why? Mr. Damon decided not to assign any form of work whatsoever. It's not like anyone had even planned to do work in the first place, but still, how much more freedom did my *peers* need? Before the chaos could break out, I hastily opened my physics binder and pulled out the novel I had been reading. *Lord of the flies*. Not really twelfth grade material, but definitely one of my favorites.

I sat in the first row. The people who sat beside me weren't so bad. The real sources of my misery were the people who sat directly behind me, Hudson Grand and his crew.
I had known Hudson since grade nine. I remember in the first month of school he had told me that I was going to be his *personal test answer provider.*

I hadn't liked the idea, I may not have been the 'coolest' person in the world, but I definitely wasn't a pushover. When I refused, he had gotten furious. Who could blame him? A nerd had refused him, denied him his apparently royal birthright to apply no mental effort yet still succeed in school.

Surprisingly, Hudson hadn't gotten physical, but he had insulted me with words I would rather not repeat. After he had shown the class that he wasn't going to take no from a… let's just say *nerd*, he moved on to another intellectual who would show less defiance.

That didn't change the fact that he still hated my guts.

I cringed as I heard the dreaded words come out of Hudson's mouth:

"So, what are we watching today?"

His gang pretended to think about it, everyone knew Hudson's question had been rhetorical, Hudson always chose what they watched.

Hudson waited, when nobody spoke, he gave a satisfied smile. "We gotta watch *Weapons of Mass Destruction*, latest episode came out yesterday."
Miles grinned. "You serious? I thought it was coming out tomorrow! That's *crazy* man, Let's turn up the heat!"

I held back a groan; how sad could Miles get? Even *I* knew that he followed that show like a lost puppy. Everything about the way he dressed to the way he ate revolved around *Weapons of Mass Destruction*, and now suddenly he didn't know when the latest episode was coming out?
My guess is that Miles had already seen the episode at least twice. But no one ever missed a chance to suck up to Hudson, he was a king.
Jode, the calmest member of the gang spoke. "This better not be a waste of ti—" he eyed Hudson and decided to rephrase. "They better have explosions!"
Hudson whistled. "You got that right."
Immediately all his gang members laughed as hard as they could, as if he had told the funniest joke in the world.

Sycophants.

Miles wiped a tear from his eye and punched Hudson on the

shoulder. "Yo, man you're hilarious."
Hudson stopped smiling for a second and looked at Miles. That second was all it took to make Miles go completely pale. "Man sorry, I just... I was…"
Hudson cut him off, making sure to speak loud enough for the girls sitting behind him to hear. "You don't touch me, *got it*?"

Miles didn't need to be told twice; he threw up his hands as if surrendering. "Sure, I shouldn't have done…sorry, won't happen again." The air was tight with tension. After a few moments Hudson seemed to decide Miles had been humiliated enough and grinned. "Alright let's go!"
Jode pressed play and the sounds of explosions and gunfire flooded my ears, I tried to go back to my book but the small incident that had just taken place distracted me.
Why did it even matter? I didn't know. It's not like this was the first time something like this happened, no way. Everyday Hudson had to make a huge show of himself, and everyone obeyed him like he was an official ruler. Why were these people treating him like a king or, like something higher? He didn't deserve any respect.

Was it even respect?

No. it was fear. Miles' face had paled in a second when Hudson had showed the slightest sign of anger. Maybe because Miles knew inside that Hudson wasn't a majestic king who deserved respect, he knew that Hudson was nothing more than a monster.

I tried to lose myself in my novel, but even reading wasn't helping.

I suddenly remembered the beautiful scene that I had

witnessed and the golden wonder I had the opportunity to save. It instantly made my heart feel a thousand times lighter. In the midst of all this superficiality, it was nice to be able to feel calm about something.

Had that really happened though? Was I really insane? Had I just imagined the snake? If I had made up such a real experience, how much more was I making up? What else was I wrong about?

One thing is for sure, if I was literally insane it would certainly explain why I couldn't get along with everyone else.

I went and took my seat at the front of the class. None of Hudson's gang members were in philosophy except Jode. But he didn't really qualify as a gangster. Sure, he was part of their gang, but he hardly ever did anything with them. You might even call him nice.

When everyone was settled Mr. Masiw took the attendance. I glanced at him. He was a remarkably interesting teacher, he pretended to be slack and carefree but many times he said something so beautiful it threw me by surprise.

He droned on with the attendance and I couldn't help but smile. Every day in every period the teacher called out the names of all the students and the students replied in the same monotonous way, with the same monotonous words. One thing I had observed during these sessions was that names were extremely strange. It was so bizarre how when someone else's name was called a certain image or trait instantly flashed through our heads.

The strange part was that it was usually unintentional. We didn't even realize the things we noticed about other people.

I decided to concentrate on the remaining names.

    "Frieda Rodmen."   "Here."   *A smart redhead.*
    "Robert Lee."   "Here."   *A future businessman*
    "Jode Haves."   "Here."   *A sad guy.*
    "Susan Gardner."   "Here."   *An amazing artist.*
    "Tylor Reef."   *Me.*

  "Tylor Reef?
  "Oh, present"

After my name was called, I dropped the exercise. I couldn't help but wonder what images or characteristics flashed through everyone's minds when they heard the name *Tylor Reef.*

Three

I slipped into the forest and allowed myself a few moments

to stop panting. I had practically sprinted the whole way here in my earnest desire to visit again.
Despite the fact that the snow was falling in sheets I didn't feel cold at all, in fact I kind of felt at home.
I straightened up and then began the hike through the trees.
At the beginning, the path was pretty visible, but the snow was falling fast and after a few minutes it was completely covered.
I stood still trying to conjure up a mental map from my last visit and eventually gave up; I would just have to guess my way through.
I walked in circles for about fifteen minutes and then finally found myself standing by the fork.
I took the route furthest to my right and allowed myself to fall into a steady pace.
The sky darkened as the trees began to thicken, and once again a feeling of fear began to possess me. The odd shapes and dark shadows seemed to be making themselves more apparent and the silence was piercing.

I abruptly stopped in my tracks. I was positive I had heard movement up ahead; I strained my ears.
It almost sounded as if someone was struggling to walk through the snow just a short distance ahead of me.
I compelled myself to keep walking and after a few moments the sound faded out.
When I reached the fallen tree, I climbed it as fast as I could.

No snake this time

Unfortunately, I was climbing too fast because the moment I scrambled to the top I slipped and once again found my face greeting the soft snow.
I didn't even bother dusting the snow off my jacket and immediately made my way to the gap.
The moment I entered I was enveloped with a strong sense of peace and serenity, just like the first time.

At least this part had been real, it hadn't all just been a hallucination.

I stood perfectly still, observing the scene in front of me. Standing here I could clearly remember the way the snake had wrapped itself around my body, the way it had looked into my eyes.

The lake, the tree, the clear night sky; it was almost too much to take in at once.
I trudged over to the rock by the tree and sat down. Once again, I felt like I could sit here for ages, just contemplating on the beauty that was laid out before me like an artist's painting that had come to life.

A smile spread across my face as I realized this was much better than a painting. I glanced up at the sky and let the snow fall gently onto my face. No human could have ever dreamt up something as beautiful as this. This place wasn't a piece produced by Da Vinci or Van Gogh; it was much better than that. It was much better than any piece of art because it wasn't created by mortal hands, it was created by God.

After a few more moments I extended out my hands and let the snowflakes fall onto my glove.

I leaned in closer and examined the small clusters of snow.

It was beyond fascinating.

At school we had been taught about the diverse design of snowflakes over and over again. Every ice crystal of reasonable size had a different pattern, a unique design.

My entire hand was covered in snowflakes, there were thousands of snowflakes covering my jacket; there were millions of snowflakes on the floor and even more falling from the sky. How was it possible for there to be so much variety?

Once again, I couldn't help but feel awestruck by the thought of God's infinite power.

I stood up and walked to the lake, the verse I had made last time flew into my head and before I knew it, I was reciting it out loud:

"Shimmering, glowing, moonlit beauty; forgotten is the
nature of men.
Sparkling, illuminated winter beauty; revived through
paper and pen."

I let the echo of the verse emanate in the open sky and fill my mind with the beauty I was witnessing.
Everything from the snow to the star filled sky displayed pure perfection.

I made my way back to the rock and pulled out the latest novel I was reading. I used the flashlight from my phone to see the words better and lost myself in the story. It was so wonderful, the author had written the novel in a completely different time and place, yet I felt like I was sharing their company with them here – despite being completely alone.

When my hands got too cold to turn any more pages, I got up to leave. I was only able to take a few steps before something caught my attention.
There was something on the smooth snow by the lone tree.
The perfectly smooth snow was spotted by a repetitive series of strange shadows. I raised my eyebrows and leaned in closer only to realize that they were footprints. The snow had almost filled them in completely, but they were footprints, nonetheless.
I hastily glanced at my own trail which was far to the right; I hadn't gone by the tree today, so those nearly faded footprints definitely weren't mine. For a second, I was scared.

Who did those footprints belong to?

The only possibility was that someone had been here a few minutes before I had arrived.
The strange noises I had heard earlier came rushing back to my mind and I hurriedly made my way towards the gap. Maybe now would be a good time to head home.

◆◆◆◆◆◆

If you ask me, knowledge is a man's best friend. Knowledge can be used in all walks of life, especially knowledge of the sciences. Knowledge of the sciences can open your mind to so many things. The science of nature: how are we living? The science of technology: when are we living? The science of thought: why are we living?

School is supposed to be a city of knowledge, but it isn't.

If people didn't go to school to attain knowledge, then why did they go to school? People went to school to socialize, to make cliques and to insult and stereotype other people.

Taking that into consideration you'd think a guy like me would get picked on more often. I definitely looked like a bully's first target, but for some reason I was hardly ever targeted.

Come to think of it I had never been physically hit, I had been insulted many times and more than enough people had told me I dressed like an old man, but no one had ever really hit me.

Not that I'm complaining.

If I had thought last week's computer class was bad, today's was even worse. After Mr. Damon taught for his traditional twenty minutes, he sent us off to 'implement what we learned', but there was a problem. The internet was dead.

Mr. Damon didn't find anything wrong with that, he just gave us non-internet related work and dived into his test papers before I could protest.

Too bad for me, because without the internet Hudson's gang only had two options; Do their work or pick on someone. What do you think they chose? I glanced over at them.

Miles looked miserable. "Aww man, no internet? This school sucks!"

Jode who looked slightly happier put his head on the table. "Looks like today's gonna be a boring day."

Hudson leaned back in his chair and kicked his feet onto the table right beside Jode's head. Jode quickly sat up straight. I didn't blame him; I wouldn't want my face three inches apart from Hudson's large brand name sneakers either. Hudson didn't seem to notice the look of disgust on Jode's face.

"Not if I can help it." He bragged. Miles looked at Hudson like a son would look at his father. "What do you mean? We're doing something?"

Hudson put his arms behind his head. "Sure, and it'll be fun."

Uh oh, I didn't want to know what Hudson's idea of fun was.

Actually, I think I already knew.

Hudson's loud voice filled the room. "Hey, you!"

Nobody reacted. He decided to add a swear word to gather the attention he needed. It worked.

For a second, I thought he was talking to me, but I knew that wasn't the insult he usually addressed me with.

Cory Sanders, a short guy with glasses sitting two seats away from me turned around. He looked extremely nervous.

"Is there a problem?" His voice held a slight tremor.

Hudson grinned and leaned forward.

"A *problem? A problem!*" he turned, now addressing his gang members. "He's asking if there's a *problem*!" Hudson threw back his head and laughed. His gang members laughed with him.

What was so hilarious? To me it was clearly obvious Hudson really didn't have anything to say, he had just called Cory for the sake of doing something that promised fun.

Something that promised fun, in *his* eyes that is.

Hudson stopped laughing and put on a dead serious expression. "Maybe there is a *problem*, maybe there isn't." He paused for effect. "It depends."
Cory gulped; I could see him shaking. "It de- It depends? On what?"
Hudson had an evil glint in his eye. "Did you do what I asked?"
Cory looked dead nervous. "Do…do what you asked?"
It was Miles turn to join in the fun. "Yeah retard, you deaf? Didn't hear him the first time?"
Cory tried to summon some courage. "I don't recall you… I don't recall you asking me anything."
They were playing the poor guy for a fool. Cory didn't even notice they were just messing with him. I looked in his eyes and I saw real fear, sure it was brainless of him to get so scared, but what was Hudson's problem? I looked at Hudson, and severe anger crept across my chest. I hated getting angry, I hated the feeling of losing my senses, but that triumphant look on Hudson's apparently celebrity features, that look of sheer joy that he was able to overpower someone weaker than him made me want to give in to my anger, I tried to recall a verse that would calm me down but the look on Hudson's face wouldn't let me.
Hudson stood up; he glanced at Mr. Damon, who was oblivious to all that was going on. Satisfied, he slowly

walked to the first row.

He walked past me and right up to Cory; I thought Cory would pass out.

Slowly Hudson sat on the empty chair beside Cory. He leaned in until their faces were only a few inches apart. "Don't remember?" His voice sounded deadly.

Cory was shaking so much by this point I wouldn't be surprised if he burst into tears.

Hudson's gang members were laughing so hard it was hard to tell whether they were still just trying to suck up, or actually enjoying themselves.

Hudson grinned, ebbed on by his unconditional support, and did something I couldn't believe. He pulled something out of his right pocket and held it to Cory's throat. "You don't recall me asking you anything? Well maybe some pain will help you remember."

Immediately his gang started hooting and hollering with excitement. What a bunch of animals, I looked at them, they were all *seriously* happy.

That scene was the last straw, I didn't know how to stop myself, and before I knew what I was doing, I spoke:

"Put it away".

Hudson's curly blond head whipped around to face me, and I saw the item in his hand, it was a pocketknife. My eyes widened with shock, what had he been thinking?

The second Hudson's eyes met mine, he sneered vehemently. "Something the matter? Don't tell me you gotta problem with me having a little fun."

My rage flared and I put on a mocking voice. "A *problem*? A *problem*?" I turned to the class, who had been following the unfolding scenario as closely as me. "He says: do I have a *problem!*"

A murmur of giggles swept across the class.

I didn't really notice the laughter; the only thing I noticed was Cory's heavy breathing, and Hudson's ugly tanned face. My anger rose.

"Of course, I *gotta problem*. What type of a sick person are you? If you had any integrity, any humane individuality left, you would put that thing away." I pointed at the pocketknife. Hudson blinked in shock, a *nerd,* a skinny, pale, {insert vulgarity here} *nerd* with his hair *parted down the center* had just insulted him. Sure, Hudson didn't have the slightest clue on what humane individuality meant, but he had enough sense to realize that the class had laughed, for the first time *at his expense*.

We both stood up at the same time. The classroom was dead silent.

He had more build; I was taller. Obviously, that meant pretty much nothing, but I allowed myself a swift triumphant celebration in my mind.

Hudson glared at me.

"You know what you're getting yourself into*?* "

I folded my arms across my chest as casually as possible and said absolutely nothing. It was taking everything from me just to stand my ground, let alone speak.

The tension in the room increased ten-fold. Everyone had been expecting me to have begged for mercy, to have run away from the fight, but I hadn't. It was obvious that everyone knew who the winner of the fight was going to be, height difference or not.

Miles jumped up ecstatically. "You should've gotten yourself out of this when you had the chance, now he's

gonna beat the life outta you! And we get to watch!"
Hudson stepped forward; I saw the anger in his eyes. That was twice in the time I had known him that I had defied him in one way or the other.
He pulled back his arm and threw a punch, I saw it coming; I didn't even try to move, to defend myself. There was no point. His fist connected with the side of my thin face. For a second, I saw white. I barely stumbled back but that blow had been hard enough to make blood trickle down my mouth. I blinked a few times, and despite the pain fought the urge to smile. I could see Cory in the background, terrified, but safe. Free.

I had made Hudson do what I wanted.

The rage in Hudson's eyes intensified, he had been expecting to knock me against the wall, at least make me cry, and here I was, standing where I had been before he had hit, practically smiling.
The whole class was holding their breath. Everyone knew Hudson could hit much harder than that.
Hudson's eyes locked onto the blood on my face, and a moment of sick satisfaction flashed across them.
He lunged again with intensified rage. I braced myself for the pain. I waited.
But the pain never came.
I looked up; Mr. Damon had finally unchained himself from his world and was standing a few feet away from us glaring at Hudson. Hudson still had his fist in the air, but he wouldn't hit now that he knew he was caught. The silence was almost unbearable. Slowly Mr. Damon spoke. "What in the world is going on?"

Hudson was red in the face. He was breathing hard, I could see that he was dying to let his rage lose, but he wasn't dumb enough to attack in front of a teacher.

Mr. Damon frowned and glanced at my bleeding face. "Thank God I had been informed *so kindly* just in time. I would hate to see what would have happened if I had been a few minutes late."

He turned to the class. "That does not mean that I approve objects being thrown at me; next time a tap on the shoulder will be just fine."

He rubbed his head on the place he had been hit by the object. *Thank God I had been informed so kindly just in time....*

I wasn't too surprised, people were always throwing things at Mr. Damon, always betting if he would wake from his world or not. But still I was grateful to the mysterious thrower, even if their intention had been completely different.

Mr. Damon stopped rubbing his head and quickly scribbled something onto a piece of paper, he handed it to Hudson.

"Go to the principal's office and give this to him."

He turned back to me. "You, head to the nurse and get yourself checked."

I didn't waste any time. As I walked to the nurse's office I did a mental checklist despite the pain in my lower jaw, I was thrilled. It had been a bad day for Hudson:

   1. The internet died.

   2. A *nerd* stood up to him while the whole class was watching.

   3. The IT teacher caught him.

   4. He was sent to the principal's office for making my mouth bleed.

Ha Ha.

He deserved it. My sense of thrill died as I remembered the initial look on Cory's face. What was wrong with Hudson? What made him feel like he had the right to hurt people as much as he wanted?

Maybe he had watched so many violent movies that normal life was too slow for him.

But a pocketknife? I shuddered at the thought of what he would have done to me if the fight had gone on.

I had seen something on his face that chilled me. Something unhuman.

Once again, I silently thanked the mysterious object thrower. I reached the nurse's office and opened the door. A tall lady with short brown hair was sitting at the only desk in the room, she was busy shuffling through a pile of papers in front of her, when I walked in, she looked up and frowned.

"Oh great, not another one, come on sit here." she pointed at a white chair. I sat down and waited for her to stop examining me. "Not too bad I suppose, how did this happen?"

I didn't reply.

She stared at me expectantly, and then sighed. "Okay then, I guess I'd rather not know anyways. I'll grab you an icepack while you wipe that blood."

Clearly, she loved her job.

She handed me some tissue. There was a mirror at the back of the room, I walked up to it and forced myself to look. The right side of my jaw was dark red, and blood was dripping down my chin; I ran my hand over the bruise and smiled bitterly.

So much for never being hit.

Thankfully it didn't look like it was going to last, maybe two days maximum. I continued staring at myself in the mirror, I guess I couldn't really blame Hudson for calling me a sick old man. My pale thin face and dark eyes just made me look naturally sick, no matter how healthy I ate.

Maybe not old, but definitely sick. Okay fine, maybe old. Very old.

The door of the nurse's office opened. And Cory entered; I was surprised to see that he could still stand after what had happened. He faced the nurse. "Umm, excuse me, but Mr. Black would like to see him in his office."

The nurse nodded. "Sure, he's good to go."

I'm pretty sure I wasn't but I didn't protest.

The nurse handed me an Icepack. Cory watched me get up and place the icepack on my cheek. The second I left the nurse's office he spoke. "Uh, thanks."

I looked at him. "You're welcome."

He opened his mouth to say something then thought better of it.

When he didn't say anything for a while, I decided the conversation was over.

I turned around and headed to the principal's office.

I had never been to the principal's office before. After the secretary let me pass, I entered. It was a large room with dark walls and a polished floor. It had a few shelves against the right wall, and the left wall was covered with certificates and various awards that had been presented to the school. At the very end there was a large window, and in front of that large window was a large desk with a large man sitting behind it. Mr. Black.

He spoke:
"Tylor Reef?"
I nodded.
 "Please take a seat."
I sat down.
It felt strange being in his office, I glanced beside me and wasn't surprised to see Hudson sitting a few seats away from me, he was clearly used to being here; his face was expressionless.

Mr. Black took off his glasses and polished them; he put them back on and looked at me.
"So, you are the boy that Hudson hit?"
I nodded.
"Can I see the bruise?"
I removed the icepack from my face.
Mr. Black stared. "Was their blood?"
I nodded.
Mr. Black seemed to think for a moment, and then he turned to Hudson.
"I've already explained to you, that what you've done is completely against school policy. I can't see how what you did could have been accidental in any way; therefore, you are suspended for one week."
Hudson's mouth flew open. "Suspended for a week! What th—."
Mr. Black glared at him.
"*You* are in no position to be protesting, what you did should have gotten you expelled, but I'm being generous, I could go back on my penalty and expel you if that's what you really want, especially considering your record."
Hudson slammed back in his chair but didn't speak.
"Alright then, you can go and pick up the suspension paper

from the secretary, I'll inform all your teachers, and if they want, they'll make amends for you, so you don't fall too behind, but don't count on it."

Hudson stormed out of the room. I got up to leave but Mr. Black signaled for me to sit back down. "Is anyone at home?"

I thought about it. "Yeah, my mom."

"Alright I'll call her and let her know what happened. I know you still have one class left, but you have permission to go home right now. Do you want your parents to pick you up?"

"No."

Mr. Black picked up the phone. "Alright you can leave."

I got up quickly and exited the office.

Well, that hadn't been too bad. I didn't even have to say much. All I did was nod and say one sentence. I couldn't help but feel intimidated by Mr. Black; he just seemed like such an imposing person; how would it feel to have so much authority? I walked a little way down the hallway and saw Hudson. He was standing by a locker and staring at an envelope in his hand. The second I passed by, he looked at me with such hatred I almost felt it physically. He said something, but I didn't even try to understand it.

He wasn't worth my time.

Four

I scrolled down the screen barely reading the list, who would it be today? I decided to go with the hit or miss method; closing my eyes I randomly selected a name: `PS5smylyf`

NBW: Hello.
PS5smylyf: What do you want?
NBW: Guess something.
Ps5smylife: Get lost before I report you.
NBW: Guess my age.
PS5smylife: 309. Now stop messaging me.
NBW: I just asked a simple question.
Ps5smylife: How do you expect me to seriously guess your age when I don't even know who you are?
NBW: My profile.

......

NBW: Well?
PS5smylyf: You're not planning to leave me alone, are you?
NBW: ☺
Ps5smylyf: Man, I wish this website had a blocking option.
NBW: ☺
PS5smylyf: UGH, wait.

You'd think poetry lovers would be calmer.

While testing my theories on numerous occasions I had realized that dealing with angry people was part of the procedure— annoying them was a bonus.

It didn't take very long for PS5smylyf to reply.

PS5smylyf: You're retarded.
NBW: Why thank you.
PS5smylyf: You don't like TV? I knew you were messed up.
NBW: I appreciate the constructive criticism, but can I have the answer please?
PS5smylyf: Either you're 9 or you're an old, old man.
NBW: How old?
PS5smylyf: Damn you're annoying.
NBW: ☺
PS5smylyf: 62?

♦♦♦♦♦♦

I used to have a best friend; her name was Mina Trew.
I remember the first time I met her was in kindergarten. She had been sitting down and reading a book at play time. Curious; I had walked over to her and seen that it was a book on trees. I was going to wait for her to finish, but she had looked up at me with her honey-colored eyes and smiled, a child's way of giving you permission to play with them.
Thrilled that I wouldn't have to wait, I sat down beside her, and we flipped through the brightly colored pages together. The entire playtime went by, and we were still staring with childish awe at the beautiful colors of the trees. We had loved the entire book, but there was one particular picture that had amazed us most.

It was a picture of a Japanese cherry blossom tree standing strong against a dark night sky. The light pink blossoms had been painted in a way that it appeared they were blowing in an unfelt wind, and the moon was shining bright. Both of us had agreed it was the prettiest picture, and in our immature innocence we had promised each other that we would visit one when we were older.

After that day we made a habit of reading every play time and eventually we grew inseparable.
We went through so much together. Everything I ever did in those years was related to her somehow. I wished it could have stayed that way but when it was time to apply for a high school, she moved. At the beginning we kept in contact but within a year we just stopped communicating with each other.

That doesn't mean I'll ever forget the memories we shared. Those days when we were innocent young kids had been absolutely priceless.

I guess I had liked her so much because she was quite different from the other girls at school. At the beginning it wasn't so obvious but as time passed, things became clear. As time passed and influence mounted, every girl in the class changed. Mina changed too, but in a different way.

When the girls in class started dressing more fashionably Mina started dressing more plainly, when the girls in class started wearing freer clothing Mina started wearing longer clothing. Eventually it came to a point where every girl in school was dressed in the latest style while Mina came to school with an ankle length skirt and blouse.

The girls in school were quick to point her out and insult her as much as possible. They rudely asked her why she didn't do something about her dull red hair, and why she never wore any Makeup. Her tactic was to remain silent.

Personally, I was proud of her. I loved the way she dressed so modestly while everyone else was only focused on the latest fashion trends, no matter the consequence to their decorum. Mina remained silent when she was insulted about her hair and lack of makeup but whenever any girl pulled Mina out and asked her why she *dressed* so weird, she replied by stating that she loved covering herself and she could dress however she felt comfortable. I always wondered what had made her so strong.

I think I found my answer when I visited her house. The first time I went over to her house I had been astounded.

It had been pretty normal, *but it didn't have a TV.*

I asked her what was up with that, and she simply replied that her parents had no interest in television, they thought it corrupted minds. I myself wasn't such a big fan of TV so I had just shrugged it off. I had just been in shock because I didn't know it was possible for a house to exist on earth without television.

I tried to go over to her house as much as possible because it had a rare sense of peace. It was so quiet and clean. Her parents worked, so they were hardly home but they seemed to like me a lot. Maybe it was because I didn't dress like everyone else either, or maybe it was because I got such good marks. I had no idea why they liked me, but I was happy. If them liking me meant I could spend hours at Mina's house just reading a book, I couldn't care less. I could always read at home or the library, but both places had their downfalls. At home the TV was always blaring so loud I couldn't concentrate, and the library was a fifteen-minute bus ride from my house, so Mina's house was a reading haven for the both of us.

We grew up with each other and the memories we had built were so beautiful because they were so innocent. Thanks to her, I was able to spend ten years of my life living a real life. Not a life full of pretending to be someone I wasn't. And not a life full of wishing I was someone else.

Amazingly, from all the time that we spent with each other that one promise we had made to each other in kindergarten; the one about the cherry blossom tree was stuck in both of our heads. We brought it up every year and when we were in grade eight, the last year I spent with her, we had reaffirmed the promise that one day; no matter how old we were we would travel to see a cherry blossom tree on a moonlit night.

Thinking back on those memories made me happy, but at the same time they were saddening. Was Mina as lonely as me in her new school? In the first few months that we had actually kept contact she hadn't talked much about classes, but when she did mention them, she had said that life was getting hard, she had sounded pretty depressed.

I shook off the memories flooding my head, but I couldn't help wondering how it would feel *now* to have a peer who actually understood life the way I did. Maybe they could tell me if I was really out of my mind or not.

Last week `PS5smylyf` had said that I was an old man. My profile had made most people think I was eight, I never realized it could make me look like an old man also.

But why was being older or younger an insult?

I opened *Souls-ink* and went to my profile; there were a few things I needed to add there too.

PROFILE PAGE MEMBER #3225560

Name: `NBW`

Likes:

Books `(reading= good)`
Art `(colors= wow)`

Photography (Scenery=
awesome)
Science (Newton = smart)
Poetry (words = expressive)
Peace (nature= beautiful)

Dislikes:

Romantic novels (Vampires = annoying)
Math (Einstein = evil)
Reality TV (sitcoms = pointless)
Movies (actors= ridiculously fake)
Fads(latest style= pinnacle of
hilarity)
Bullies (pain=...painful)

Age: Guess

After the quick additions I went over to my poetry page. I opened my twelfth poem entitled *'anti socialists'* it always received the most hits and most comments. Just as I expected there were five new comments. The poem opened and I read through it before scrolling down.

ANTI SOCIALIST

What goes through the minds of those who
sit and do not speak?
What goes through the minds of those
whom we consider freaks?

Don't we realize that there's a reason
for their being?
There is more to the picture than merely
what we're seeing.

What gave birth to their odd nature, and
acts of misery?
What gave birth to their lifeless acts,
is but a mystery.

Their perception of reality seems so
brittle and weak
But could *wisdom* be the reason that they
scarcely speak?

Is sacred realization, what they
comprehend?
Have they understood that which we've
failed to apprehend?

Do they see the world the way that it
should really be?
Should we all see the world the way that
they do see?

What goes through the minds of those
who sit and do not speak?
Is it them who are odd, or are we the
true freaks?

I mean did a person have to be loud and social to be
considered normal? Didn't people realize that silence and
solitude were essential in building one's character?

I scrolled down to the comments.

JH: man that was nice, I never thought about it that way

Freak4lyf: o yeah! That's what I'm talking about!! Nice interpretation, you're amazing!!

Typicalgal: wow. There's a creepy girl in class who's always so quiet, I never really thought about what she was thinking. Maybe I'll say hi tomorrow.

Uplifter: you're a poet; you should sell your work

Ihatefreaks: Please. It's so obvious that freaks are just quiet because they're freaks. Why get poetic about it?

The last comment was interesting; there was always someone who disagreed with my work.
I stared at the screen for a while then curiosity got the better of me. I passed my mouse over Ihatefreaks and I was given the option to click. I obliged and I was immediately taken to their profile page.

PROFILE PAGE MEMBER #27890000

Name: Ihatefreaks

Likes:
Movies
Clothes
Shoppin
Makeup
Jewelry
TV, TV, TV!!!
Magazines
Celebs (list 2 long 2 type)

Dislike:
School
Freaks
Work
Family

Age: 12

Dislikes: family? Interesting. I scanned through her poems, she had 45 poems up. Just glimpsing their titles was more than enough to educate me on how she thought.

'Life is a hole unless you're a celebrity'
'More, more, more'
'I want to be a star'
'Size 2 is 2 fat'

I tried not to laugh. Maybe I would read them when I was in the mood for some comic relief.

After reading the comments again I couldn't wipe the smile off my face; I loved it when I got a positive reaction to my poems, when I was able to make a difference in someone's life. I loved it most when I didn't get the credit for it, why? Because then the people who were affected didn't feel like they owed anyone anything.

They felt like they had come to their conclusion all on their own.

Five

I stared at my computer screen and tried to work on the design assigned to us by Mr. Damon. As usual it was simple, but the conversation of the gang behind me was distracting. They were much calmer than they would have been if Hudson had been around, but Hudson wasn't going to be around until Monday, so the class was safe for a while.
Miles stretched. "So, what d'you wanna do?"
Ryan who was sitting to Miles' right shrugged. "I dunno, Weapons of Mass Destruction?"
Jode sighed. "No way, it's getting boring; we've been watching that show for a month."
Miles went on the defensive.
"Hey what d'you mean boring? It's a different episode every day!"

Jode raised his eyebrows. "Okay, so they bomb a different place every day, but nothing else ever happens."
Miles grinned. "Hey, it's still different; don't tell me you're turning soft? Can't handle the blood?"
Ryan jumped in. "Naw, I know what he's saying it's getting boring now, how about something else?"

Miles thought about it then shrugged. "Okay, any ideas?" there was silence as everybody thought.

Was it just me or was 'The Gang' actually happier, more relaxed, without Hudson's presence looming over them?
None of them had even bothered threatening me or showing attitude to Mr. Damon. Maybe it was possible they didn't really feel bad that Hudson had been suspended.

Or maybe they were just saving it for later.

I tried not to think in that direction and concentrated on the work.
Today's task was to create a website on anything you wanted and add as many effects as possible. Sure, it was preliminary, but it was part of the curriculum. After much thought I had decided that I would base my website on the ocean.

Mina used to love the ocean. I remember one time she said that she would do anything to be able to live inside the ocean. I had laughed at her, but she was dead serious. She claimed that technology had advanced so much so why was living daily underwater impossible? I guess you could say it was her dream, so I had stopped laughing at her.

Everyone had the right to dream, even if it was about crazy things.

I searched up *ocean* on the internet and opened up the first site, in big bold letters it read: 'fun ocean facts.' I read the first 'fun' fact:
The ocean is a large body of water
How informative. I scrolled down to the middle and read a random fact, hoping to find something useful.
Ocean water is salty

I didn't even bother reading the rest. I closed the site and decided to choose another topic, maybe something above first grade material. I searched up *interesting topics* and scanned the search engine.

The Occult: Supernatural or magical principles that range from simple metaphysical beliefs to satanic practices that include dark rituals such as human sacrifice.

Definitely above first grade material.

I began reading and instantly regretted it, gruesome images of strange symbols, and ceremonies filled the screen. Nevertheless, I was glued to the screen, reading fact after fact, hardly daring to believe any of it was true yet knowing it was a very actual reality.

I snapped out of my trance by the sudden sound of gunfire in the background.

So, they had decided on another show, maybe with a different title but the same storyline. I creased my brow trying to cancel out the annoying sounds and continued searching until I finally found a few decent facts, then I set about fixing the layout of my website.
As I searched for a family-friendly picture I could use, I

remembered that I still hadn't developed the photo I had taken on my first visit to the *Natural World*. I didn't know why I had stalled so long, but I decided I would go as soon as class was over.

◆◆◆◆◆◆

I opened the door of the small Photography room. Raymond High had a poorly financed photography club; the facilities offered weren't exactly magnificent. They had a few old computers for uploading and editing photos. They also had outdated cameras for rent but there was one strong point, the photo printer. The printer had such accurate colors; it could practically make any photo come to life.

I walked over to a computer and without hesitation, took my camera and USB cable out of my bag and plugged them in. A pop up appeared asking which photos I wished to upload. I had twenty-four on my camera in total. I scanned through all the scenery pictures, and in the end decided to print all twenty-four. Thank God for Government funding.

As the pictures uploaded, I took some time to examine the familiar room. It was quite small, the size of an average bedroom. The walls were bare, and it had two industrial printers on one side, four computers on the other side and a desk at the front.

I think the desk was supposed to be for a teacher or supervisor, if the room ever got busy enough to need one that is. The photography room was a place I visited often, and I had noticed that hardly anyone else ever visited.

Well, it made sense. Most students had printers at home, and the photography room was located at the back of the school, surrounded by old broom closets and locked doors. Come to think of it, nobody even bothered walking through the hallways near the photography room, forget entering the room itself. Even now, I was the only one in the room, maybe even the only one in this part of the school.

The pictures finished uploading, another pop up came letting me choose whether I wanted to edit the photos or print. I selected the second option.

In a few seconds I heard the familiar buzz of the printer going about its work. I leaned over, watching the printer slowly eject each photo and place it in a neat pile. The first photo came out. I had taken it two months ago, a sunset. Instantly a poem popped into my head, it was the poem I had written when I had taken this picture. I had a habit of doing that, every picture I took came with a poem. This particular photo had been taken after I had found someone plagiarizing my work.

Two months ago, we had to hand in a poem for philosophy. The day after I handed it in, Mr.Masiw called me and told me that someone else had the exact same poem as me, he told me that he knew I hadn't copied but he just wanted me to be more careful next time, he hadn't even done me the favor of telling me the person's name. The sunset symbolized the disappointment and sinking shock I had felt. I hadn't put it up on *Souls-ink* yet, but I was intending on doing it soon.

I watched the remaining photos print; it was an agonizingly slow process. After the first ten photos I began to get impatient. Why did I have to print all of them? The last photo was the one I wanted to see.

By habit, my hand automatically went to my jaw. Gratefully, the bruise had healed only two days after the incident. Whenever I thought about the event of that day I automatically smiled. I couldn't help but feel that even though I had gotten hurt, the day had been a victorious one.

My thoughts were interrupted as the silence was broken by voices. Once again, hardly anyone came to this part of school, so I couldn't help but feel slightly curious. I walked closer to the door and the voices came into focus. They weren't *voices*, rather it was just one voice: definitely a guy.

There was something weird about the way he was talking. He was saying something, not just random words but sentences *with a rhythm.*

It took me a while to realize that he was reciting poetry. A verse from a poem. I walked closer to the door and strained to hear. What I heard shocked me beyond belief. He was repeating the same verse constantly. At first, I only heard the last part of the verse, but as I continued to listen, I heard the entire verse. My heart sped up, and started beating hard against my chest as I began to realize what his words meant:

"Shimmering, glowing, moonlit beauty; forgotten is the nature of men.
Sparkling, illuminated winter beauty; revived through paper and pen."

I doubled back in shock and stayed that way for a while. Those words, I had made them, read them aloud only *twice* when I was…
I threw the door open and scanned the hallway. No one was there. I had taken too long to react. I couldn't even hear footsteps.
The printer beeped then turned off.
Still dazed I walked over to the printer and looked at the top picture. It was that beautiful scene, that beautiful place. The picture I had taken on the first day.
That was two weeks ago.

The way I saw it there were only two possibilities. The first and least likely possibility was that the person had made the verse himself. Somehow thought up of the exact same words I had recited.
The second and more likely possibility was that someone had heard me.
The strange noises and unknown footprints from my more recent visit filled my mind.

So, someone *had* been there. But who?
Was there someone else in the school who also knew about the *Natural World?*
Staring at the perfect photo with the thought that someone else may know about it too, gave me a new feeling, and with that new feeling came new words. The beauty of the photo motivated me, and I spoke:

"Glowing calm, overwhelming peace, man's nature calls him back.
Illuminated stars, garlanded trees, our old forgotten track."

I stood there for a few moments and soaked in the verse. Just like the first verse this one matched the essence of the *Natural World* perfectly. Satisfied, I collected the photos and put them in my bag.
I pushed open the door still trying to digest the fact that someone else knew about the *Natural World* and they had gone as far as to memorize the verse I had recited. My mind flew back to that time someone had plagiarized my poem in philosophy. But this was different; this meant that someone had been in the forest at the same time as me. I had always liked being alone, but I didn't have anything against having someone who thought like me around.

The only reason I never bothered talking to people was because I had just figured that they would never understand me. But now, the idea of having a friend, a companion who knew about the *Natural World* whether I knew who he was or not brought peace to my heart and a smile to my face.

I sped up my pace. There was only one thing I wanted to do right now, and that was to visit the *Natural World*. I promised myself I would go tonight; I had a feeling that someone might be waiting.

◆◆◆◆◆◆

I thought night would never come, but when it did come it felt like no time had passed at all. I buttoned up my jacket, and walked over to the mirror, as much as I was dying to get out of the house, I had to follow procedure.

I picked up the gel and covered my hair with it, after I had placed a substantial amount on my head; I parted it directly down the middle. It took a while to tame my dark unruly hair, but eventually I succeeded.

It was amazing how one little action could make a person look so different.

I double checked to see if the camera was in my pocket, then I headed out the door. My head was packed with the day's events. Questions chased themselves around in my mind.

Who was that guy? If he had heard me reciting, why hadn't he shown himself? Had he even seen me? Did he know who I was?

My questions overwhelmed me. I pondered over them for a long time. Anxiety was starting to grab hold of me.

My feet came to an abrupt stop along with my questions. I was standing in front of the forest. I had been so distracted I hadn't even noticed the walk.

I held my breath and then slowly walked into the forest. On

my first two visits I had been scared. This time I felt much calmer. I walked slowly through the maze of trees, trying to follow the snow-covered path. It was strange how I didn't even have to think twice about knowing the exact location of the *Natural World*.

I reached the giant fallen tree, taking time to remember the embarrassing way I had gotten scared when I first saw it. I carefully pulled my way up the branches and struggled to the top. When I reached the top I wobbled, trying to keep the unpleasant memories of last time's experience out of my mind. Closing my eyes, I jumped down. I landed on my feet, but after a few seconds the impact hit me and caused me to lose my balance. That was one thing I would never get used to.
After I recovered, I tried to walk a little faster.
I could see my breath coming out in the form of fog. I could feel the cold air biting my bare face. I could feel the piercing silence; the only sound I could hear was that of my pounding heart. When I saw the gap of light behind the tree my heart began racing faster, my anxiety built as I walked closer and closer to the *Natural World*.
The questions came back to my mind, whirring around in circles. Would it be possible that their answers would be mine in a few moments?
I stopped directly in front of the gap, panting. I tried to catch my breath, and then I squeezed through.
As soon as I got to the other side, I brushed off the snow that had accumulated on my jacket, too scared to look up. I could feel someone else's presence, slowly I lifted my head.

I stared for a few moments trying to comprehend what I was seeing. A red-haired guy was leaning casually against the large tree in the center, hands in his pockets. His head was facing the other way. It didn't take him too long to notice me, he turned around and my shock nearly turned into trauma.

It was Jode Haves.

Jode seemed as shocked as me. We both stared at each other for a while, both of us uncertain of what to say. He spoke first.

"Tylor, right?"

I nodded. "Yeah, and you're Jode." It was more of a fact than a question.

We stared at each other.

He straightened up. "So, you been here before?"

I didn't need to know why he was asking that. "Yeah, I have, have you?"

He kicked the floor lightly. "Yeah, a few times."

A few times.

I walked over to a rock by the tree and sat on it. So, it had been Jode. Jode had been reciting the verses at school. Who would have guessed? I looked at him.

"So, you heard me, two weeks ago?"

He seemed taken aback by the question.

"You mean the poetry?"

I replied. "Yes, I mean the poetry"

Jode unpocketed his hands and stared down at them. "Yeah, I heard it, how did you know?"

It was my turn to find something to stare at. "I was in the Photography room, and I heard someone reciting the verse, I figured they must've heard me."

He seemed embarrassed "Oh."

Oh. What else was there to say?

I realized that I had been quiet for an uncomfortably long time. Maybe I should say something. Jode saved me the trouble.

"Did it hurt?"

For a second, I was confused, and then I remembered the incident with Hudson. I grinned, my hand automatically going to touch the place I had been hit. "Of course, it hurt."

He raised his eyebrows. "You don't look too upset."

I tried to stop grinning. "I don't?"

He stared at me amused. "I guess you do have a right to be happy, that was one point up for you."

Confusion swept through me. What was he talking about? Through *his* eyes it should have seemed like I was an idiot to have challenged Hudson. His king.

I feigned innocence. "One point up for me?"

Jode stopped leaning against the tree and walked forward. "It's simple. Hudson didn't hurt Cory because of you. You basically, bent him to your will, even if you did get punched for it."

I observed his face, looking for hints of sarcasm and found none. Come to think of it, I had never really seen

him sucking up to Hudson. Did he even think of Hudson the way his other gang members did? I decided to test him. "You must be mad about him being suspended."

He shrugged.

"Aren't you upset?"

He resumed his old position by the tree. "No, not really."

So he *didn't* like Hudson. Then why did he hang out with him? I considered asking him, and then thought against it. The last thing I wanted to do was start a heated discussion about Hudson, especially when I was in the *Natural World*.

For a few moments both of us just spaced out. Jode looked up at the sky. "Did you make it?"
I glanced at him.
 "Make what?"
"The verse, did you make it?"
I thought about it for a second then I shook my head. "No, I didn't make it." I looked around at the winter scenery. "I didn't make it. This place made it."
He stared at me with a look in his eyes that I couldn't exactly put a finger on. "I think I get what you mean, this place is so…"
His voice trailed off, at a loss for words.
I was surprised that he had understood me. It's not like I thought Jode was dumb; it was just that he seemed so normal. He was good at sports, hung out with a huge crowd and always kept up with the latest trends. He was a go with the flow person. At least that's what I thought.
Until now.
I glanced at him and couldn't help but remember what trait had flashed in my mind when Mr. Masiw had read his name in attendance.
A sad guy.
Why had I thought that? He was one of the most well-known guys in school.
Maybe it was because I barely ever saw him smile.

A few minutes of peaceful silence passed. I looked up; the moon was at its last quarter.
"I wonder how this place would look in a full moon."
Jode turned his eyes up to the sky. "The next full moon is on February first."
I was impressed. "You keep track of the

moon?"
Jode shrugged. "Yeah."

Bizarre. I was sitting in the *Natural World* beside Jode Haves. One of the most media-oriented people I knew. Well, I didn't really know if he was media oriented, but he was popular, and that automatically made him media oriented, right? I furrowed my brow, more bothered by my premature judgement than anything else.
Looking at him right now with that peaceful look on his face I couldn't ever imagine that he believed in the fake world. I looked down at the snow, it was practically sparkling. Those words I had said in the Photography room, when I had seen the photo, came flooding into my head. I was so tempted to say them out loud and test the way they sounded in the large empty forest. I glanced at Jode, he was still staring at the sky.
"Hey, you don't mind if I say something I've been working on out loud do you?"
Jode looked in my direction. "No, go ahead."
I could tell he was curious.
I stood up, and walked up to the lake, I positioned myself at an angle where I could see the entire area clearly.
The words came flooding out:

"Glowing calm, overwhelming peace, man's nature calls him back.
Illuminated stars, garlanded trees, our old forgotten track."

Yes. It had been perfect; I knew it would suit the place perfectly.

My sole voice had sounded astounding in the large empty forest. Peace enveloped my heart, and I forgot about all the

ridiculous things my peers did. I forgot about the sad way everyone I knew and loved were wasting their lives. I forgot about my deep worry that I had hallucinated the startlingly realistic experience of saving the golden wonder.
The glowing calm produced by the snow, the overwhelming peace emanating from the enclosed place. How did people fight the urge to return to their nature?
The stars hanging like lamps in the sky. The trees decorated with icy snow. Nothing like this could be found in the fake world that men had created, we had forgotten our true way of life.

I closed my eyes and stood by the lake; arms folded across my chest, and just listened. An eternity later, I awoke from my standing meditation, and reflected on the peculiar events of the day.

I didn't need to turn around to know that Jode had already left.

Six
JODE

Jay's room door was open. I slipped inside and made my way

over to the back where he kept his enormous tank. Sure
enough, he had left Mr. Snake at home again today.

"Hi there Mr.Snake. It's me again."

The snake immediately lunged forward and bared its fangs,
hissing in rage. I felt braver knowing there was a thick layer of
glass between me and him.

I didn't blame him for being angry. The last time I had taken
the stunning reptile out, he had gotten lost in the forest.

In winter.

A death sentence for a snake.

I was sure that would be the last of him, but he didn't die. Like some divine miracle, he was found outside the house in the morning.

Lucky for me, Jay didn't realize it was my fault, he just thought he had been careless and left the tank and door open.

"Can we try again? I really want to be your friend."

I carefully opened the tank and tossed in a savory snake snack, hoping to pacify him. The deadly viper hissed again and returned to a coiled heap in the corner where it had been resting before I interrupted it. Clearly it wouldn't let me hold it again. What a shame, I had been making so much progress.

I supposed I deserved it.

I returned to my room and slumped against my pillow thinking about what had just happened in the forest. That had been really weird.
Tylor Reef had been the poet? The voice I had heard? I would have never guessed.

But the more I thought about it, the more it made sense. Tylor wasn't exactly a loser. He dressed like a nerd; that was for sure, but he didn't act like one at all.
At school he just seemed so confident. You could tell he felt he knew what life was about. Come to think of it if he just

changed the way he dressed he'd be...normal.

The incident with Hudson last week flashed through my mind. Tylor had done something no one ever dared to do. He had stood up to Hudson. He had gotten punched too, but if you ask me, it was worth it. If anyone deserved to be suspended, it was Hudson.

 My mind went back to the day I had heard Tylor reciting poetry in the forest.

The night had started off typically, I had a huge disagreement with my brother, and before things could get violent, I had left the house. This time though, I decided to sneak his pet snake with me due to my rage. Maybe I had wanted to punish Jay by taking away what he cared about most. I had never intended to lose it though.
Just like every other time I didn't really know where I was going, but my arrogant body carried me wherever it wanted. This time I found myself sulking around in a forest, in *that* forest.

I had eventually cooled down, and was about to head back home, when the most miraculous thing happened. I heard a clear, loud voice echoing through the forest.
The fact that there was someone else in the forest at such a late hour didn't amaze me as much as what that person had been saying. He had been reciting poetry.
After I heard the voice, I went crazy trying to locate it, and I eventually fell upon that place. I closed my eyes for a moment trying to remember the exact way the place looked. It was covered with snow, with a lake on the side and a large

tree directly in the center.

The second I saw the area I knew the voice had come from there, but the person had disappeared.

I had gone back for two weeks after I heard the voice, hoping he would come back, with no luck.

Until today that is.

It wasn't easy spending two weeks there; of course, I went home to sleep but those crucial hours were the hours I usually went out with my friends. The first few days I had told them I had to finish some work so I couldn't catch a movie, they had been pretty cool about it but by day three they had gotten fed up. I had to hold my head to prevent a migraine when remembering the constant questions being tossed at me from every guy in the gang.

 Miles' annoying voice echoed in my head.

You're turning into an old man! What could be more important than bloody war 4? An old man? *He* was the one who couldn't even kick a ball properly and *I* was the old man? All I had wanted was a few days of peace, but all they wanted to do was play video games and catch movies.

They had absolutely no meaning to their lives. They just walked around and did exactly what they saw on TV. They actually used dialogue from movies in normal conversations without realizing it. They had forced me into watching so many violent movies I was starting to hear gunshots everywhere I went.

How could killing people be entertaining? I admit it was exciting at the beginning but after seeing it a hundred and one times, I got sick of the constant gore. What was up with today's youth?

Okay maybe I did sound like an old man.

But was being an old man necessary to get some peace? *Peace.* The scene of Tylor reciting the poem by the lake came back to my head. His words had brought peace to my heart. That new verse he had recited:

"Glowing calm, overwhelming peace, man's nature calls him back.
Illuminated stars, garlanded trees, our old forgotten track."

It was just like the first verse. It did something to me. The feeling was unexplainable, it was beautiful. It was poetic.

I was a sucker when it came to poetry. I didn't write much but I would search the internet for hours, looking for poems. I couldn't help but smile as I remembered the poem that I had read the other day, *Anti socialists* by some guy named NBW.

That poem had been so well thought out.

Could wisdom be the reason that they scarcely speak?

Only someone who understood how hard it was to sit and listen to people trying to impress each other all day could have written such truth.

I pulled myself up from bed and sighed, there was school tomorrow. I would have to go back to sitting with *them* again.

I shuddered as I thought about the gang.

They hadn't always been so bad. I had known Hudson since I was in grade six. The first day I had come to school Hudson was sitting at the back of the class quietly doing his work. When our teacher asked who would like to sit with me, no one raised their hand, so she just seated me beside Hudson. He had been a noticeably quiet person. He never really talked much, and he paid full attention to whatever the teacher said. I had liked that about him because I was quiet too. After a few days we discovered that we shared the same interests; from sports to food, we had the same taste. We spent all our lunches together, we visited each other's houses after school, we basically became inseparable.

One thing we loved doing was going to the old park at the end of town. It was a deserted broken-down place, but we didn't mind because we had the place to ourselves. We would spend endless hours on the swings, just letting our hair and clothes flutter in the wind, it was the best way to forget our problems, and back then we had some pretty big problems.

One problem was much bigger than the others.
At that point in our lives there had been a bully in school. Bully was too sane a word to describe him. I think he was mental or sick because he definitely wasn't your average guy, or even your average bully.

Everyone called him Beef, maybe it was because he was huge, or maybe it was because he made you feel like dead cattle after you had an encounter with him. I wasn't sure and seriously it didn't matter. What mattered was that the guy was in grade seven and he weighed two hundred pounds, let me just point out that he wasn't chubby.

Yeah. 200 pounds of muscle.

Sound like an exaggeration? Well maybe the fact that he had failed elementary school five times would clarify things. He was really sixteen. The school said if he failed one more time he would be sent to a school for mentally challenged students. You'd think he would at least try changing after that, but instead he took out his rage by intensifying his hatred towards the kids in school. Some said he failed on purpose, just so he could continue his sick reign of tyranny.

Beef had a habit of patrolling the hallways at recess. Any kid that was caught by him during those crucial minutes was immediately attacked. That might sound stupid, but when you're twelve and a six-foot tower of muscle is coming towards you to slam you against the nearest wall, you wouldn't ponder the stupidity of the act, you would just concentrate on not wetting your pants.

That hadn't been the worst part. I wish it had been the worst part. The worst part had been lunch time. Apart from Beef's daily recess patrols he also had a lunch patrol. Now the average bully would spend lunch stealing snacks from innocent kids. Beef on the other hand spent his lunch *making* snacks.

One time me and Hudson were eating lunch, and he came up behind us. Immediately we had both stopped talking. Too scared to open our mouths too scared to breathe. We knew what was coming, he did it every lunch, but this was the first time he was doing it to us. Grinning widely, he had rubbed his huge hands together and started his daily routine. He picked up Hudson's glass of juice. Hudson was transfixed with horror, so was I, and so was everyone on the table.

Beef had looked around the room, and spotted *Emile Furte*, the girl who always had a cold. He called her over and snatched her clutched tissue from her trembling hand. Then with pure pleasure he dropped the snot-soaked tissue into the glass.

Disgusting.

He didn't stop there; he had gone on for about ten minutes throwing disgusting stuff in the glass, which included mold from an old piece of bread, hair found on the floor and gum scraped off from the bottom of a table. He had finished up his repulsive routine with his signature move. He pushed around the saliva in his mouth for a while then with great triumph spit straight into the glass. I'll never forget the way the spit sounded when it landed in that cursed glass. It was horrible.

Hudson was close to tears; I was close to tears. We knew what came next. When Hudson took too long to pick up the glass, Beef grunted, and that grunt was all it took for Hudson to pick up the glass and swallow the whole thing; tissue and all. The sight had been too much for me and before I knew it, I had vomited, a few seconds later Hudson threw up too. The average bully would at least be scared that he would get in trouble, but Beef just grinned. As if that whole episode hadn't been enough, He walked over to Hudson and still grinning punched him in the stomach.

That day we had gone to the park, and as usual sat on the only thing that wasn't falling apart, the swings. In our frustration we made up a game where every time we thrust our legs out to go higher, we would be kicking Beef in the stomach, the person who could kick higher won. Even though I was taller Hudson always won the competition. The game turned into our favorite and anytime we visited the park the first thing we would do would be jump on the swings and pretend to extract revenge on Beef.

The satisfaction was great, and so was the feeling.

But I couldn't help noticing that what Beef had done that day had changed Hudson forever. I saw how Hudson watched Beef's every movement. He followed everything Beef did and knew every place Beef went. At first, I thought it was paranoia, but as time passed, I realized that Hudson was actually warming to Beef's behavior. He wasn't looking at him with paranoia but with something else and at that point in time I hadn't understood.

The following year the prayers of all the students and teachers in school were answered when Beef got kicked out for academic reasons. Things couldn't have been better, but one thing I learned was that, that perfect feeling doesn't ever last long. In this case it lasted three months. Everything was just right until a new student came to school and that student was Miles.

Miles was definitely not a bully; he was just a bully maker. When he came, he immediately took to Hudson and followed him around like a puppy dog. He did everything Hudson wanted, and I guess in that sense he created Hudson's love for power. Because he followed Hudson around, he instigated the humiliation Hudson had hoarded in his proud heart, and once that was set off things began to change. As time passed Hudson began to allow his pride to overtake him. He took peoples' money, hit whoever he didn't like and insulted anyone who was a little different. The only difference between him and Beef was that he was loved by the popular people. Beef junior.

By the time it was graduation day Hudson was horrible. He was loved by the cool people, but he was hated by the others. It was sickening to watch the way he treated some people; it was saddening to watch his transformation.

Eventually it was time to apply for high school. When we applied, we ended up applying for the same one, both of us made it into Raymond high. Miles applied for Raymond high also, but due to his low average got rejected.

It was then that I realized how much Hudson had really changed. With Miles around I couldn't really tell, but now his transformation was clear. He no longer bothered talking about anything unless it was about a movie or videogame; he spent

his time making fun of people who looked weak. He spent his time destroying lives.

The first semester of grade nine was torture. I had to do everything he did; I had no courage to fight back. When second semester came, Miles got transferred to Raymond high. I was actually happy, sure I hated his guts; he was the one who had destroyed my best friend, but I was happy because I no longer had to be the only one dealing with Hudson.

It was clear that I didn't share the same interest as those two anymore, but I was too scared to leave them especially when we had just entered a new world. I mean there was no way I could just walk away from my only friends in my first year. Now, standing here so many years later, I wish I would have just walked away from them on the first day, but I hadn't so I was left here, hating everything they did, hating myself because I did it with them. When I had reached high school, I had realized the way Hudson looked at Beef had not been paranoia or fear, but it had been admiration.

Hudson loved the way that Beef was able to control so many people, strike fear into the heart of whomever he willed. I don't know where he got the idea that Beef's actions were esteem worthy. But the point was it had transformed him into something horrible.

I walked over to my window and sighed; I missed the good times before everything had changed. My thoughts were forced back to the awkward conversation in the forest. Had it really been awkward? I think I had felt pretty much at home. More at home than I felt with my friends or even with my real family. But still, it was Tylor, how could I have anything in common with him?

After he had recited that new verse, he had gone completely quiet for fifteen minutes. I myself had dazed out for a while but as soon as my mind came back to reality I had bolted.

My logic had told me that standing in the forest listening to a nerd recite poetry would make me lose my sanity. That if I stayed there longer, I would turn into someone crazy. But now looking out my window at the intense night sky, pondering on my past, I couldn't help but wonder if it was possible that my logic had been completely wrong.

Seven

I checked my watch; four minutes until the bus came.

I had been dying to get my driver's license since the second I turned sixteen, but fear of failing combined with procrastination had stalled me for a whole year. It was times like this that I regretted slacking off most. I threw my bag over my shoulder and on my way out caught my reflection in the hallway mirror.

I was disgusted, my hair looked repulsive. I had woken up late, so I hadn't gotten a chance to gel it up. I hastily ran a hand through it in an attempt to make it look better, but it still looked completely flat.

How did everyone else get their hair to look so perfect? Frustrated I tossed a random hat on and bolted out the door.

The cold winter air hit my face hard, but I compelled my athletic figure to push me down the street. My breath was coming out as tiny clouds in the cold winter air.

The nearest bus stop was a seven-minute walk from my house. I pumped my legs as hard as I could; this was one bus I couldn't miss.

 I couldn't care less about being late for school, but today, we had soccer practice, I usually didn't care about that either but this time I was in a fix. Mr. Zen had told me that if I was late one more time, he'd kick me off the team, no matter how valuable I was.

I didn't like waking up an hour early to go to the school gym and practice, especially in winter, but I loved playing soccer and I'd do practically anything to stay on the team.

One minute left and I could barely see the bus stop. My shoulders sagged and I stopped running, there was no way I'd make it. I would be late again. The only reason I had to take this bus was because it took me thirty minutes to get to school. It was 7:35am right now and practice was at 8:00am. My only hope was getting a ride from a friend, but who would give me a ride at this time?

I made it to the bus stop a good four minutes after the bus pulled out. Boy did I feel stupid, the next bus was in fifteen minutes.

I couldn't afford that much time; Mr. Zen had sounded pretty serious with that last threat. I dragged myself to the bus shelter and sat down.

I loved playing soccer. It was a passion I had held since I was a kid. I was the best player in my team since grade three and even now in Raymond high I was the best. I thought back to all the victory goals I had scored for my team. Maybe Mr. Zen wouldn't kick me off.

My thoughts were interrupted as I saw someone walk into the stop with me. It was Tylor.

We stared at each other for a while. After a few moments he walked over to the bench and slowly sat down.

Last night's event played through my mind. Had that actually happened? I remembered the peace I had felt and then looked back at Tylor. Yeah, it had definitely happened.

I opened my mouth to say something but then caught myself. What was I thinking? I wasn't supposed to talk to someone

like him. Yesterday at that place it had been different, but now in public, no way. I frowned and closed my mouth, I shouldn't talk to him; he was too different; sure, he wasn't a complete loser, but still, I couldn't get myself to accept the idea. The air grew extremely awkward. How much time was left until the next bus? I glanced over at him; he was resting his head on his hand and staring outside. Once again, I remembered yesterday's conversation and oddly enough felt like I should say something. Yesterday had been special, as weird as it sounds, I knew that we had established some sort of link and even stranger, I wanted to keep it alive. I tried to imagine how it would be like hanging out with Tylor at school but couldn't even think of it. Maybe I should start with being able to have a normal conversation. Once again, I opened my mouth but this time I was cut off.

"Jode!" I looked up and saw Hudson in his black Audi waving at me. It had been a while since I had heard that voice; I forced myself to grin and jumped off the bench.

"Hey man! Good to see you again!" I almost frowned as I realized that his suspension had ended today.

I casually walked over to his car. He had the window pulled down. "Get in; I'll give you a ride."

I opened the door and sat down. "Thanks man you saved me." As soon as I saw his face up close, chills ran down my spine. Something was different.

Hudson pushed down on the pedal. "Was that Reef with you?"

I nodded. "Yeah, it was…"

Hudson frowned. "I didn't know he lived around here."

Shrugging I pulled down my seat belt.

He continued driving for a while then at the next stop he turned to me. "Did you guys do anything to him yet?"

I looked over at him innocently. "Who? You mean Tylor?"

Hudson almost growled. "Who else?

I had been afraid of this. I turned to look out the window, avoiding direct eye contact. "Yeah, we pushed him around a bit, but we didn't go too far, I mean it wasn't his fault if you think about it."

That had been a pure lie, we hadn't even gone near Tylor, but I knew all the guys would say the same thing. Everybody would make it seem like they were real mad about Hudson's suspension, but the truth was they didn't want to do anything to Tylor because he wasn't someone you could push around. No one wanted to be embarrassed like Hudson had.

Hudson tightened his grip on the steering wheel. "Yeah, I'm gonna let him slide but it was that guy's fault who threw the pencil at Mr. Damon. Did you see who it was?"

I tried not to laugh and transformed my innocent look into one of severe anger "no man, but when I find out who it is—" I slammed my fist into my other hand. "He's dead". This violent gesture seemed to satiate Hudson, and he stopped asking questions.

Obviously, I knew who threw the pencil because it had been me. The fight had been getting worse and the fact that Tylor hadn't given up was more than enough to get me to act. Sure, it was traitorous but what Hudson was doing hadn't been any better.

Hudson relaxed a little. "What were you doing out this early anyways?"

I looked up at him. "Soccer practice."

Hudson grinned. "I have hockey practice today too."

Nodding my head, I turned back to the window. This was the first time I was actually happy to get a ride from Hudson, despite the strange aura around him. Maybe I wouldn't be late after all. "Hey, you mind going faster? I think I wanna get their early."

He sped up slightly. "So, how've things been in school? The guys told me it's been dead boring.

I thought back to all those peaceful classes of pure relaxation with no fear or exaggerated fakeness and forced myself to look upset. "Yeah, dead boring."

Hudson seemed satisfied.

We got to school in thirteen minutes and me and Hudson went our separate ways.

I took my time walking to the gym and changed into my soccer gear. It was annoying having to practice indoors, but until winter was over, we had no choice. Most teams stopped practicing in winter, but Mr. Zen said we couldn't afford to waste any time.

I walked into the gym; there were already two guys there

plus Mr. Zen. Mr. Zen looked at me and smiled "Ah, Jode. Glad to see you've learned your lesson, first time in all the years I've known you that you actually bother to show up early."

I ignored him and walked over to a soccer ball, I wasn't in the mood to pretend to be happy. I was starting to feel extremely irritable; the fact that I hadn't said anything to Tylor was driving me up the wall. I don't know why it even mattered, but when I had talked to him yesterday, I had felt normal, like I was my real self, not the fake person I always pretended to be. I kicked around the soccer ball for a while until the whistle blew and Mr. Zen started Practice.

My first class was chemistry. After running around for forty minutes I really didn't feel like sitting down and studying chemical formulas. But nevertheless, I dragged myself to class and slumped down in the first row. I liked sitting at the back, but for chemistry I forced myself to sit up front. It was already complicated enough; I didn't need any distractions and the best way to ensure that I paid attention was to be in row one.

I pulled out my textbook and tried to follow along. After fifty minutes of lecturing, Mrs. Reedmen told us to partner up with our lab partners and answer a few questions. I stood up and walked over to Susan Gardner. She was extremely annoying, and I couldn't stand her guts, but Mrs. Reedmen had chosen the pairs. I had even asked if I could trade partners many times, but I had been told that Susan Gardner being an *extreme pain* was not a valid excuse.

Bracing myself I sat down beside her and set my pen. "Shall we get started?"

Susan tossed her light highlighted hair behind her shoulders; just like she did every time a guy talked to her and fluttered her eyelashes. "Sure thing *Jode*."

I looked down at my textbook and flipped through it. "Alright the answer to question one is on page one fifty-nine, do you remember Mrs. Reedmen mentioning that diagram to help us understand Orbitals?"

She didn't reply for a while, so I risked looking up, she was putting on lip gloss. I stared at her in disbelief, she caught my annoyed look and misinterpreted it. "What's wrong? Too much?"

I sighed and resisted the temptation to bang my head against my textbook.Twenty-five more minutes of this? How would I survive?

Luckily, I didn't have to find out the answer to that question because a few minutes later Mrs. Reedmen's voice filled the room. "Everybody, can I have your attention?"

She waited for everyone to stop talking and then began: "I was finally able to get your project guidelines printed. I'll be handing them out in a few minutes, but I'll brief you on everything once: As I mentioned to you last week this is your Creative Application project. You chose a topic related to chemistry and compare it to anything that's relevant. The

more relevant the comparison is, the better your marks. It'll be five percent of your grade and you *will* have to present it. It's due this Friday and you will be working in groups of four."

A girl at the back raised her hand. "Can we choose our own group?"

Mrs. Reedmen frowned and shook her head sternly. "Absolutely not, as usual you'll be working with your lab partner, and another set of students."
My heart sunk at the thought of spending more time with Susan and I silently prayed that the other members would make up for it.
Mrs. Reedmen started calling up groups to take their paper. I drummed my fingers impatiently until I heard our names.
"Jode and Susan?" I got up and dragged my feet to the front, Susan didn't even bother getting up. Mrs. Reedmen gave me a small smile. "You will be working with Tylor and Hume." She faced the class. "Tylor and Hume?"
Tylor. What a coincidence.
I watched them both make their way to the front. Tylor looked absolutely exhausted; on the contrary Hume was practically bouncing up and down on the balls of his feet, as usual, it looked like he had drunk one too many cups of coffee.
I observed his odd frame and couldn't help but groan. Hume was probably the most hyperactive person I had ever met. He always had a substantial amount of extra energy, and the saddest part was he didn't ever use it to do work, I didn't even know how he was passing.
Mrs. Reedmen handed us the papers and turned back to calling out groups.
The three of us just stood there perfectly still staring at our papers; well Hume was kind of vibrating, but that was definitely as still as I had ever seen him.
I scratched the back of my head. "I guess we should get started, Friday is only two days away."

Tylor opened his mouth to speak but Hume cut him off. "Hey,

really? That's just way too awesome, I'm going skiing a day after that."

Tylor continued on as if he hadn't been interrupted. Clearly, he was used to this. "We obviously won't have enough time now, how about we meet up in the library at lunch?"

I nodded my head. "Yeah, there's only a few minutes of class left, the library it is."

Hume waved his sheet in the air. "Man, the library? I hate that place, it's so quiet. I'd rather chill outside, oh! That reminds me, did you guys hear? Yesterday Dylan pushed Abejith into the wall by accident and they ended up getting into a scrap, they're having the real fight today. "

I glanced at Tylor and now understood exactly why he looked so exhausted. He sighed slightly.

"Susan is still sitting, maybe we should go discuss over there so she won't have to catch up later."

I stared at him. "You're kidding right?"

He raised his eyebrows. "What's there to kid about? She is in our group."

It took me a while to realize that he had probably never had a conversation with her before, because if he had he definitely wouldn't be thinking of her as an asset.

Before any of us could make a move, she joined the group with a phony smile on her face.

"So, do you guys know what we're doing it on?"

Tylor didn't hesitate. "What do you mean *you guys*? I believe you're part of the group as well."

She spun around sharply, her smile turning into an ugly frown. "Did you say something?"

Tylor stared at her unnerved "Yes I did, and I think you heard me well enough."

She raised an eyebrow. "Whatever, as long as I get a good

mark I don't care. You guys better have it done on time, okay?"

Tylor frowned "No, not okay. We're meeting in the library at lunch; if you're not there you're not part of the group." She looked like she would explode; she turned back to me making a horribly disfigured pouting face.

"Jode, I know *you* understand. I don't understand chemistry, I can't be expected to deal with this stuff. You'll cover for me, right?"

I stared at her blankly. What was I supposed to say? I couldn't side with her because she was obviously wrong, but I couldn't side with Tylor either because that would make it seem like I was on his side. If word got out that I had sided with Tylor against Susan; I didn't even want to think about it.

"Well, actu–"

My words were cut off by the bell.

"Guess I'll see you guys at lunch," with that I collected my stuff and shuffled out of the room as fast as I could without actually having to run.

I let out a sigh of relief as I sunk into my chair in the computer lab. God did I love that bell.

I kind of felt guilty for leaving Tylor with the likes of those two but hey, what choice did I have?

Mr. Damon came into the classroom and started writing on the board. Computer class used to be my favorite Subject because we got to sit back and relax for most of the time, but lately I was going crazy with the stupid shows the guys always put on. It was the same thing over and over again, sure there were a few days when they decided to dedicate the day to watching video game trailers or playing an online game but most of the time it was the exact same thing. I looked around, most of the class was in now but the guys weren't here yet. That wasn't weird, they usually came in late so they wouldn't have to listen to the first twenty minutes of class in which we actually learned something.

I attempted to listen to the lecture, but boredom overpowered me. Information technology was a subject I couldn't care less about. The field I wanted to go into was chemistry; I was just here because I needed IT to get into the program I was going into.

I estimated that the guys wouldn't be here for a good ten minutes, so I had some time to myself. I turned back to the computer and typed in *www.Souls-ink.com.* That was one site I absolutely loved. It was packed with poems, thousands and thousands of poems. Most of them were real trash but there were a few that were actually worth it. I signed in as *JH* and went to my favorites list. I had a couple of favorite authors, but my all-time favorite was NBW. I clicked his name and was immediately taken to his profile page.

I grinned; it was hilarious. He had put stuff on it that made him look like an immature kid; I would even guess he was a kid if it weren't for the fact that his poetry was so breathtaking. Skipping his profile, I went to his poems. He had one new poem; it was entitled *Forgotten Songs*. Curious I clicked it, and when the page loaded, I allowed myself to be taken in by the strong words.

FORGOTTEN SONGS

```
From deep, deep, memories rise, memories
hidden far too long.
Forgotten thoughts, long held sighs, a
piercing guilt trodden song.

Voices sing reminding me of all the
deeds I'd done.
Deeds larger than the open sea, larger
than the sun.

My memories remind me of my dream to
erase all my tracks.
My memories increase my will to
scream, to take my actions back.

These voices seem to eat my mind, they
quietly torture my soul.
They claw and gnaw at my injured
heart; to change them is my goal.

These voices play with my sanity, my
thoughts trapped in a net.
These voices sound like a song to me,
the songs of guilt and regret.
```

I blinked. Wow.

I *did* have voices in my head. Regrets that were singing to me, trying to remind me of the things I did. They were calling me, but I always pushed them back. I never heard what they were trying to say.

Maybe I was so restless at school because the songs were louder. Everything around me reminded me of all the wrong decisions I had made.

Still deep in thought I commented on the poem and then closed the screen. A few minutes later, Hudson and the gang walked in triumphantly. They didn't even bother giving an explanation about their lateness and Mr. Damon didn't seem to care. They walked over and sat beside me. "Man, you actually came early. You should've stayed with us."

I smiled. "I didn't know where you guys were."

Miles turned on the internet. "Yeah? Well, you missed out! Some kid bumped into Hudson, and he beat the life out of him!"

No wonder they looked so happy.

I put on my most convincing frown. "Man, I always miss the fun."

Hudson looked at me. "Maybe you'd witness more fun if you actually hung with us after school."

I laughed. "Yeah, maybe. But I just got so much to do."

Ryan looked at me suspiciously. "What's so important that you've been gone for two weeks, huh?"

I tried to make my frown look more convincing. "I was working on the chemistry ISU."

Ryan raised his eyebrows. "Isn't your ISU topic on the

Aufbau process? How could such an easy topic take you that long?"

I tried not to groan; I had forgotten Ryan was in my chemistry class. Couldn't it have been Miles? Ryan may be known for his laziness but unlike Miles he was actually smart.

"Okay maybe I wasn't working on the ISU."

Miles nudged me on the arm. "Then? You better not be hiding something"

These guys were so annoying; I was going to have to play my trump card.

I put on a serious face. "Family stuff."

These words were followed by a solemn silence. Miles spoke: "Oh, your brother again?"

I shrugged. "All I know is it isn't gonna be over soon. Maybe I'll hang with you guys till eight, but after that I have to get straight home."

Hudson shrugged. "Sure, thing man."

I wanted to laugh in their faces, but I kept my serious face on. Sure, I felt bad about lying but I knew that the only way they'd shut up was if I said *family stuff* was happening. That was one thing they didn't pry into. Especially with me.

Ryan nudged me and grinned. "Yo, you got partnered with Reef and that hyper kid?"

I cringed; I was hoping he hadn't noticed. "Yeah."

Miles immediately started laughing. "You serious? Man, you suck! You got stuck with the old man and the retard? That's priceless!"

I tried not to sink lower in my chair as his laughter washed over me. "Yeah, it really does suck."

Ryan grinned wider. "Hey, Reef is pretty smart. At least you won't have to do any work."

Hudson frowned threateningly. "Reef is smart?"

Ryan instantly sat back in his chair "I meant stupid."

Hudson stared at him for a while, then decided to let it go. He faced the computer and turned on the latest episode of 'Weapons of Mass Destruction'. As glad as I was for the distraction, I zoned out again as I always did when the mindless shooting began. The entire episode probably had around six seconds of actual dialogue. I rolled my eyes as an actor did impossibly exaggerated gymnastics move in order to avoid a bullet. If that had been real life the bullet would have killed him before he even thought about moving a muscle. Forget jumping eight feet into the air and ricocheting skillfully in six different directions before landing.

I glanced at everyone's expressions and to my great disgust, they seemed utterly impressed by his moves. What type of people did I hang out with?

I looked one row ahead and saw Tylor; he was saving his work. I watched him for a while more and saw him log onto a site. I was too far away to read what site he was on, but the format looked impossibly familiar. My eyes widened when I realized he was on *Souls-ink.*

Why was I surprised? He *was* a poet. I saw him go to his profile and start reading. His profile name was big enough for me to make out that it had three letters. The first one looked suspiciously like an N. I grinned, Somehow, I had a strong feeling I knew who NBW was.

Miles punched me on the shoulder. "What's wrong with you? He just got shot! What's the smile for?"

I hadn't even noticed what was going on in the movie. I leaned back trying to look casual. "I'm excited to see what happens next?"

Miles eyed me for a moment then grinned. "Yeah, he'll win, you're right."

I looked at the screen and not surprisingly the hero staggered up and pulled out his 'secret weapon' the gang started hollering and high fiving each other as the hero maneuvered the weapon with amazing skill. Someone shot at him, and he flipped in the air while slashing the shooter across the throat. Apparently, a bullet in the leg was doing nothing to falter his performance.

I forced myself to watch the rest of the episode and nearly hopped with joy when the bell rang.

I pushed ahead of everyone and fast-walked to the door hoping no one would stop me; for once things actually worked in my favor. I made it to the library without getting spotted even once.

As soon as I entered, I saw Tylor sitting on one of the tables. After making sure no one I knew was in the library I walked over and sat down. He had a notebook and pen with him, and he was staring at the sheet we had been given.

I pulled out my own sheet and stared down at it. "The others didn't come yet?"

He glanced up at me and for a second, he seemed surprised. "Oh, I didn't even see you come in."

I half smiled. "You thought I wouldn't show, didn't you?"

He smiled awkwardly. "Of course not." Then after a brief pause, he added: "Well, kind of."

I tried not to smile again and glanced at his blank notebook. "So, you didn't think of a topic yet?"

He frowned. "It's proving harder than I thought. The project guidelines are so vague: It basically says that we have to select any topic on chemistry that we covered this year and put a new spin on it."

I raised my eyebrows questioningly. "New spin?"

"Yes, like look at it through a different perspective. And the more relevant the analysis the better mark we get."

I stared at the paper. "What kind of a project is that?"

Tylor shrugged. "She did say Creative Application…how about we do it on amides?"

I thought about it. "Okay, so what would we relate them to?"

His eyebrows furrowed in thought. "We could relate amides to…the way…wow this is hard. Maybe we should look at what an amide really is first." He thought for a while more. "Okay, so amides are organic compounds that have a carbon atom double bonded to an oxygen atom…What could we possibly relate that to?"

I smiled sarcastically. "That's easy."

Tylor grinned. "No seriously, I think we should relate it to something in our life. Maybe… maybe the carbon atom can stand for peace and the oxygen atom can stand for life and the double bond can signify the bridge that separates the two yet binds them together to form the place we live in today…?"

I stared at him for a long time and then despite myself snorted with laughter. "Please tell me that was a joke."

He grinned. "Of course, it was, I'm not planning on failing."

We spent the better part of an hour flipping through our textbooks and trying to think of something, but in the end, we came up blank. Tylor sighed "We only have two da—"

"Hey! Sorry we're late. The fight was crazy outside, but Mr. Black came, so if he asks, we were here the whole time, okay?"

We both looked up simultaneously to see Hume standing there with a soft drink in his hand and Susan standing behind him.

Tylor glanced at his watch. "There's only twenty minutes left."

Susan gave him a satisfied smile. "Well, I showed up so whatever, now my part is done."

Tylor looked like he was going to argue and then he just shook his head. "Well, if you don't work now, you'll just end up failing the presentation."
She glared at him. "Was that a *threat*?"
Tylor stared back calmly. "No, it was a fact."
Susan's face contorted with such rage it looked comical.
She looked like she was debating on what to do, then she slowly pulled up a chair and sat down. Hume followed.
"Okay, so what are we supposed to do again?"
Tylor started explaining everything to them. Why was he wasting his time? Neither of them knew any chemistry at all.
Hume furrowed his brows trying to focus "So like, we have to pick any topic in the book? And then relate it to life?"
Tylor nodded "yeah, any ideas?"
Hume pulled Tylor's textbook towards him and started flipping through it. Susan leaned forward and joined him. I was sure they were only pretending to read the actual words.

As expected, at the end of 20 minutes, we still had nothing.

But Susan was looking at Tylor differently. "You're actually good at explaining stuff. Do you think you could help me out? I need the help."
She really looked distraught "I can't afford to fail this; I'm going to be in so much trouble. I need this to pass the class."
Hume nodded in agreement.

5% made no difference to me. I was already doing well.

Tylor scratched his head. "I'd be happy to help. And don't

worry about the project, we'll figure it out, *together*."

Susan and Hume didn't look very happy when he said *together but* nodded and got up and left.

Tylor put his papers away and pulled a novel out.
"What are you reading?"
He seemed shocked I was still there, or maybe he was surprised I was talking to him.
"*The Picture of Dorian Gray*, I'm rereading it."
"Sounds boring."
He half smiled "You should try it, it's a real mindbender."
He closed the book and slid it over to me. "Seriously, try it out and let me know what you think."

I stared at the black cover of the novel but didn't pick it up.

Once he left the library, I picked up the novel and flipped through it absentmindedly, it couldn't hurt to try it out, right?

♦♦♦♦♦♦

The next few days, we gathered in the library every lunch to try and get some work done. We weren't making much progress because Susan and Hume both starting using that time for homework help instead.
I was surprised at how patient Tylor was with them both. I was also surprised at how smart Susan was when she actually focused.
Friday came faster than ever and before we knew it, we were waiting for Mrs. Reedmen to enter the panicked classroom. Tylor was pacing back and forth frantically, shooting out random thoughts that to my great dismay weren't making

much sense. "Alright, alright, what about this? Maybe we can talk about Chemical equilibrium? The way… No that doesn't make sense. What about oxidation numbers?"

I frowned. "Why'd this have to be five percent?"

Tylor stopped pacing. "No, why did the project have to be today? I was busy studying for physics for the past two days, and we spent all our library time on homework that I almost forgot about this completely."

"Yeah, I've been going crazy with that physics test too. How about we say something abou—"

Mrs. Reedmen chose that moment to enter, and the class went dead silent; the type of silent that could only be born on presentation day.

She walked up to the front and put her textbooks onto the table with a thud. "Good morning students, I believe you all know what day it is."

The class mumbled a reply and Mrs. Reedmen smiled.

"Alright, so who wants to go first?"

Nobody raised their hands. Mrs. Reedmen sighed and pulled out the attendance sheet. "I guess I'll just have to choose myself."

I tried not to disappear in my seat as I silently prayed that she wouldn't pick us. Maybe if Tylor had 10 more minutes, he would figure something out. At that instant, the classroom door burst open, and Hume came barging into class. "Sorry I'm late! I actually woke up early today but there was so much snow the bus got held up, you should've seen the bus driver's face he looked like he was gonna explode!"

Mrs. Reedmen looked up from her paper and smiled. "Well Hume since you're here why don't you start with your

group?"
I resisted the temptation to run across the room and strangle
him.
Hume didn't look worried. "Man, this isn't my day. Alright
I'll go first. We are ready right?"
Now he was facing Tylor. Tylor looked equally stressed, but
he just sighed and stood up. "Yes, I guess we'll go."
All four of us walked up to the front and stared at the class.
I glanced at Mrs. Reedmen and knew asking for another day
would be futile. She never gave second chances to anyone.
It would be better to just wing it instead of making it look
like we knew nothing.
All eyes were on us.
Mrs. Reedmen frowned. "Anytime now, you have five
minutes."
Susan leaned forward, she had tears in her eyes. "I can't fail
this, please tell me you guys have something ready."

Hume looked livid. "Do you want us to fail? Just say
anything!"
Mrs. Reedmen shook her head and wrote something down.
I bit my bottom lip thinking fast and took a risk. "Sorry about
that, actually the comparison we chose was based
on…amides."
Tylor coughed to cover his shock and then looked up with an
extremely serious face. "Yes, the topic we chose was on
amides." He walked up to the board and drew the structure.
"As you can see, an amide consists of - "
Susan cut him off "a carbon atom, an oxygen atom and a
double bond."
Tylor beamed and continued "But how, may I ask, can this be
related to our lives in any way possible?"
I walked up to the board trying my best not to pass out and

burst out laughing at the same time. "It's actually quite simple when you think about it. You see we figured that for an amide to exist it requires these three components: The carbon atom, the oxygen atom and the double bond."

Tylor nodded in agreement. "Yes, and if even one of these were missing it would cease to be an amide."

I braced myself trying to remember what Tylor had said that day in the library. "So looking at it through that perspective we decided that the carbon atom could easily be a symbol of peace, the oxygen atom a symbol of the world or life as we know it, and the double bond was a signification of the bridge between life and peace; holding them apart yet binding them at the same time."

I risked a glance at Mrs. Reedmen, she looked like she was buying it.

Tylor labeled the three on the board and turned to face the class.

"If you really think about it, it's true. The world, the notion of peace and the bridge between the two are all correlated. Would the world still exist if there was no notion of peace? Would the notion of peace exist if there was no world? Would the world and the notion of peace exist if there was no link between the two?"

He paused for effect.

"The answer is no. Just like the amide, all of them are a reflection of one another. "

Mrs. Reedmen seemed impressed. "So, tell me, what is this link between the world and the notion of peace?"

Tylor smiled easily. "The link between the world and the notion of peace? That's simple, it's contemplation."

Mrs. Reedmen raised her eyebrows, but Tylor continued. "If we humans failed to contemplate then we would never be able to understand how to attain peace. If we didn't ever stop to consider the miracles around us what could possibly enable us to comprehend this majestic notion? If we failed to observe the way the rain falls and in doing so causes greenery to rise, how would we understand to respect the life around us? If we never contemplated on the ever-gentle stars in the sky and the humble clouds moving by, how would we ever understand that the purpose of the world is more than what we've made it? That it is possible to coexist without devastation, just as other things do."

The whole class was transfixed. I took advantage of the moment and jumped in. "Yeah, and contemplation represents the double bond because just like our thoughts it can be broken, not as unlikely as a single bond and not as easily as a triple bond, but on average. It's easy for us to get distracted by everything but under the right conditions we stay on track and in doing so…produce an amide."

Tylor stared for a while and then smiled slightly. "Thank you for listening to our presentation, we hope you learned something."

There was a moment of awkward silence and then the class clapped.

I let relief flood me and I almost sank to the floor. Mrs. Reedmen smiled at us. "That was absolutely wonderful! That's exactly what I was looking for. Excellent work!"

Susan signed in relief and smiled at Tylor, for what I was sure was the first time ever.

"Th..thanks."

He nodded and smiled back, then turned to me and grinned. "Amides? When you said that, I almost laughed out loud."

I grinned back and shrugged. "Hey, desperate times call for desperate measures."

I sat down and watched the remaining presentations distractedly, all the while accepting the dawning realization that this was the most fun, I had in a very, very long time.

Eight

Cool people were expected to have cool nicknames.

Since I hung out with Hudson, I was apparently cool, but if anyone ever heard my nickname and understood what it symbolized, I would probably fall fifty levels down on the social ladder.

My nickname had been given to me by my *loving* brother, Jay. When I was seven years old my cousins from my dad's side of the family called and said they were coming to Canada for a month, so they needed a place to stay. My parents graciously offered to let them live with us. My first impression of them when they walked into our house was that they were a perfect family. Two parents, two daughters and two sons.

They all had the exact same shade of blonde hair except the father, whose hair was slightly darker.

We had a three-bedroom house, so me and my brother had to sleep in one room with the two guys and the girls got my brother's room. All of them were loud and friendly; I couldn't help but like every member of their family. Well, everyone that is, except one.

There was one particular cousin who drove me insane. This cousin was a little four-year-old girl who probably weighed more than me and always had snot running down her face, they called her Jo. The first day she entered I had immediately noticed her; she just emitted this weird aura. Everyone else thought she looked innocent enough, but after a week of living with her we all discovered that she was probably the most repulsive creature to have set foot into our house — and that's a compliment.

 A good example of her habits would be this thing she would do whenever we sat to eat. Every time we sat down for breakfast, lunch, or dinner she would take an empty glass from the kitchen and waddle up the stairs. She would come back down after a minute or so and oddly enough her empty glass would be full to the top. The first few times we ignored it, but after two days we began to get curious.

The next time we sat to eat we watched her carefully and sure enough she went with the glass upstairs. Me and my brother followed her and poised ourselves on the top stair in a position so we could see exactly where she was heading. We watched her go past all the rooms and into the bathroom; she paused in front of the sink and held the glass with both her pudgy hands, then she walked right past the sink and straight to the toilet. We watched in disbelief as she dipped the entire glass inside the toilet and brought it out, full of water.

Disgusting.

I don't know how other people would have reacted, but me and Jay reacted by laughing until we hit the floor. I mean come on, when there was clean, safe drinking water downstairs why would someone come all the way upstairs just to get bacteria infested water from a toilet? It didn't matter that she was only four; she should still have some form of common sense.

We were laughing so hard that we didn't notice that she was now standing in front of us. Our laughter immediately turned into fear and we doubled back, trying to distance ourselves from that thing she held in her hand. For a while she stared then she turned to me and in a squeaky voice said: "hey your name is Jode right?"
I had nodded my head. This positive gesture caused her fat face to break out into a huge grin. "Hey that's super! My name is JODE-ette!"

It didn't take Jay very long to pick the name up and start ruining my life. It was horrible. I didn't really mind the name in itself, but the thing it symbolized sent shudders down my spine. Who would want someone who drank toilet water and always had snot running down their face to be linked with them in any way? I mean what if she started idolizing me or something because her name was immediately connected to mine. It was a scary thought.

It became a family thing for all the guys to call me Jodette wherever they saw me. I guess it wasn't that bad since it was mainly domestic. I just had to keep praying that my cousins or my brother wouldn't show up at school. The thought of Jay at school sent shudders down my spine. Jay *had* come to school before, in fact he had met Hudson and the gang many times, but he hadn't let the name slip, I hadn't given him an opportunity.

Jay and I had never really gotten along. I was constantly reminded by my parents (whenever they were home, that is) about the way we hated each other's guts since we were barely old enough to walk. It may sound like an exaggeration, but I knew it was true. When I was just three years old, I developed this thing, that whenever Jay came into the same room as me, I'd throw the nearest object at his head for no apparent reason. One time I was in the family room watching TV and Jay came in the room. Unfortunately for him the nearest object to me just happened to be a glass. Keep in mind that I was three and that I didn't really care to consider the difference between *throw-able* and *non-throw-able*. So, I threw the glass at his head and immediately regretted it, I'd rather not go into the details of the scenario but let me just say there was blood.

I had begun crying and my parents came running only to see their eldest son fainted on the floor and their youngest son bawling his eyes out while standing beside a pile of broken glass.

After that incident my parents had forced me to stop throwing things at him, and by the time I was nine I had grown out of the habit.

Yeah, I might sound pretty evil to you right now but it's not like Jay was some sort of saint. I may have had the odd habit of throwing something at his head whenever I saw him, but he had a habit of breaking every new thing I got. When I was thirteen and he was fifteen, I received my fourth soccer trophy. Jay was thrilled, not because he was happy his little brother won. No. He wasn't into sports. But he was happy because there was something new of mine to break. I had known that he had this annoying habit, so I hid my trophy at the top of my closet the second we came home. The next night I came home from school and checked up on the trophy. My heart had sunk as I saw that in place of my trophy was a brown paper bag; I pulled the bag down and opened it to see the trophy smashed to pieces, under the shards of plastic was a crumpled piece of paper.

I pulled out the paper and opened it. Green crayon filled the paper, it read: 'UNTIL NEXT TIME JODETTE.'

My parents scolded him for the better part of an hour and in the end when they asked him to apologize. He just grinned and said *no*.

He had gotten grounded for three weeks after that, but eventually things returned to normal, and everyone forgot about the incident.

Personally, I believe that my parents should have paid

more attention to his actions because if you ask me, his rebellious behavior then, had set the base for what he had become now. Now his pranks were much worse of course. Most of them involved his deadly viper. I shuddered thinking about those glistening fangs. I was so tired of being scared of the snake, I had to overcome my fear so the next time he left it under my blanket or in my backpack, I wouldn't freak out completely.

I got off the sofa and flipped off the TV. Both my parents worked, and they were never *ever* home, they just showed up at night and by then they were too tired to talk —forget discipline their children.

These old memories always made me feel melancholic. I walked over to the kitchen and while pouring myself a glass of juice, glanced at the time. It was 8:00pm. The guys were going to a movie tonight; I was praying they wouldn't remember I was supposed to go with them.

Speak of the devil.

I pulled my ringing phone out of my pocket and read the caller ID; it was Hudson.

I considered allowing it to keep ringing but after the fifth ring I picked up.

I tried to sound cheerful. "Hey, Hudson, what's up?"

I barely finished my sentence before he replied excitedly. "We're waiting for you! What time'll you be down?"

I feigned innocence. "Huh? Waiting? Oh yeah! The movie was tonight! Aww man I forgot."

Hudson groaned. "Are you serious! You haven't even left yet?"

I tried to sound sad. "Yeah, there's no way I'll make it before the movie starts."

"I guess I could pick you up." He offered hesitantly.

I pushed harder. "No, you'll miss the beginning of the movie, plus I have to stay home after eight for a while, remember?"

There was a pause from Hudson's side then he sighed. "Yeah, okay man but next time you better come."

"Yeah, sure" I turned off my phone. That was close.

I threw my bag in my locker and headed to the cafeteria. The morning had been rough. The gang had gone crazy talking

about the movie and re-watching clips of it on the computer
and their phones. Once again, the theme had been exactly the
same. Shooting, fighting, and killing.
The only reason I hadn't gone crazy by now was because I
was leaving for a doctor's appointment right after lunch.
I joined the line of people waiting to get their lunches and
scanned the cafeteria. Like every high school our school was
divided into cliques, like every high school everyone judged
you by the people you hung with, and not for the person you
were. All the tables were practically full, except one. This one
table had three people sitting on it. I didn't recognize two of
them. But the third was Tylor Reef. Tylor was reading a book,
and the other two were eating their lunches. All three were
sitting far apart from each other.
I glanced at the table I was supposed to sit at and cringed as I
saw a table full of loud, annoying people trying to impress
each other. I looked back at Tylor's table and my pity turned
into envy as I wished I was sitting there quietly reading a
book instead of sitting with the 'cool' people and acting
fake. Looking at him instantly caused the last verse from his
poem,
'anti socialists' to play in my head.

*"What goes through the minds of those who sit and do not
speak?*
Is it them who are odd, or are we the true freaks?"

He was always so quiet, yet he didn't seem unsure of himself
at all. My thoughts were interrupted as I was pushed forward
in the line. I got some fries with a drink and then headed down
to the table. I sat down beside Miles and picked up a fry, but
the fry never made it to my mouth because my hand had

frozen with my gaze as I realized that Jay was in the cafeteria making his way down to my table. Ryan caught my stare and looked up. "Everybody, it's Jode's bro!" Whoever heard him immediately stopped talking.

Jay walked over to the table and stared at me dully. "Where's your phone? I've been calling you for thirty minutes."

I shrugged. "Must've left it off. Shouldn't you be at college?" He ran a hand through his maroon-colored hair and shrugged back. "Yeah, but mom said to take you to the doctor's office for your appointment."

I raised my eyebrows. "Since when do you ever listen to mom?"

He rolled his eyes. "Come on and get up already, I don't have all day to stand around and have your stupid friends stare at me."

I looked back and sure enough everyone on the table was gawking at Jay. The second they realized they were being discussed they immediately looked down and started whispering among themselves. They all knew his reputation, and nobody wanted to say anything to offend him. I glanced at Hudson. He was the only one staring Jay in the face and there were clear signs of anger ebbing into his features — once again, I felt a vibe that sent shudders down my spine. He had always hated Jay. Whenever he came over to my house or met Jay outside, he only had bad things to say. I stood up, "Miles, throw my stuff away for me?"

Miles nodded quickly. "Sure."

The second Jay walked out the cafeteria door the air of awkwardness immediately evaporated, and everybody resumed their original loud conversations.

I pushed my way out after Jay. I could have gone myself,

why did *he* come to pick me up? I was sure it had something to do with the junk I had hidden. It was either that or he had a test that he wanted to skip. "Hey, I'm signing myself out, okay?"
He ignored me and kept walking. I sighed and assuming he would wait for me, made my way to the office.

I walked through the familiar floors. This was the route I always took to get away from people, the route that took me right by the Photography room. I felt embarrassment possess me as I remembered that Tylor had heard me reciting his verses in this hallway. I had been reciting those verses because whenever I experienced solitude all I remembered was that beautiful place. I signed myself out and then jogged back to the main doors, as soon as I stepped outside, I caught sight of him. He was sitting in his red Chevrolet honking his horn at no one in particular. I ran up to the car and waited for him to open the door, he pretended not to notice me.
I waited for a while more and then knocked on his window impatiently. He stopped honking and I felt relief as I thought he would finally let me in, boy was I wrong. He pulled down the window, reached over and flicked on the radio. In an instant the entire parking lot was filled with loud vulgar music. I held my head and resisted the temptation to break the windows. After a few minutes of torturing my ear drums, he turned to me in mock surprise. "Oh, hello there Jodette didn't see you. Can I help you with something?"
I glared at him. "Open the door."
He pretended he couldn't hear and cupped his hand to his ear. "What's that Jodette? *Louder*? You want the music louder?"
He grinned and increased the volume by at least ten. I had to cover my ears in order to stop them from exploding. This guy

was mental. Why did he even come to school if he didn't like picking me up? Whenever mom asked him to do anything, he always ignored her, but today was different. As the music got to me, I realized that he had probably just come to annoy me to death. I opened my eyes and started pounding on the door. "Open the door you retard! Why'd you come to pick me up if you didn't even want me in your car?!"

Jay turned off the music and put on a serious expression. "Hey, man, I think you're right, maybe there is something wrong with me. Maybe I *am* mental; you know I think some

crazy kid smashed a glass on my head when I was five that must've really messed me up." That stupid grin was back on his face.

The bulge on the front of his sweater started moving, and Mr. Snake stuck his head out, peering at me curiously. The reptile seemed to have cooled off and didn't bare his fangs as it set its deadly gaze on me. Feeding it every time Jay left seemed to be paying off.

Jay grinned "Mr.Snake, you want to say hi to your uncle?" before I could protest, Jay passed the snake over, and it coiled itself onto my arms with an iron grip. It slowly slithered up my arm until it was face to face with me. There was no glass to protect me this time.

I was sweating "c..come on Jay, please, just get this thing of me and leave…I'll go myself. Just get this thing off me."

Normally I wouldn't be this scared, but now me and Mr. Snake had serious history between us. I couldn't predict what the reptile would do. Did it even remember? It had always been eerily intelligent…looking at its intense eyes I knew it did remember.

After about two minutes of paralyzing and frightening

silence, the car door opened, and Jay gently eased Mr.Snake back into his arms, grinning as if he was holding a small infant and not one of the most poisonous reptiles in the world. "And that's what you get for messing with my stuff again." Mr.Snake disappeared back into his sweater.

I took a deep breath of relief and slipped inside the car without looking at him. "So, you found them?"

He raised his eyebrows "Under the patio? Come on you already tried that like ten times."

I gritted my teeth and couldn't help but wonder what was worse, a car ride with Jay and his loyal pet or a lunch period with Hudson? That was a hard one, but I think I'd go with the car ride. At least Hudson didn't have poisonous fangs he could sink into me at any given moment.

At least not literally.

I stared out the window and did some calculations. The ride from my house to the doctors was around fifteen minutes. The school was in the opposite direction, and it was a seven-minute car ride to school. So, getting from school to the doctors would take about twenty-two minutes. Twenty-two minutes in a car with Jay. All the horrible possibilities flooded my head. I tried to distract myself but was interrupted by Jay's voice. "So, why do you gotta go to the doctors? Gained too much weight?"

I rolled my eyes. Jay had serious problems with fat jokes, I was nowhere near fat, yet he always called me fat, it probably had something to do with Jodette. I looked out the window. "No, it's just an annual checkup."

Jay grinned. "Ah, I remember those."

I looked at him disgusted. "Yeah, it wouldn't hurt you to get

one yourself."
Jay grinned. "Me? I'm the flag of life, I don't need checkups."
I tried not to punch him. "You seriously believe that? Now I know you need a checkup more than anything."
He shook his head wisely. "Jodette, Jodette, Jodette. If I got a checkup I'd be sent to jail, surely you know that by now."

I avoided eye contact. "Maybe that's a good thing."
He grinned. "Aw, I'm not that bad am I?"
I didn't reply. He *should* go to jail, if that's what it would take to get him off of his addiction. I examined his face. He wasn't really skinny, but his skin had a really unhealthy glow. His eyes were drooping, and his hair was unkempt. Right on top of his nose he had a thin scar and another scar stretched from his chin to his left cheek. His jacket sleeve was pulled up enough for me to catch sight of another long thin scar stretched across his arm. All these scars were a result of his constant fights. It was a wonder they had healed so well considering that he never saw a doctor.
That stupid *thing* he did had ruined his life. Ever since he had gotten hooked, he stopped associating with normal people, he started spending all his time outside and his grades had suffered horribly. In grade ten he was an honor roll student, sure he had attitude problems, but he had been extremely smart. But now… he was barely passing his courses. I stared down at my feet. How much time was left until he completely caved?
Jay stopped at a red light and impatiently drummed his hand on the steering wheel. "So, how's school?"
I nodded. "Normal."
Jay grinned, "And what about that Hercules guy? How's he?"
I looked at him confused.
His grin widened. "You know, curly blond hair, big muscles,

stupid expression on his face?"
I couldn't help but smile. "Yeah, him…he's still the same."
The red light turned green, and he continued driving.
"Every time I meet him, he acts like I killed his mom, what's up with that?"
Then in a fake nagging voice he added, "Has Jodette been telling lies about me?"
I rolled my eyes. "No *Jodette* has not been telling lies about you, Hercules is just messed up. He hates who he wants to hate."

Jay didn't reply to that.
The silence didn't last long as a few minutes later he pulled into the parking lot of the clinic and in a British accent announced: "We have now reached the fat camp for obese people. Will all obese patients please exit the car and enter the building, be warned that all chocolate bars and candy will be confiscated."
I jumped off the car and turning to him, allowed myself to smile. He may be annoying, but he was also funny, I'd give him that much.
"Are you dropping me home?"
He pretended to look shocked. "Don't you think you've weighed down my car enough for one day?"
I smiled, "come on…"
He shrugged "Too bad, I got somewhere to be. Take the bus," and with that he drove off. I watched his car go and my smile evaporated. How could he act so normal when he was going through so much? I made my way to the clinic door and tried to erase the image of the scars on his body from my mind.

I paused outside Jay's door and once again glanced at my watch. He would probably be home around nine, so I had some time.

I pushed the door open and hastily stepped over the maze of clothes and garbage that littered his floor. Mr. Snake wasn't in his tank today, Jay had taken him.

 I reached his bed and dug under it until I found the box I was looking for. Bracing myself I lifted the lid and glanced inside, it was full of needles.

My heart rate increased tenfold, and my hands began trembling slightly, but I forced myself to work fast. I pulled them all out and stuffed them in a brown paper bag; I had to get rid of them before he got home. But how? The last time I had thrown them in the garbage he had found them in a second, and the time I had buried them he had just beat the answer out of me. Not this time I thought, this time I had had enough.

"What d'you think you're doing?"

I froze at the sound of his voice and then turned around indignantly. "What does it look like I'm doing?"

Jay looked furious. He walked over and made to grab me, but I was too quick. I ducked and made a break for the door. It didn't take him long to catch up and before I knew it, I was pinned to the wall. "You're so annoying, how many times do I have to tell you not to mess with my stuff?"

I struggled to break free. "You're ruining your life."

He glared at me. "What's it to you? Now give me the bag before you get hurt."

I stared at him defiantly and tightened my grip on the bag. "You don't even know what you're doing! I swear you'll regret it one day."

He snatched the bag out of my hand and despite my efforts got it easily enough. "Do you think I'm that stupid? These things won't be the end of me if that's what you're trying to say; now get out."
I tightened my fists and glared at him. "Why don't you just stop?"
He threw the bag onto his bed and turned away from me. "Why do you care?"
I resisted the temptation to hit him as hard as I could. "Why wouldn't I care? Now stop changing the subject and just answer for once. What's so bad about life that you're trying to end it?"
He turned to me furiously. "Who said anything about ending it? That's not what I'm trying to do."

His voice took on a strange tone, "I guess you can say it's a way out of life… without dying"
My blood boiled and I took a step forward. "Do you realize how dumb you sound? That's the stupidest thing I've ever heard."

In a split second he grabbed me by the collar of my shirt and pushed me out of his room. "You need to get out of my life and get your own."
With that he slammed the door.
I stared at his closed door and trying not to swear kicked it angrily. If only my parents would bother staying at home; they both ran a business, so they were always travelling across borders. Whenever they were home, I always tried to tell them what he was doing but they never took me seriously. They thought Jay was just 'going through a phase'.

I almost spit on the floor at the thought and Tylor's words rushed back into my head. *If we humans failed to contemplate then we would never be able to understand how to attain peace. If we didn't ever stop to consider the miracles around us what could possibly enable us to comprehend this majestic notion?*

Jay said he did what he did because it made him feel at ease, but it was clear he only did it because he didn't know what peace really was. He hadn't contemplated on life enough to know what he was doing to himself.

I frowned and stared at the ground; the only thing that could make him understand would be some sort of miracle.

Nine
TYLOR

I climbed down the stairs as quietly as possible. Praying that nobody would hear me, just a few more steps and I would be out. I could almost feel the cold night air against my face.

I heard stirring.

Uh oh, it was a commercial break; they were coming to the kitchen. All hopes of stealth abandoned, I ran down the remaining stairs and dived for the door, maybe I would still make it. My hopes were drowned as I heard a sharp voice come from behind me. "Where do you think you're going?"

I turned around slowly to see my mom standing there with her hands on her hips and eyebrows raised.

I coughed. "I was just…checking if I left my… bag here."

She looked at me skeptically.

"Oh really? I didn't know you had to wear your jacket and shoes to do that."

I glanced down at my winter gear and smiled at her. "Okay I was just going out to get some fresh air."
She raised her eyebrows higher. "At 10:40pm?"
I scratched my head and pretended to look innocent. "Is it really that late? I thought it was nine."

Mom looked like she was about to lose it. She tapped her foot against the floor. "Tylor, I don't know what's wrong with you! You never come and spend time with us, and you're always out late at night. I thought I told you yesterday that you can no longer go out after nine."
I thought back to yesterday, she had seen me come home at midnight and when I told her I had just been prowling, she had refused to believe me and canceled my late-night walks.
I frowned. "I already told you that I was just on a walk, I've been walking at night since I was in grade nine in case you hadn't noticed."
Mom caught the bitterness in my voice and immediately raised her own. "YOU WERE OUT FOR THREE HOURS! YOU EXPECT ME TO BELIEVE YOU WALKED FOR THAT LONG?"
I looked around and when I realized that she was waiting for a reply I quickly nodded my head.
She held her head in her hands "OH MY GOSH WHAT DO I *DO* WITH YOU?!" she took a deep breath and then looked at me sadly. "Sometimes I wish you would just be more normal."

She said it so offhandedly, as if it were a fact. All of a sudden, I felt drained.

I saw a flash of golden scales in my mind and my eyes filled up with tears. How had I made that up? What actually was wrong with me?

I was abnormal, wasn't I?

She had hit my weakest spot. It wasn't my heart that broke, but my spirit.

The tense silence was broken by Siara's loud voice. "MOM, HURRY UP! YOU'RE MISSING THE BIG SCENE!"
I was actually glad to hear those words, maybe now I'd be left alone. My mom stared down at me and after a few moments let out a sigh. "Whatever. Do whatever you want because I know family doesn't mean anything to you."

She looked at me for a second more, then turned around and went back to the family room. I wonder if she had been expecting me to follow. I chewed my bottom lip and recited a few verses that I had read earlier regarding patience.

But it didn't help. I felt a dizzying sense of confusion. I forced myself into the family room. The TV was blaring at its maximum and my sister and my mom were sitting there with their eyes bulging and mouths slightly open. The way every person looked while watching TV, once I had actually recorded people on a school movie night. I had gotten them from an angle where you couldn't see the screen, so it looked like an ordinary person sitting on a chair. The lighting had been horrible, but the effects were exactly as I had predicted. When I uploaded it and muted the volume the severity of their expressions became clear. It looked like they were either being brainwashed, or they were mentally retarded. I deleted it afterward of course; it was far too scary to watch. I glanced at Siara and my mom; they were completely absorbed in the fake story that was being played in front of them.

Was this actually normal?

Pity overwhelmed my being as I saw how they watched, so desperately as if wishing they could be in the show. Maybe they thought that if they paid enough attention, they might just become a part of the show. In a way they were right.
Making a quick decision, I turned to my mom. "There's a place I want to show you."
My mom didn't take her eyes off the screen. "Maybe later Tylor, not now."
I stared at her dumbfounded. "Please? I'll show you where I go."
My mom spared me a glance, "Tylor I *said* not now."
It was as if she hadn't even heard what I said. I turned around and nearly ran outside; I pulled the door open and let the wind slam it hard behind me.

My family was so desensitized it was sad. Did they really think spending time sitting in front of the TV was quality family time? I frowned and continued walking down the road. My mind filled with thoughts of all the countless times I had tried to tell my family about the dangers of excessive TV watching. I had even written a speech on the very topic and presented it at school for the annual speech competition. Sure, I had won, but I highly doubted that my words had caused even a single person to change their ways. Why was it so hard for people to stop watching TV? I mean if *I* could live without watching it, why couldn't everyone else?
The cold night air bit at my bare face and hands. In my haste to leave the house I had forgotten to wear gloves. Shivering slightly, I dug my hands into my jacket pocket in an attempt to warm them and pondered my question. Maybe people didn't want to stop watching TV because they realized that

if they stopped spending their days watching TV, they would have to start spending their days actually dealing with their lives, and the many problems that came with it.

Clearly nobody wanted to do that.

It was getting colder, and my hands stubbornly refused to warm up. Maybe a hot chocolate would help. I changed my course and a few minutes later, found myself pushing through the doors of the *ChocoChurn.*

A burst of warm air along with the smell of coffee and chocolate greeted me as I cleaned the snow off my shoes on the brown doormat. Even though it was practically eleven the place was still bustling with activity.

"Hey, Tylor!" I looked up and saw Mr. Gret, the owner of the store waving and calling me over. He was a middle- aged man who loved discussing politics and government conspiracies. Even though I wasn't the type to enjoy such topics I had always allowed him to discuss whatever he wanted with me, sometimes even for hours, he was too nice to avoid. I pushed my way to the counter, and he handed me a hot chocolate without even having to ask. I always ordered that, just one medium sized hot chocolate. I dropped two dollars onto the counter, and he smiled at me. "Can't talk today, too many customers. But drop by some other time and we'll discuss something that's been on the news for quite a while."

I accepted the thirty cent change he replaced my coins with and smiled. "The election?"

He smiled back but didn't get a chance to reply as a group of people called him over to place their order.

As soon as he left, I turned and scanned the large room in search of an empty table. All the tables had at least one person sitting on them except one on the far left. I walked over and sat down, carefully placing my cup on the table. The

ChocoChurn was one of my favorite places to stay, mainly because I could just sit and think.

I looked out of the large glass window and let the buzz of people talking carry my thoughts to a different place. The snow was falling in giant cotton ball chunks, and after a few moments of staring I couldn't help but notice that the streetlights looked like small moons floating in the sky.

It had been a while since I had seen the moon.

I almost groaned out loud as I realized I had missed February first. Jode had said the full moon would be out on the first, but I had been so busy with everything I hadn't visited the *Natural World* at all. I couldn't believe I had missed it. When would the next one be out?

My thoughts were interrupted as the front door of the coffee shop burst wide open and I saw a flash of red hair. I grinned and raised my hand to wave, but abruptly stopped myself.

He was with Hudson and his crew.

They made their way to the counter and placed their orders. Hudson was clearly having trouble walking straight.

Miles looked around and made eye contact with me and grinning, nudged Hudson in my direction. You didn't have to be Sherlock to know that things were going to get ugly, fast.

Hudson locked eyes with me and sneered. A few seconds later, he was standing in front of me. There was definitely a stagger in his step.

Without hesitating he grabbed the front of my jacket. I could smell his disgusting breath—definitely intoxicated. His eyes told me he hadn't let the computer lab incident go. He was hungry for revenge.

"Well, isn't it my lucky day…it's pretty empty in here right now, isn't it? Who's going to save you today?"

I couldn't help myself, "actually, it's pretty full."

He pushed me hard, and I fell hard on the floor. Maybe silence would have been smarter. I prepared myself for his next assault, once again, I wasn't even going to try and defend myself.

The following events happened so fast I couldn't process what was going on. All I saw was Hudson lunging again, a blur, and now Hudson was on the floor with me. As the scene in front of me began to make sense, I went pale. I couldn't believe what had just happened.

Jode pushed Hudson off me.

Everyone else was equally shocked.

Hudson spat.

"You serious right now?"

Jode didn't back down. "Just leave him alone."

In a single moment Hudson had Jode pinned to the wall. "I've been seeing you at school with him as well, what's wrong with you? It's about time I put you in your place."

Miles interrupted.

"Umm, Hudson?"

Hudson looked up and now it was his turn to go pale.

I followed his gaze and saw some guy with maroon hair and black clothes placing his drink beside a brown bag across from me. He looked up at me and I realized that he was the person who had come to pick Jode up today. I believe someone had mentioned he was Jode's brother.

 I had only glimpsed him in the cafeteria but now I could see him much clearer. In the brightly lit café, I could see that he looked sicker than me and there were two scars running across his nose and chin. I couldn't help but wonder what had caused them. The one across his nose was extremely thin, but the one on his cheek was worse, it looked newer.

Hudson backed away from Jode, still furious—but now with obvious fear stunting his bravado.

"You're going to regret this, Jode."

Miles stepped in.

"Yeah, this place sucks anyways, let's go to the Den." For once, Hudson took Miles's advice and they disappeared without even waiting for their orders to arrive.

They were scared out of their minds.

The maroon haired guy didn't even look at me and turned to Jode. "Karma's awesome, isn't it? You saved this guy here, and I come swooping in to save your sorry b-"

Jode pushed past him.

"Shut up."

We watched Jode leave.

Snickering, he proceeded to sit across from me. "The least he could have done is say thank you, you know? Look at me, I'm literally a hero."

 Maybe not a hero, but I couldn't help marvel at how he had done nothing, yet Hudson went running for the hills.

I guess I had been staring at him really hard because after a few moments he looked up at me with an annoyed expression on his face. "S'there a problem?"
I quickly shifted my eyes back to the window, trying to pretend that nothing had just happened.

"You're Jode's brother, right?"

He didn't seem surprised. "Yeah,
why?"

I shrugged. "You looked familiar."

He chewed on his bagel for a while then with his mouth still half full he asked: "You a friend of Jode's?"

I didn't know how to respond to that. The magnanimity of the event that had just taken place still hadn't sunk in yet.

Jode risked his entire reputation to stand up for me.

I was humbled.

Apparently, he didn't need a response. "Yeah, I didn't really think Jode would hang out with someone like you."

"I'll take that as a compliment."

His smile widened. "Hey, I didn't mean it in a bad way; in fact, if you're not a friend of Jode then I like you all the more. I mean that Hercules guy, what's up with him? I only met him like five times, yet he still drives me crazy."
I smiled. Hercules? That was an obvious reference to Hudson.
"I think that's something we can both agree on."
He leaned back in his chair and cocked his head knowingly. "I think that's something *every*one can agree with."
I couldn't contain my concern. "What's he going to do to Jode now?"
Jay grinned widely. "Don't worry too much about Jode, Hercules was completely drunk, almost out of his senses, he probably won't even remember what happened." He paused to take a sip of his drink.

" Jode acts so tough, but I have enough stuff on him to make him the biggest laughing stock in this part of town."

 "Most brothers usually do."

He picked up his cup and sloshed it around for a bit. "Yeah,

well I have more stuff on Jode than normal brothers, especially when you consider his reputation."
I couldn't help but feel curious. "What do you mean?"

He stared at the contents of his cup for a while, and then put it back on the table. "He's actually Jod*ette*."
This time I actually laughed out loud. "*What?*"
He grinned. "Yeah, I'm serious, you wanna know what he does on the computer all day?"
I bit my bottom lip to prevent myself from bursting into laughter. "Sure, why not?"
He leaned back in his chair. "All day long he sits on the computer searching up poems. He's a total girl."

I stopped laughing.

Poetry was not strictly a female subject. In fact, a large majority of famous poets were male. I looked at him, my grin now a frown. "*I* write poetry"
His smile left his face and he chewed on his bagel thoughtfully. "You know what? I take that back. Maybe Jode would hang out with someone like you."
I smiled. "Yeah maybe"
He drained his cup and looked at me.

"What's your name?"
"Tylor"
"My name's Jay."

I nodded. Just as I began to drift off again, his words broke into my thoughts.

"Why don't you think Jode likes Hercules?"

I turned to face him. "He hangs out with him in class, but clearly after today's display, there's something wrong. Are you sure Hudson won't do anything to him?
"Yeah, for sure, those guys've been friends for ages…
no idea why though. Jode's a sad kid, he doesn't know anything about life, he just does what he sees."
I couldn't help but raise my eyebrows "I think everyone is like that nowada—"
He cut me off with a cocky grin. "Not me, I'm the flag of life, *I* know why I'm living and how I'm doing it."

His statement caught me by surprise. "The flag of life?" He grinned and shrugged casually. "Sure, I live my life doing what I want, nothing can stop me, when it comes to living, I'm way up there." He paused to point at the sky, "Nothing can bring me down."
"What about death?"
Jay froze in mid-bite and looked at me, an odd expression crossing his face. "What about death?"
"You said that when it comes to living, you're way up there, but obviously you know that you won't live forever... so what about when you die?"
He swallowed his bagel slowly. "Wow. You're really slow, *life* is about *living*, when I die then I *disappear forever* which is why I'm *living* my *life* now, because it'll only come once."
"But what if you don't disappear forever?"
He stared at me, sarcasm apparent on his features. "What do you mean?"
I smiled slightly. "What if there's a life after death?"
Jay rolled his eyes. "Sorry kid I don't believe in that reincarnation stuff."
I smiled. "You don't believe that people will be judged for their actions?"

He shrugged. "When we die, we die. I prefer science over fantasy."

I held back a skeptical laugh. "Really? You're a man of science? A modern man? Then all the more reason for you to believe in it."

He looked severely confused. "What do you mean?"

I took a sip of my hot chocolate. "Imagine if there was a tiny village in the middle of nowhere, and this village had a small community of people living in it; imagine that these people had no idea that a world existed outside their community. Now how do you think these people would live?"

"What does this have to do with anything?" I continued smiling. "Just answer."

"I dunno, they would be poor, no TV, no life"

I ignored the *no TV* part and nodded. "Basically, they would live like animals, at the peak of barbarianism. Now imagine that a brutal act of injustice such as a murder occurs in this village, how do you think the people would react?"

"They would, well it depends on who they liked more. They'd probably be happy if they didn't like the guy who got murdered."

"But what if they *liked* the guy who was murdered?"

Jay raised his eyebrows. "Then they would kill the murderer."

I took another sip of hot chocolate. "Exactly, they would base their verdict on whom they liked more, favoritism. They wouldn't use any form of proper reasoning; they would punish whom they wanted and spare whom they willed. There would be no justice. Now would you call this a modern way of thinking?"

Jay shook his head, now fully absorbed into the story. "Of course not, now we have courts everywhere, if any judge made an open decision based on whom he liked more he'd be fired, hands down."

I continued staring at him, now with a hint of amusement in my smile. "So, you agree that not having a proper justice system is purely barbaric and non-modern?"

Jay's half smile was frozen on his face. "Yeah..."

"And you also believe that everything that happens must have a reaction?"

Jay nodded slowly.

I grinned widely. "Then how does it make sense that your life ends with death? Modern ideology proves that justice must be served for every action, that every action has a reaction, so how is it possible that someone who spent their whole life doing horrible things but had everything they ever wanted can end up in the same position as someone who spent their whole life praying but lived in the poor house? How can both people end up in the dirt? Is that Justice? If you, being a modern man believe in justice, then don't you think something must come after death? Something like a final judgment which will determine whether we should be rewarded or punished?"

His smile vanished and I could tell he was debating something in his mind. "I see what you're trying to say, but the rule of 'an action followed by a reaction' only applies for someone that's *living*."

"A person's body decays after death, isn't that a reaction?" Jay gritted his teeth "Okay, but nothing happens after that."

I frowned slightly. "Alright, then tell me this. When a person is born, he comes into the world with extreme difficulty, right?"

"Yeah, the mother suffers, so what?"

I ignored his impatience and went on. "And when a person

passes away, he suffers a lot right?"
Jay nodded.

"So, if there's so much pain in coming into this world, and so much pain in leaving it, how can whatever occur in the middle be purposeless? Common logic tells us that something that requires effort and loss has at least *some* purpose. We came into being and will die with so much suffering so how can everything just end after death?"
Jay stared at me with his mouth slightly open. "Yeah. but...wait that doesn't..." his eyes glazed over, and he bit his bottom lip thoughtfully. "Maybe that's something to think about."

We spent the next few minutes eating in silence. Silence that was broken by a sudden sharp hissing sound. I glanced up and for a second, I thought I was seeing things. There, coiled calmly around Jay's neck was a beautiful golden snake.

The golden wonder.

"Staring again? Seriously?"

I didn't say anything, I couldn't. I had never been so at a loss for words. The reptile made eye contact with me, and I saw an alarming glint of recognition. In an instant it crawled across the table and was coiled around my shoulders.

Jay raised his eyebrows, astonished. "I guess there's a first time for everything. He usually hates people."

I stared down at the glistening scales and resisted the urge to

kiss the snake out of sheer ecstasy.
It was real. I wasn't insane.

I felt so relieved, so happy. This whole time I had been doubting myself, thinking I was half-insane for making up the whole snake-in-the-forest incident. But it was real. It had happened. This beauty was still alive, and I had helped it.

I couldn't control my smile as I passed my hands over the snake in fascination. "It remembers me."

"Pardon me?" Jay leaned forward, curious. "You've met Mr.Snake before?"
"That's quiet an original name, very creative."
Jay smirked. "I know right? But seriously, where'd you meet him? Is this some sort of joke?"
I was about to tell him, but something was off. If this was his pet, what had it been doing by the *Natural World*?
"I… did you ever leave your snake near the forest?"
"Of course not. That area of town is dead, and it's winter, you think I'm insane?"
It didn't take me long to realize this probably had something to do with Jode.
"I, uh, I saw it at your place… Jode showed me."
"In my room, seriously?" he looked like he was going to get mad, then he smiled.
"Well, if he likes you this much, that's enough for me too I guess."
He eased Mr.Snake back into his arms and stood up. "Alright, I gotta run."
"Sure, but tell me, what species is he exactly?"
Jay ginned. "You can't tell?"

I stared at him blankly.

"*Bothrops insularis,* The Golden Lancehead."

My face turned pale. The golden scales were a dead giveaway, why didn't I realize sooner?

Jay saw my expression and winked. "Your face tells me you know a thing or two about snakes. That's right, he's one of the most venomous pit vipers in the world. One bite, and it's over…you're lucky he likes you."

With that he tossed his leftovers in the trash and walked somewhat solemnly towards the exit.
I was stupefied, I would have never guessed I would come so close to such a deadly animal, let alone actually form some sort of a bond with it. As soon as he left the café I glanced at my watch. It was 11:20pm. If I came home at twelve again my mom would kill me, but I was dying to go to the *Natural World.*
After throwing my stuff in the garbage I waved to Mr. Gret and pushed my way out the door.

The cold winter air greeted my face for the second time in the same night as I trudged through the fresh layer of snow. He had seemed like a nice person, but I couldn't help but notice that there was something weird about the way he looked. Everything about him looked dead except his eyes. His deadly preference of pet didn't help liven his aura either. I pushed him out of my mind and focused on the decision I had to make. Either I turned right and headed out of town and into the forest or I went left and headed back home. I paused for a minute and stared in both directions. After a moment of debating, I decided that getting yelled at by my mom was better than going to sleep without seeing that peaceful scenery. I turned right.

The forest path was unusually hard to walk through. Maybe it was because every time I attempted to walk my feet kept sinking into the thick layer of newly fallen snow. My vision slightly blurred as an unusually strong gust of wind sent snow flying across my body. I carefully made my way through the remaining path, my feet stopped abruptly, and I groaned out loud as I saw the fallen log in front of me.

I had completely forgotten about that. I paced around for a while looking for the area with the branches. The log was covered in a thick layer of snow, and it was extremely dark, but eventually I found the area and began making my way up. I climbed two feet up without hesitation and then I lost my grip and fell backwards onto the floor. I let myself lay on the floor; at least the snow was soft.

I opened my eyes to stare up at the sky and my heart skipped a beat as I saw someone's head staring down at me. As my vision cleared, I saw that it was Jode standing there with a worried expression. "Two times in one night, you, okay?" Embarrassed I stood up and brushed the snow off my jacket. "Uh, yeah…"

He looked at me for a while then his expression of concern transformed. He was trying to bite back a smile and failing miserably. I could see why he wanted to laugh; I must have looked really stupid sprawled on the floor like that; I couldn't help but go on the defensive. "What's so funny?"

He allowed his smile to break lose. "Nothing, you just…Nothing."

I stuffed my snow-covered hands into my pockets and stared at him challengingly. "I'd like to see *you* do any better."
At the sound of the challenge, he grinned and took a few steps back. "My pleasure."
With those words he ran forward and with one hard jump soared over the five-foot log.
Wow, wouldn't that be useful.
There was silence for a while and then I saw the top of his smiling head appear from the other side. He looked at the floor and pretended to cough. "Came first in high jump three years in a row…. you were saying?"
I smiled, feeling stupid for the second time today. "Okay, you're athletic, I get it." I walked over to the branches and struggled to the top of the log. Bracing myself I jumped down, thankfully I landed on my feet.
For a while both of us stood still in the winter snow; then I turned to him.
"Thanks, for the… you know, back at the—"
He cut me off. "Don't mention it. I've been wanting to do that for years. Thanks for giving me an excuse."

Silence.

 I cleared my throat, "You were going to the *Natural World* right?"

He looked confused for a second then he smiled as he realized what the *Natural World* was.

"Yeah, the *Natural World.*"
It felt weird hearing those two words that I had only said in my head be spoken aloud.

I turned to my right, and made my way to the gap of light, I could hear Jode a few steps behind me. I squeezed through the tight space and waited for my eyes to adjust to the bright light. As my vision cleared and the lake and tree came into view,

 I felt peace and calm flood my body. It was the peace that only came when I was here. I walked forward, hating the fact that my feet were destroying the perfect snow. Jode was stepping carefully too, but he was moving faster than me, he walked over to the tree and leaned against it.

 I saw his expression ease and his body relax. I walked over to the same rock I had sat on last time and seated myself. The snow had decreased, and it seemed like the temperature had dropped a little. I looked up at the sky and saw a thin outline of the moon. Jode looked up at the sky too. "We missed the last full moon."
I nodded in dismay. "Yeah, I guess I got too caught up with school, do you know when the next one is?"
"Around the twenty eighth."

He looked at me for a while then he grinned. "Do you always have that much difficulty getting across the trunk?"
I frowned and looked at the ground. "Yeah, me and that log go way back."
Jode laughed a little. "That's hilarious, you should work out more."
I tried not to feel too injured; maybe it was time I played on

his pride a little. I smiled at him. "Yeah, maybe you could show me where the gym is one day *Jodette*."
My grin widened as his eyes filled with shock and his face began to color. "You talked to Jay, didn't you?"
I nodded my head. "Yeah, after you left"
His embarrassed expression turned into a dreading frown, and he looked like he was trying not to cringe. "What else did he tell you?"
I rubbed my hands together in an attempt to warm them and thought back. "Well, he did mention that you love reading poetry."
Jode let out a sigh of relief. "Well, I guess that's not so bad. Also, that reminds me…"
He pulled out *The Picture of Dorian Gray* from the bookbag he had been carrying and handed it to me.
"It was amazing. Got any more?"
I grinned. "Yes, an entire library full. I'll send you a list?"
Jode smiled and nodded "As long as they're as good as this one, I'm in."
I pulled out the novel I had in my oversized jacket pocket and handed it to Jode.
Jode raised his eyebrows *"Frankenstein?"*
"Give it a chance, trust me, it's nothing like the movies."

"Why'd you bring it with you here?"

I laughed "I like to read here sometimes."

Jode looked around. "It's definitely quiet enough."

For the next few minutes, we lost ourselves discussing the plot and bone chilling implications of *The Picture of Dorian Gray*. As we spoke, I couldn't help but notice that he looked exceptionally like Jay; except Jay's hair was longer and darker; Jay also had those scars on his face. Curiosity possessed me and I decided to ask. "How did Jay get those scars?"

Jode looked at the floor and kicked the snow lightly. "Fights..."

I looked down too and frowned. Jay didn't really seem like the gang type. He had seemed too nice. I thought back to the abnormal sick air that had been hovering around him. If he had the capability to get into fights, I had a strong feeling I knew what had made him look so sick. I glanced up and regretted asking my question. Jode looked like he was in a completely different world, staring into space with a faraway look in his eyes.

I decided to change the subject.

"Hey Jode, did you ever bring Mr.Snake out to the forest?"

Jode turned pale. "What, why would you ask that?"

I smiled, "just curious."

Jodes brows furrowed, then his eyes widened. "You saved him, didn't you?"

"I took him home after seeing him here the first time I ever found this place. He was freezing and looked like he was right about to die."

Jode's face fell. "I didn't mean to leave him. I was just trying to befriend him. I guess I was also sort of trying to teach Jay a lesson. I really messed up."

"Hey, that night messed with my mind too, when he was gone in the morning... I thought I was crazy and that I imagined the whole thing."

Jode grinned. "Yeah, he is known for slipping away. We found him in the yard in the morning. He must have escaped your house and made his way back home when someone opened your front door...he's a very smart snake."

I raised my eyebrows "—eerily so."

There was silence for a few more minutes.

Suddenly he turned to me, "Why are you always so quiet?"
I couldn't help but smile a little. "Why? Is there something wrong with not talking excessively?"
He shook his head. "I've been told I'm too quiet myself, I just wanted to see your point of view."
I thought about it for a while and then looked up. "I feel people don't reflect on anything, they just do what they see without even considering the intent or implication of their actions."
Jode nodded slowly. "Like a herd of sheep following whatever the leader does and not knowing why."

"Is that why you pushed Hudson today?"

Jode shrugged "he's changed. Something is seriously wrong, but I can't put my finger on it."

 "Maybe he just needs to give himself some time to sit and think."
I looked up at the starry sky and allowed myself to take in the scenery again. The snow was reflecting the light of the stars, and the lake was shimmering as if someone had poured a large amount of glitter across its surface. The lone tree looked strikingly beautiful standing erect in the middle of the plain empty field. Icicles hung from its branches and sparkled, like the snow catching the light of the stars. I looked down at the perfect snow and noticed for the first time that among all the perfection there was a path of engraved footprints in a straight row, leading to the large strong tree. They were Jode's footprints.

As I continued to stare at them, surrounded by perfection they seemed to hold a deeper meaning. A symbolic blemish in a sea of flawlessness.

Smiling I stood up and allowed the new verse that had formed in my mind to flow out into the silent forest.

"The silent soldier stands alone, contesting natural with fake. He finds true joy to be a standing tree, true peace a shimmering lake."

My smile widened as the words left my mouth; the verse had captured the scene perfectly once again.

I heard stirring behind me and remembered that I wasn't alone. I glanced back and saw Jode pacing back and forth with a solemn expression on his face. I watched him for a while, then he looked up at me. "Wow you made that on spot?"

I pocketed my hands. "Yeah, I guess you could say that."

He watched my face for a while then looked down. "That was nicely said."

There was silence for a while then Jode stopped pacing. "You should write these verses down somewhere"

I smiled. "No need to, I just…" my voice trailed off as I realized I had no way to explain that I didn't write them because I just knew that I would never forget them.

His next statement shocked me. "Yeah, they kinda stick in my head too."

I was taken aback; a feeling of absolute peace overcame me.

I stared at his genuine expression and remembered his determination to defend me at the risk of almost everything he had. Something told me that my question on how it would feel to have a companion who thought like me had finally been answered.

I pushed my key into the door and slid inside. Hopefully everyone would have gone to sleep by now. I took off my wet shoes and listened carefully. The downstairs TV was off; maybe I would be able to go to my room without getting yelled at. I tiptoed up the stairs keeping my head turned so I could see behind me. I made it up 12 stairs until I had a feeling someone was watching me. I looked in front of me and my heart sank as I saw mom standing there in her sleeping clothes nearly in the exact position she had been in when I had left. This time though she looked much angrier. "Tylor! Did you just come home now?"

I looked down and didn't speak. Maybe if I stayed silent, she wouldn't blow too hard. Boy was I wrong.

"DO YOU KNOW WHAT TIME IT IS? IT'S ONE O' CLOCK!" She glared at me waiting for a reaction; I continued looking at the floor. I was seventeen, yet I still got yelled at like a little kid.

Mom continued to raise her voice. "YESTERDAY YOU CAME HOME AT TWELVE, TODAY YOU COME HOME AT ONE! I DEMAND TO KNOW WHERE YOU WENT!"

I sighed. "I went to get a hot chocolate, and plus Siara stays out late too, why don't you yell at her?" I knew I sounded like a baby, but I was tired of getting yelled at. What was it to her if I stayed out late? Okay she was my mom, but she spent all her time living in the television, so I barely even knew who she was.

She sighed. "Siara can stay out late because she tells me where she's going"
I felt my anger rise. "I already told you, I go on *walks*."
My mom exploded again. "WALKS! WALKS? WALKS FOR THREE HOURS AT NIGHT?" she paused for breath then continued in her loudest possible voice. "GO TO YOUR ROOM RIGHT NOW! AND DON'T YOU DARE COME OUT UNTIL MORNING!"

I slid past her and walked into my room heaving a sigh of disappointment. She was my mom; shouldn't I be able to respect her more? I felt my heart sink further as I realized the relationship, I had with her. It consisted of me being sulky and her yelling. I *should* be able to respect her more and I *wanted* to.

We needed to spend more time together. I wanted to know who she really was, and I wanted her to know who I really was too.

But she was always so distracted.

Remembering my recent banishment to my room caused a guilty smile to creep across my face.
I *had* just gotten off with just a yelling; on top of that I hadn't really been banished to my room because technically it was already morning.

Ten

The screen finished loading and the familiar list of names popped open. I had planned on clicking randomly, but as I scrolled down, I caught sight of a name that promised entertainment: *Mediaholic*. With a smile I clicked it and began typing.

NBW: Hello.
Mediaholic: Hey.
NBW: I need you to guess something.
Mediaholic: Huh??
NBW: Guess my age.
Mediaholic: ummmmmm 23?
NBW: No, I mean go on my profile page read it and then tell me what age you think I am.
Mediaholic: I don't get it.
NBW: What's there not to get? Read my profile and guess my age.

Mediaholic: What if I guess wrong?
NBW: I don't care, I just need an

estimate.
Mediaholic: Estimate?
NBW: ***Just check my profile***, trust
me you'll be surprised.
Mediaholic: okay now I'm curious BRB.

Sighing I glanced at the clock, it was 6:00pm, I still had a chemistry lab to fill out and a philosophy essay to complete. I didn't have to wait long, a few seconds later *Mediaholic* replied.

Mediaholic: Wow.
NBW: Well?
Mediaholic: That's amazing...
NBW: What?
Mediaholic: You're only nine yet you use such big words, and you even wrote seventeen poems, are you some sort of genius?

That's a laugh. But then again it *was* expected.
Asking people to guess my age had been something I had been doing since I was in grade eleven.

Why did I keep asking?

I pondered over this for a while then concluded that maybe I was just hoping that, for once, someone would guess it correctly.

◆◆◆◆◆◆

I braced myself and walked down the hallway. Chemistry period had flown by, and now it was time to go to the place I hated most the computer lab. Maybe there was a way I could miss out on it today.

As much as I would like to miss class, I knew that I wouldn't allow myself to skip a lesson, even if it was only a few minutes long. I walked past two more doors and then entered the large room. I was early as always. There were only four other people in the room. I walked over to my computer and turned it on; maybe I'd check my profile to see if I had received any new comments.

"Hey Tylor." I turned around and saw Jode sitting in the row behind me, for a second, I was shocked. He had greeted me in *public*. That one, common phrase could have instigated his immediate social death. I quickly looked around and realized that none of the gang or anyone who could spread believable rumors was around; it was just us and a couple of *intellectuals*.

I sighed; well at least he had even bothered to say hi. "Hey." Jode smiled awkwardly and opened his mouth to say something but was interrupted as the door opened and the entire class filed in. After everyone was seated Mr. Damon pulled out the attendance and started reading out names. I had listened to the attendance so much that I practically had it memorized for every class. It's not like I sat there trying to memorize it, it's just that I had played that *associating a name with a trait* game so often that it had made me memorize every name on the long list. As I contemplated the lists, I realized for the first time that Jode was in all of my classes. Weird how I hadn't noticed that before.

Mr. Damon stopped calling out names and wiped the board. He turned back to the class and began his lecture. "Okay class today we're going to be looking very briefly into CSS. For those of you who do not know, CSS is something like HTML,

for a better definition please flip to page one hundred and for—"

The whole class jumped as the computer lab door flew open and slammed hard against the wall. As soon as the door opened Hudson and his gang stormed into the room. They had solemn poker-faces on; they were clearly upset about something. They stormed past Mr. Damon without bothering to explain their lateness and stomped to their seats. All eyes watched them fearfully as they walked down the aisle; they were obviously enjoying the attention.

I stared at them for a while more. Sure, it was obvious they were trying to put on a show, but for what reason? Something must have happened to make them feel the need to act so upset. Miles tried to add to the effect and slam down in his chair angrily but ended up stubbing his toe on the leg of the table and stumbled clumsily instead— his facial features distorting with pain. I bit my bottom lip trying not to smile, these guys were so sad.

A few moments of awkward silence passed; then Mr. Damon coughed. "Um, yes. Page one hundred and forty-seven." There was a shuffling of papers as everyone quickly flipped to that page in hopes to eradicate the awkwardness that had followed the gangs' entrance.

Twenty minutes later Mr. Damon concluded his lecture and released us to our computers. In a few seconds the silence that veiled the class was replaced with laughing and talking as everyone began discussing the shows, they had seen last night. The angry entrance had been forgotten. I frowned and once again wondered what had made them so angry. I glanced back at them. They were sitting in a huddle and discussing something in quiet voices. All of them had odd expressions of anger on their faces except Jode who remained expressionless. A few seconds later they resurfaced, now all of them looked pale, even Jode. I turned back to my computer screen itching with curiosity. Okay so it was none of my business, but still, I wanted to know what could be bad enough to have made Hudson go pale— other than Jay that is. I stared at my computer screen contemplating the possibilities when Hudson spoke.

"I can't believe it's actually going to happen." His voice sounded strange and quiet.

There was a silence and then Miles grinned. "Yeah, you're rolling with the big boys now."

Hudson looked down and chewed his bottom lip thoughtfully. "Yeah."

Ryan leaned in eagerly. "So, when's it gonna happen?"

There was a pause as Hudson thought about it. "There's still some time."

Jode who had been staring at the ceiling for the past few minutes turned to Hudson. "How much time exactly?"

Hudson shrugged. "A little more than a month."

There was a long pause after his words. Then Jode spoke: "Why'd you get yourself into this?"

Hudson looked at him challengingly. "'Cause it's something I wanted to do since forever, something wrong with that?"

Jode looked like he was going to blow. "Of course, there's something wrong with that! You're so stupid! Do you know how dumb that was?"

Hudson's voice began to rise. "Relax man; I know what I'm getting into."

Jode shook his head. "No, *you* don't know what you're getting into, *I* know what you're getting into because I've seen this happen before."
Miles jumped in. "Don't be stupid Jode, Hudson did something smart."
Then grinning he turned to Hudson. "Your dream finally came true man."
Hudson grinned back. "Yeah, I guess it did."
Jode frowned. "Oh, so you're saying that that *thing* they asked you to witness doesn't sound a little extreme?"
Hudson looked down as if thinking about Jode's words.

Before Hudson could say anything, Miles turned to him, "Aw, come on man, it's nothing *you* can't handle"
Hudson looked up with new confidence. "Yeah, it's nothing."
Jode turned solemnly towards Hudson. "You're trapping yourself, what you're doing is beyond dangerous."
Hudson snorted. "What's the point of life if there's no danger in it?"
Miles and Ryan nodded their heads in agreement.
Jode raised his eyebrows. "You were scared half to death a few seconds ago, don't tell me you think it's okay now?"
Hudson shrugged. "Maybe I *was* scared, but now I know it's something I gotta– something I *wanna* do."

I shuddered, what in the world was going on? Hudson had done something he shouldn't have, that much was clear. I frowned and tried to make sense of what I heard. After a few moments I shrugged it off. Why was I worrying? This didn't have anything to do with me.

A group of prisoners have been confined to a cave since birth. They are chained by the leg and neck so they can't see each other; they can only see in front of them.
In front of them is a wall which is reflecting the light of a fire that is behind them. In between the fire and the prisoners is a parapet one similar to those used for puppet shows. People are walking past the parapet carrying different objects over their heads.
The prisoners watch day and night as the shadows of the objects are reflected onto the cave wall.
One day a single prisoner is unchained and taken out to the light. He is told that what he had seen in the cave was an illusion. He is shown the fire and the real objects that had projected the images, but he fails to make connections.

Slowly, he starts adjusting to the real world first by observing the shadows, then by observing at night. Eventually he realizes that his life in the cave had been an illusion and goes back to tell his fellow prisoners.
His fellow prisoners laugh at him and mock him saying that he went up to the light only to come back blind.

I put down my pen. That was my summary of Plato's Allegory of the Cave. I frowned; I knew I should have done it for homework. But I had fallen asleep instead. Now I was paying the price.

Now all I had to do was write my analysis. I tried to concentrate then scowled. The noise of the cafeteria was overwhelming and the odd conversion I had heard in computer class was still fresh in my mind.

How was I supposed to concentrate with so many distractions?

I glanced up at the clock. I had spent so much time eating and writing the summary that lunch was over.

Sighing, I gathered my stuff and headed out the cafeteria door. Mr. Masiw hated it when homework was incomplete.
I pulled the door of the philosophy classroom open and stepped inside, it was nearly empty. I walked up to my seat in the front and sat down. Mr. Masiw hadn't come in yet so maybe I still had some time to write my analysis. I pulled out the sheet I had been working on in the cafeteria and started writing. I only got a few words down before I was interrupted.

"Is that the homework?"

I looked up to see Jode standing in front of me. "Yeah, I fell asleep last night, did you do it?"

He took a paper out of his binder and threw it on my desk.

"Yup all done"

I looked at it, the paper was blank.

I grinned deciding to play along. "Lucky you, it took me *all lunch* just to get the summary done. Good thing you completed it."
Jode's eyes widened. "All lunch? Are you serious?"
I nodded my head. He quickly sat down beside me and pulled out a pen. "We just have to write a summary of Plato's Allegory of the Cave, right?"
I smiled. "Yeah."
Jode quickly began writing away. I looked at the time, there was three minutes left until Mr. Masiw came in. I looked at my own paper and wrote the first words that came to my head:

Plato's allegory of the cave displays a prominent flaw of man. It explains how a man lives his life in an illusion, and only when he receives help from outside does he understand what true reality is.

I put my pen down a second before Mr. Masiw entered the room. I glanced over at Jode. And was surprised to see he had filled half a page. I leaned in closer and realized I could barely read what he had written. He stopped writing and paused to frown at his work. "Do you think I'll get a zero?"
I tried not to laugh. "It's just homework, who cares what you get?"
I walked over to the front and handed both our papers in.
Mr. Masiw flipped his book open. "Alright, today I have an important job to attend to, so after you've handed in your homework please proceed to reading about our next topic: *Existentialist Ethics* on page one hundred and ninety-two. We'll have a discussion on it tomorrow." He wrote the page numbers on the board then seated himself at his desk.

I flipped to the page, after rushing on the homework at lunch I honestly didn't feel like studying more philosophy. Jode was staring at his own book, but it was clear that he wasn't reading.

Now was the best time to ask about what had been happening in the computer lab.

I coughed. "Hey, I know it's none of my business but what happened in the computer lab?"

Jode snapped out of his trance and looked at me. "What do you mean?"

I looked down at my textbook. "I mean that Hudson seemed unusually mad."

Jode looked at me for a while then smiled. "You heard us talking, didn't you?"

I nodded my head guilty. "Yeah."

Jode grinned. "He wasn't mad. I guess you could say he was scared."

I looked at him curiously. "What could be bad enough to scare Hudson?"

Jode looked down and frowned. "It's a long story."

Then, after a short pause corrected himself. "Okay, maybe it's not a long story, it's just something I'd rather not talk about. And to be honest, nothing makes sense to me either."

I frowned; I guess I would never know what that mysterious conversation was about. Maybe it was better that way.

I turned back to my textbook when Jode spoke. "Have you heard of Outbreak before?"

It definitely sounded familiar, but from where? I thought for a while then looked back at him and shook my head slowly. "No, I haven't."

Jode bit his bottom lip, "What about Spades, have you heard of him?"

Once again, I shook my head. Jode stared at the ceiling for a while then turned back to me. "When you find out what that stuff is then ask me again, maybe I'll tell you more."
I smiled. "Okay sure if I ever find out what that stuff means."
Jode shrugged. "The sooner you find out the sooner I'll tell you."
I turned back to my textbook in deep thought. Hudson had said something was going to happen in a little over a month. I

had no idea what it was but for some reason I found myself hoping that whatever it was would happen far away from here.

The next few weeks were a blur of schoolwork and being banished to my room. My mom still refused to let me go for late night walks.
The only thing keeping me going was the new two-people bookclub me and Jode had created. We were currently going over the original Sherlock Holmes series. I had forgotten how good the story was.
I threw my bag on the kitchen table and pulled a pear out of the fridge. I was about to take my first bite when Siara burst into the kitchen excitedly. "Tylor! Come to the family room! There's great news!"
I looked at her suspiciously. "What do you mean by *great*?"
She smiled widely and, in a sing,-songy voice added. "Come to the family room and see."
Sighing I put my pear down and followed her to the family room.
I wasn't too excited or curious because through experience I knew that things Siara found great were usually things I

despised. Last time Siara had gotten this excited, it was just to tell me that she was having a celebrity guest at her sweet sixteen.

I walked into the family room to see my mom, dad and Siara sitting on the sofa discussing excitedly with each other.

I looked at them unsure of what to do.

The silence grew and nobody spoke, eventually I broke the silence.

"Well, is someone going to tell me what's going on?"

Dad's smile widened. "I thought you'd never ask." and with those words he pulled out a thin stack of papers from his pocket and handed them to me.

I tried not to let my heart sink too low. They looked suspiciously like concert tickets.

With a heavy heart, I reached forward and accepted the papers. I looked down at them expecting my doubts to be confirmed the second I read their contents, but to my great surprise my heart didn't sink, in fact I felt my excitement begin to rise.

They weren't concert tickets; they were *plane* tickets, for a week in California.

I smiled. I loved California. Not because of the attractions, but because my grandfather lived there.

I had cousins all across the States, but I was drawn to him in particular. He was always so quiet, and when he spoke, he always offered the best possible advice.

Still smiling, I handed the tickets back to my dad. "So, when do we leave?"

My mom smiled. "We leave on the seventh!"

I started getting excited. "Oh, that's great, our March break starts around then so we won't miss any school."

Siara jumped up and threw her arms in the air. "Yeah! My holidays start then too! Let's celebrate with a movie!"
Mom smiled. "Great idea, but which one?"
I turned and made my way to the family room door, happy times never lasted long.
I was about to make it out when dad called me back. "Hey Tylor! Get back here, where do you think you're going?"
Frowning I turned around. "I umm can't go. I Have way too much work."
Mom raised her eyebrows; her jolly expression had evaporated. "No, not this time, this time you're spending time with us whether you like it or not."
I turned to my dad in protest. "Dad! I have work to do, tell her I can stay."
Dad looked down at the sofa. I knew he hated problems; there was no way he would force me to come.

He glanced at my mom then looked up. "Tylor, can't you make one sacrifice for your family?"
My mouth flew open. "You guys should be proud of me, I want to miss a movie to do work!"
Dad looked at me angrily. "We would be proud of you, but you do this every time, this time your work can wait."
I looked at the floor angrily. "Can't we go out to eat or something? Why a movie?"
Siara jumped in. "Because when we're eating, we aren't really spending time with each other, but when we watch a movie then we all feel the same things at the same time!"
I looked at her skeptically. That had to be the dumbest thing I had ever heard. "If that's the case, then standing here staring at a wall would also be a great way to spend time together because we'll all be feeling the same thing. Bored."

Siara frowned. "You're so dumb, you know that's not what I meant."

I looked at my dad and tried one more time. "I don't want to go."

My mom pursed her lips and stared at me for a while. "You really know how to ruin a good moment don't you?"

I decided it would be best not to reply to that. *They* were the ones who had ruined the good moment by bringing a movie into it.

When the silence grew overwhelming Dad stood up. "Okay, everyone gets dressed, we're going to the movies." He paused for a while then looked at me. "And by everyone, I mean you too Tylor."

A few minutes later I found myself walking to the shoe closet with my jacket on. My excitement had died completely. Going to California *did* sound like it would be fun, but if it meant I had to go to a movie, I'd rather not go. I mean I couldn't stand it when I *heard* people watching movies, how would I react when I actually went inside a

theater? Come to think of it I hadn't been to a theater since I was twelve.

Sighing I pulled my shoes on; my dad had never forced me to do anything before. He was always busy doing something, and whenever he was free, he watched TV so he barely even talked to me. But now that he had, I knew he was serious.

I pushed the door open and walked to my dad's car, A few minutes later I was joined by everyone else chatting excitedly about what movie we were going to see. Dad rubbed his hands together and smiled. "Okay, so who's going to drive?"

All of us looked at each other, nobody volunteered. Dad looked around hopefully. "Anyone… Siara?"

Siara frowned. "I'm not going to drive, ask Tylor."
I didn't miss a heartbeat and immediately shook my head. "I don't feel like driving."
Dad sighed. "Even though every member of our family can drive, it's usually me who ends up doing it."
Mom smiled. "Aww, so what's so bad about driving?"
We all looked at her. The person who drove had three backseat drivers driving him crazy, that's what was so bad about driving. Dad threw the keys to her. "If it's not so bad, why don't you drive?"
Mom threw the keys back at him as if they were on fire and laughed nervously. "Okay, fine. Maybe this time we'll try not to be *so* critical."
All of us piled into the blue Honda, and dad started the ignition. "All seat belts on?"
Mom and Siara simultaneously nodded their heads. There was silence as everybody waited for me. Frowning I pulled my seatbelt on. "Yes."
Satisfied, my dad pulled out of the driveway. "Alright, we'll be there in ten minutes, so just kick back and enjoy the ride!"

His optimism was short lived as he stopped at a stop sign and moved forward a bit too slowly.

Siara frowned. "No dad! You should've gone a little faster; you didn't have to go *that* slow!"
Mom nodded her head. "Yes, Siara's right you *always* do that."
I saw dad grit his teeth through the mirror and I couldn't help but smile, *less critical my foot.*

After a few more minutes of criticizing, Mom and Siara began discussing the movie we were going to see again, and I sunk back into my seat.

Maybe I should be optimistic. Maybe I wasn't giving the theaters a fair chance.

I had never liked movies, as I mentioned before they just didn't make sense to me. Sure, I had only seen about six movies in my whole life, four of which I saw in kindergarten. But it was enough to give me a basic concept of what movies were.

I knew for a fact that if anyone ever sat down and contemplated about the concept of movies, they would conclude that they've never heard of anything stupider.

Sure, there were documentaries and movies that had historic significance. Those movies were fine. But the movies I was referring to, were the ones that were actually popular; the movies that people actually watched.

My thoughts were interrupted as the car stopped a second time. "Okay everyone out! We're here!"

I looked out the window and saw the huge white building towering a few feet away from the car. I waited for the last possible moment and then forced myself out into the open.

Maybe this wouldn't be so bad?

Eleven

Movie

I shuddered. I never wanted to hear that word again. I closed my eyes and scenes of what I had just seen flew into my head. Those had been the most useless storylines I had ever witnessed in my seventeen years of life.

But there had been something strangely pleasant about the experience. Sitting with my family, watching their reactions, and most importantly, discussing the potential deeper meaning behind the film on the way back home had been fantastic, fun even.

One of the movies had been about a loner with no friends who changes himself completely to fit in. It had hit my sorest spot. *Would changing myself make me happier? It had certainly made the protagonist happier.*

 If I needed anything right now it was a visit to the *Natural World*. I glanced at the time, and frowned, it was only 9:00pm. I could easily go and visit.

I walked over to my window and stared outside, it wasn't snowing today, but even from the safety of my own bedroom, I could tell that it was freezing. I wiped the window in an attempt to see clearer, but even the beautiful natural scenery wasn't enough to make me forget how I had spent my last three hours. I creased my brow and attempted to wipe the scenes from my mind, maybe if I concentrated really hard, I could forget everything I had seen. I smiled at the sadness of my reasoning; I highly doubted that the power of selective memory could be that strong, but still; desperate times called for desperate measures. My attempts to erase the useless images from my mind were proclaimed futile as there was a loud knock on my door.

Can't I have some privacy!

I shuddered again, that had been a quote from one of the movies I had seen. I frowned as I walked to the door, how long would I be seeing the scenes in my mind whenever something related came up in real life? I pulled open the room door and saw Siara standing there with the cordless in her hand. "Here, it's your call." she stuffed it in my hand, "I need it, so you better finish with it quick, got it?"

I put the phone to my ear and closed the door, who would be calling me now? Or at all.

"Hello?"

There was a brief silence on the other side then Jode's voice broke through. "Uh…hi."
The brief silence jumped in again, then Jode coughed awkwardly. "You have the chemistry test review?"
I smiled. "Yeah, I do have it, why?"
"Soccer practice extended, so I missed chemistry class." he sounded embarrassed.

I picked up my bag and pulled out the review. "Okay sure, it's pretty long so how about I just scan and email it to you?"
"Yeah sure, sounds great. My email address is—"
His voice was cut off by a squeakier   voice.
"It's *Jodette_sucks@imagirl.com.*"
I blinked; then grinned as Jode's next words made everything clear.
"Jay put the phone down."
Jay laughed aloud into the phone. "Ah, I crack myself up; who are you talking to anyways? Hercules?" He sounded hopeful. When Jode didn't say anything for a while Jay spoke again. "Hello? Anybody there?"
I smiled broadly. "Uh, it's Tylor"
Jay's voice amplified enthusiastically. "Tylor ol' pal long time no talk! How are things going? How's Marianna doing? You been feeding her well?"
This guy was too much. "I've only spoken to you once so technically I'm not an old friend. And our conversation had nothing to do with feeding a Marianna."
Jode   butted   in.   "Okay,   my   email   address is *Fifahaves@hotmail.com.* Email me as soon as possible, okay?" I opened my mouth to reply and this time I was interrupted.
"Aww the two witto itsy bitsy babies are discussing

homework! Isn't that absolutely adowable?"
"Don't you have something to do?" Jode snapped
Jay laughed. "No need to get feisty Jodette, and don't tell me
I don't have a life, *you're* the one discussing homework."
Jode sighed. "If you discussed homework more often maybe
you'd spend less time repeating your courses."
Jay's voice turned serious. "Hey, I haven't failed once yet, I
may not be Einstein but I'm definitely not failing."
I scratched my head awkwardly. "Okay I'll email you the
review,"
"Yeah okay, I'm waiting."

Jay sounded disappointed. "Aww, leaving already?'
Jode didn't give me a chance to reply. "You're such a pain,
I swear you're mental."
Jay's serious tone returned. "You wanna say that to my
face?"
Anger fueled Jode's voice. "Yeah, okay sure."
There was a brief moment of footsteps as Jode climbed the
stairs then I heard him speaking to Jay. "You're *mental.*"
Jay still had the phone to his ear and his playful tone
completely dropped. "You'll wish you never said that."
There was the sound of Jay hanging up and then rapid
footsteps as if both of them were running; apparently Jode
had forgotten to turn off his side of the phone. I pressed the
off button on the cordless resisting the temptation to fall on
the floor laughing. I wondered what would happen when Jay
caught Jode.
After my laughter subsided, I walked over to my laptop and
placed the review in the scanner. After a few moments of
clicking and loading, the paper was scanned. I sat down on
my chair and attached the review to an email. I grinned as I
typed in the topic: *did it hurt?*

I'm sure he would understand I was referring to the brawl that had obviously resulted after I had shut off the phone. After the message was sent, I decided it wouldn't hurt to check my profile. I signed into my account and saw that I had two new comments on *Forgotten songs*. I clicked and the page opened.

J.H: it's true, I think all of us have songs of guilt and regret calling us... once again nicely written

I smiled, J.H commented on all my poems, and he had even bookmarked me. Now that was someone with a sensible taste in poetry. I moved onto the next comment.

Perker-q: umm are you emo? Cuz that was reaaallly not...something that makes people happy...

I frowned, not all people had sensible taste in poetry, once again I had someone who didn't agree with my point of view. My frown turned into a guilty smile as I realized I was acting arrogant. Obviously, everyone had different poetic tastes; I had no right to say that Perker-q didn't have sense.

I closed the screen and as I did, I got a notification that I had received a new email. As expected, it was from Jode, I grinned at his topic: *Just a little*.

I scrolled down to read his message:

"Thanks for the scan, have fun studying..."

Sighing, I closed the screen. I still had to study for my chemistry test.

What you're studying? What about our plans!

Shuddering, I pulled out my chemistry book. If only we hadn't gone to that *place*. How was I expected to study when every other word reminded me of the three hours I spent in that cursed building?

I flipped through the pages for a while and then eventually gave up. I already knew most of the stuff anyways; paying attention and actually doing my work really did help. I closed the textbook with a thud and threw on my jacket which was sprawled by the foot of my bed. After pocketing my camera, I climbed down the stairs not caring to go quietly. I had gone with them today, they owed me enough to at least let me go to the *Natural World*. I think I had been going down the steps too noisily because a few seconds later mom came to stand in front of me.

"Where are you going?"

I tried not to scream; this was starting to get annoying. "I'm going for a walk."

She stared at me for a while then sighed. "No, you can't go."

I closed my eyes to build patience. Despite the fact that she was being unfair I had to consider the fact that she was my mom. I was sure I hadn't been easy to deal with when I was a kid either. So, if she had been able to bear patience with me at that point in time, what right did I have to show her attitude now? I decided I wouldn't argue and went back to my room. Was I being unreasonable or was she really being unfair? Did she have a reason to worry about my late-night walks? It's not like I was into drugs or in a gang. I almost laughed at that. Me in a gang or doing drugs? That's hilarious, if that's what my mom was suspecting then it's clear she didn't know me at all.

I walked over to my bed and threw myself on it. Now what? My heart sank as I caught sight of the chemistry textbook.

As much as I liked chemistry, I didn't feel like looking at the material now, what I felt like doing was going to the *Natural World.* The vision of the scene flew into my mind. It was so peaceful.

My retained anger began to rise; now I couldn't even go to the one place I found solace? How was that fair, I didn't stop them from doing what made *them* happy, in fact I could hear the blare of the TV from my room right now, but I wasn't stopping them. What gave them the right to stop me from doing what I found peace in? Frowning, I realized I had to distract myself; I walked over to my window. I couldn't help but smile bitterly as I contemplated the wide selection of emotions, I had just undergone in less than ten minutes. Excitement for leaving, disappointment for getting caught, anger for realizing. Maybe I should just throw happiness into the picture and complete the list. I pulled open the window and looked down.

If I couldn't leave the house through the door, then why not leave through the window?

There was no way I was going to stay inside. I contemplated my options, if I really wanted to escape from the window, I would need a practical way down. I glanced to my left. A few years ago, my dad had installed a trellis on the left side of our house for some new plants my mom wanted to grow. It had always looked pretty useless to me considering the fact that nothing had actually grown on it, but now it may just come in handy. I leaned out of the window and reached for it. My left hand just reached it, not enough for me to grasp though. I pulled myself further out of the window and I was able to grab the wooden structure.

I rattled it and to my great surprise it barely shook, it was fastened firmly against the wall.

Satisfied I began lifting myself onto the window ledge but stopped midway, contemplating. I knew I was supposed to respect my mother, but I wasn't doing anything wrong, and it's not like she would ever know. I frowned at my lame justification and looked down again.

I gulped; I was on the second story, maybe it would be smarter to stay inside. A picture of the *Natural World* flew back in my head, and I smiled, who cared about fear? The peace that came with the *Natural World* was something I couldn't miss out on, especially after I had spent those long hours in *that* place.

Before I could change my mind, I forced myself fully out of the window until I was hanging on the ledge. I hung there for a while and blinked. I couldn't believe I had just done that. What had I been thinking? That was probably the stupidest thing I had ever done. Two seconds ago, I had been safely inside and now I was hanging out of my window, holding on for dear life. My hands began to get tired, and I knew that I would have to move, there was no way my body was strong enough to lift me back up to my room.

Slowly I edged to the left. After hanging for a good three minutes, I reached out my hand to grasp the trellis and held on tight. Despite the fear I couldn't help but smile, I was hanging with my arms spread wide apart, my right arm holding the ledge and my left arm holding the wooden frame. I felt sorry for anyone who saw me right now, I probably looked crazy.

Without thinking I let go of the ledge with my right hand and immediately regretted it, because as soon as I let go my body was pushed back with such force that I began swinging pendulum-like against the wall. I kicked and flailed resisting the temptation to scream, and after a long time finally stopped swinging. My heart was racing impossibly fast. That had been the scariest experience of my life.

I braced myself, my smile long gone and slowly made my way down. To my great surprise the way down didn't require too much athletic ability. Sure, I was going down at the pace of a snail, but the point was I wasn't breaking any bones, or even a sweat. Fifteen long, exaggerated minutes later I was steadying myself on the ground. I let out a sigh of relief. That had been extremely stupid of me, but it was also satisfying. I couldn't help but smile smugly. I had successfully made it out of the house without getting caught. My smug smile evaporated as I realized that I would have to get in somehow. I quickly checked my pocket. I had my key with me, but I was pretty sure mom wouldn't exactly be thrilled to see me walk in through the front door. I glanced back at my house and shrugged, no point of crying over it. I was outside now, might as well do what I had intended on in the first place. I straightened up my jacket and made my way to the *Natural World.*

◆◆◆◆◆◆

I squeezed through the gap and allowed the peace and calm to engulf me. My small worries and problems flew straight from my head and my heart felt like it was melting even on this freezing night.

I walked over to my place by the rock and sat down. Today was exceptionally cold. I pocketed my bare hands and looked down at the shimmering snow. After staring at the snow for a while I sat up straight, something was different. I looked around once again, everything *did* look different. For a second, I thought I had come to the wrong place, but I immediately crossed that thought from my mind. I was definitely in the Natural World, but there was something different about it. Not *bad* different, but *good* different. Everything just looked so…

I looked up at the sky and my mouth felt open. How had I not seen it before? It was the twenty eighth, the full moon was out. I blinked twice then stood up to look around again, no wonder it had felt so different. The entire area was bathed in eerie white light. Everything looked as if it were glowing. I looked back up at the sky and a smile stretched across my thin face. The moon perfected the scene which I stood in. Turning around my eyes caught sight of the giant tree in the center. It was bathed in white light and at that moment I couldn't help but believe it was the most miraculous thing on earth. Slowly I walked up to it and when I got close enough, stopped. It was so large, how did it get here, all alone in the middle? Separate from every other tree? I reached my hand out and touched its cold trunk. It was just so perfect. I took a few steps back and looked at it top to bottom. It was so beautiful, so organized and strong. A tiny seed made that tree. A tiny little seed. Something so small that it could fit in the palm of my hand, had turned into *that*. I stared for a while. It was obvious that this was all created by God. Who else had the power to make something as small as a seed into something as large as a tree? Science and technology may have the power to explain how it happened, but they did not have the power to create

something so great.

I pulled out my camera and took a picture of the lone tree. I turned and positioned my camera to face the moon, it took a while to get it directly in the middle of the picture but eventually I got it. As I pocketed the camera, I heard footsteps behind me and turned around. Jode had just entered, and he was staring wide eyed at the sky, a lost smile playing on his face.

I smiled. "Hey"

He looked at me, his smile widening. "Hey, the full moon is out."

I walked over and sat on my rock. "Yeah, time flies."

He slowly made his way to the tree, observing everything around him. "This place, it just looks so…"

"Different?"

"Yeah, I guess."

There was a long silence as both of us lost ourselves in thought. I had always wanted to know how this place would look in a full moon and now I knew. It was so stunningly beautiful, and to think I had been debating staying at home.

"You done studying?"

I looked up at Jode and grinned. "Not really, but I kind of knew everything, maybe I'll review in the morning. What about you?"

Jode smiled. "Yeah right, Jay was driving me crazy, I had to get out of there."

I stood up and my grin widened. "Do you guys always fight that much?"

Jode pocketed his hands and looked away. "Yeah, ever since we were little."

I smiled slightly. "Yeah, I don't get along with my sister either."

Jode didn't say anything for a long time after that, then he turned to me uncertainly.

"You ever see someone change completely in front of your own eyes?"

I raised my eyebrows. "What do you mean?"
"I mean, have you ever known someone who was close to you, but one day they just turn into someone you wish you never met?"

I stared at him for a while. "No, not really, have you?" He continued staring into space and laughed bitterly "Yeah, one too many times."
I waited for him to continue, when he didn't say more, I allowed myself to get lost in my thoughts.
The silence of the area was overpowering. It was strange how when silence came into play, we were able to think so clearly. I looked up at the moon with its glowing light, it was beyond breathtaking. Nowadays people had made artificial things that they felt were depicting the same image. But I knew it would be impossible to capture the beauty of the moon.
I guess it was because man was so into trying to make things perfect *his* way, he ended up destroying true perfection. My mind went back to the scene of Jode's footprints standing alone against the perfect landscape. Sometimes perfection was not what we thought it to be. *The silent soldier…*
I stood up and walked over to the lake. The verse had been building in my mind and now in clear strong words I recited it.

"He sees the moon as a smaller sun perfecting an icy night. He neither speaks, nor does he say, but his vision is his light."

As soon as the words left my mouth, peace engulfed me. Not everyone could see the moon as a near perfect orb that further perfected the world. Not everyone could see that the moon was a perfect creation of God, and that contemplating its beauty was necessary to understand.

The silent soldier.

Only when a person practiced silence would their eyes open and their vision broaden to observe the miracles around him, the miracles of God's creation and in turn receive guidance.

"The silent soldier?"

I broke from my daze and turned around to see Jode standing right behind me.

"By *he*, you're referring to the silent soldier, right?"

I nodded my head smiling slightly.

Jode got a faraway look in his eyes. "*He* doesn't need words to convey what he's thinking…"

I nodded. "Exactly, sometimes silence is more than enough."

For a second, we stood there; then simultaneously we made our way to the gap in the trees.

The moment we exited the forest Jode went a separate way and I walked home alone. The bitter cold of the night was making my arms and legs feel numb, but I forced myself to continue walking. A few minutes later I found myself standing a few feet away from my house, contemplating whether I should go in through the door or find another way in. The thought of my mom's expression pushed me to choose the latter.

I walked over to the side of the house and looked up. I was surprised that it looked much higher from down here than it had looked from up there. Frowning I felt the steadiness of the trellis, it seemed like it would be strong enough to support me, but honestly with my body numbed from the cold I didn't know if I would make it.

For a brief moment I felt like something was wrong, I glanced at my window and tightened with fear. Mom was standing

there glaring down at me. I stood frozen. "What do you think you're doing?" unlocked anger present behind every word. I continued looking up. "Walking?"
She lost her nerve. "GET INSIDE THIS SECOND!"
I tried not to cringe and slowly made my way to the door. This was embarrassing. Could I do anything without getting caught? I inserted my key and the door creaked open. I felt like I was in a horror movie. What was going to happen to me now. I hoped she wouldn't go Asian on me and bring out the rolling pin.
I closed the door behind me. The house was dead silent. The TV wasn't even on.
Uh Oh, I was in serious trouble. I didn't get a chance to think of a good excuse because before I knew it mom and dad were standing in front of me, arms crossed, angry glares present on their faces.
I smiled weakly. "I'm home"
"What were you doing outside?" Dad frowned
I shifted uncomfortably. "Can I take off my jacket?"
Mom sighed and looked at dad, "I told you, he's impossible"
"Not if I have anything to do with it." Dad glared at me, "I said: what were you doing outside?"
I looked back at him. "I went for a walk"
Dad glanced at the hallway clock. "It's five to eleven."
"So?" I shrugged.
Mom butted in. "So? *So*? I told you, you can't leave the house after nine! That's what's *so*! It's not normal for people to walk for three hours!"
Dad nodded.
I sighed. "I've told you before and I'll tell you again, I take long walks outside at night, I don't know why. Maybe it's some sort of disorder or something, but that's just what I do."
I knew my answer sounded lame but what else could I say?

That was the closest to the truth I was willing to get.
Dad raised his eyebrows. "Okay, where do you go?"

I sighed and looked down. "Why does it mat—"

I was cut off with dad's now rising voice. "I said *where did you go?*"

I scratched my head; fine I'd tell him the truth. "The forest."
His glare intensified. "What? You expect me to believe you go to the forest *at night*!? To do *what*?"
My own anger began to rise. If they wanted the truth, I would give it to them. "To observe nature."
Both of them stared at me obviously stunned. They hadn't been expecting this. For a second, I thought I saw dad's expression soften but mom jumped in. "Do you really think we're that gullible? What type of freak goes to the forest at night for hours on end just to observe nature?"

My anger came out. "No, I think the real question is what type of freaks drive to a building and pay just to see people wasting their lives for hours on end?"

Both my parents were taken aback, they looked hurt. Dad looked at me disappointed. "I thought we had a good time at the movies?"

My heart sunk and I immediately regretted what I said, "what I actually meant to say was I'd rather spend time with you guys doing something else other than watching movies."

My mom shook her head. "You know, you could actually learn something from what we watched."
She was obviously referring to the loner guy who changed himself entirely.

Now it was my turn to be offended. I pulled my shoes off and slumped past them. "I'm going to sleep."

Gratefully they didn't try to stop me. I reached my room and sat inside. It was still cold from the open window. Sighing I walked over and laid down in bed. The house was dead silent. It had never been this silent before. For the second time in the day, I found myself contemplating silence. It was so strange how it could mean so much. In the *Natural World* it meant peace, but over here, in my house, it meant something else.

For some reason I was reminded of Mina. What was she doing right now? Did she get along with *her* parents? I wondered what she would think about my situation. What she would think of the *Natural World*.

My thoughts were interrupted by my parent's conversation downstairs. Either they were talking really loudly, or the quiet atmosphere was amplifying their voices because I could hear every last word.
Mom sounded extremely upset. "What are we supposed to do with him?"

Dad spoke. "I bet he's gotten himself addicted."

"Don't say that!" Mom gasped.

Dad sighed. "Face it! Did you see how sick and pale he looks? He hardly ever talks and he's out all night. It's obvious what's going on."

Mom started sobbing quietly.

I bit my bottom lip in thought. So they seriously thought I was some sort of drug addict? I glanced into the mirror. My dark eyes stared back at me. I did look incredibly sick.

I sat up and held my head in my hands. How little did my parents know about me? I didn't even like going to the movies and they were saying that I was a drug addict. This was proof, pure evidence of the ideology that people only judge you based on what they see on the outside. Had I ever said anything similar to that of a drug addict? Had I ever been caught bringing home mysterious packages? And now just because I looked slightly sick and didn't talk much my mom was sobbing downstairs with the thought I was corrupted beyond belief.

I had to distract myself.

I pulled out my phone and started searching up Spades and Outbreak, Jode's words were echoing in my head and now was a good time as any to try and figure out what he was talking about. Maybe that could get my mind off things.

My parents fell asleep a few hours later; I tried to follow but ended up staying up the whole night reading up and watching the full moon fade into the morning light.

Twelve

"The occult."

Jode looked up from his textbook, clearly puzzled.
I raised my eyebrows. "You said you would tell me more if I figured it out. The answer is the occult."
Jode continued staring at me blankly.
"You seriously don't know what I'm talking about? I'm talking about Outbreak and Spades of course. They're part of the occult, and not one of the lower level one's either." For a second Jode looked scared, then he snorted. "No, you've got it all wrong, nice try though. They're just gang members."
"Trust me, I did my research, and I did my website project on it, they conduct human sacrifices and everything."
This caught Jode's attention, and his smile disappeared in a second, "human sacrifice?"
"Yeah, it's all there online, Spades is their head man. They believe in human sacrifice to appease evil demons and spirits."

Jode was visibly shaken.

"Wait, what? Why though?"

"Apparently, they believe they get power. Things like the ability to control minds, unlimited money, and influence. The better the sacrifice, the better the prize."

Jode slumped down in his chair. He looked sick to his stomach.

"You okay?"

He didn't look up at me but pulled something out of his pocket. "You know what this is?"

I peered into his hand. He was holding a piece of paper with markings on it, grids with numbers and what looked like blood stains on the top.

Chills ran down my spine. "Yeah, I think I do, this looks like some sort of talisman or sigma."

"Come again?"

"A contract many occultists write up in a state of possession, it's an agreement with the devil basically. Where in the world did you get it?"

Jode looked down shaking his head. "Susan told me she saw Hudson putting something in my locker, I went to see what it was and found this." He looked up at me in utter disbelief. "I thought it was a dumb joke …"

For a few moments we stared at each other, realization dawning on him at the same time it dawned on me, I didn't need him to tell me more. "He's finally lost his mind."

A few more solemn moments of silence later, we both burst out laughing at the same time. What else was there to do?

♦♦♦♦♦♦

 No one ever passes me the ball.

People who use this quote are often termed as losers or wimps. Sadly enough, this quote is one that applies directly to my life. I frowned and observed the heated game of

183

basketball being played in front of me.

I hated sports, the only reason I was even standing in the middle of the gym pretending to play was because of our school policy. You see, our school has something like house leagues. At the beginning of the year, you're randomly put into one of six houses and for the rest of the year you have to play sports and compete with each other. There's no prize at the end but it's mandatory to participate. So once a month it's my turn to stand in the middle of the field and do nothing, and if I don't, I lose my team points. Honestly, I wouldn't have cared, but there was something inside me that told me that I shouldn't let my team down. I moved to the side as one of my team members whizzed past me with the ball, as if I were invisible.

It's not like it even made a difference if I played or not anyways. It was thirty minutes into the game and as usual I hadn't even laid a finger on the ball, *once*.

The sad part was, I wasn't half bad at basketball. Even though I wasn't into sports my dad had put a basketball hoop in the backyard and occasionally, I liked to go out and play.
The challenging idea of having to score the ball into that one small hoop seemed appealing to me, and over time I had gotten fairly good. Not that my team knew. I had been standing in practically the same spot for twenty minutes, I bet they wouldn't have even noticed if I went and sat down. I decided to give it one last shot before quitting. I waited for the ball to come my way, a few moments later a member from the opposing team was running towards me with the ball. I found an opening and lunged for it, finally after so long I felt the hard ball beneath my hands. I felt my heart rate increase as I

dribbled the ball.

This was my chance to prove myself, but before I could even move one inch, the ball was swept from under my hands. My mouth fell open, I hadn't been near anyone on the opposing team, I watched the guy run with the ball and realized he had been on my own team.
Sighing I walked over to the bench and sat down. Weren't house leagues supposed to promote teamwork? My *own* team member had swept the ball from under me, that wasn't teamwork, that was *bullying*. I looked at the field, Rick. K the basketball star on my team shot and missed.
If I had ever made a mistake like that, no one would ever pass me the ball again. I leaned back against the wall and lost myself in thought.
A few moments later Jode jogged up to me, his forehead dripping with sweat. He had been on the opposing team. He grinned and looked at me mockingly. "You were on fire out there; you should go for pro."
I smiled sarcastically. "Yeah, I'm thinking about it."

He wiped his forehead and continued to grin. "Well, I'll see you in class."
With that he headed out the door, ten minutes later I was the only one in the gym.
I pulled myself up and smiled, not being an active member in the team did have its benefits, at least I wouldn't need a shower. I walked towards the door and on my way felt my foot hit something hard. I looked down and saw the basketball by my feet. I picked it up and after throwing it up and down for a while faced the net; I was a little closer to the net than half court, which was about the size of the unprofessional court in my backyard.

My team would have never given me a chance to take a shot like this. I jumped to the side and couldn't help but laugh as the ball hit the rim and bounced back so hard it almost hit my face. Maybe I did need a little more practice.

◆◆◆◆◆◆

I froze in my tracks and pulled my bag off examining its contents, good I had all my books with me.

I would need them considering that the March break was starting tomorrow. As I pulled my bag on, the front door burst open and hundreds of high school students flooded out shouting and screaming with glee. A whole two and a half weeks of doing nothing but staring at a screen and maybe hanging out a bit, it was practically a dream come true.

I ran to the left to avoid being jostled around. It was like watching a herd of wild buffaloes running from a lion. Except in this case, their lion was knowledge.
The crowd forced me back a few feet and I bumped into someone, I turned around to apologize and saw that it was Jay.

leaning against his red Chevrolet, staring at the crowd with a bored expression on his face.
He caught me looking at him and his bored expression turned into a grin. "Man, you're really creepy."
I raised my eyebrows questioningly, taken aback by his statement.
"I always catch you staring at me; seriously it's starting to freak me out."
I smiled slightly. "You have maroon hair; shouldn't you be

used to it?"
His grin widened. "Point taken."
"What are you doing here
anyways?"
He scratched the back of his head. "Waiting for
someone." "Jode?"
He snorted. "Yeah, he wishes he were that important, the guy
I'm waiting for isn't from this school, and before you ask
again, we just decided to meet here 'cause it seemed the most
convenient place."
I nodded, but I was saved the trouble of trying to continue the
conversation as Jode came up behind me with a bag of Chips
in his hand. "What are *you* doing here?" he directed his gaze
to Jay.
Jay resumed his bored expression and ignored the
question. Jode turned to me. "Ready for the break?"
"Yeah, my family has plans."
 "Oh, what are they?"
I frowned. "We're going to California."
Jode crunched on a handful of chips. "Cool, when are you
leaving?"
"Day after tomorrow."
Jay reached over and grabbed the bag of chips from Jode's
hand. Jode looked like he was going to protest but then he
thought better of it and settled with a dirty look.
Jay grinned and chewed loudly. "So wathca gonna do there?
Wait lemme guess, write poetry?"

I shrugged. "Maybe."
His eyes lit up. "Are you serious? Aww, you and Jodette
really are *just* like each other!"
There was a brief break in conversation as Jode tried to grab
the bag of chips but missed. "So, what exactly do you write

poems about?"
The question seemed innocent, but I could tell it wasn't serious. "About anything, I guess."
Jay smiled maliciously as if that were the answer he had been hoping for. "Anything?"
I shrugged. "Yeah, sure"
Jay's expression turned dead serious. "Don't tell anyone but I kinda have a poem of my own. It might not be that great, but I've been working on it for some time."
I glanced at Jode, he was staring at Jay suspiciously. Jay stopped leaning against the car and stood up straight, holding the bag of chips as hamlet held the skull in all plays. He spoke:

> *"Oh, potatoes why do thy taste so chippy?*
> *Is it 'cause Jodette's a hippy?*
> *A soccer ball he thinketh he can kicky But truly*
> *my boots he does licky..."*

At this point he dropped the bag and burst out laughing. I tried to bite back my smile, had I really thought Jay was going to recite a serious poem? I didn't even bother pointing out his grammatical errors.
Jode's expression of disbelief had turned into a look of disgust but I could see that even he was trying to refrain from smiling.
"You're so clever." He said sarcastically.
He picked up the bag from the floor and moved a safe distance away from Jay. Jay stopped laughing and looked up, he had been laughing so hard there were tears in his eyes.
"Man, you guys are so-"

Suddenly he stopped smiling, he was looking directly behind Jode. It didn't take me long to figure out why.

"Hey Jode!"

Hudson and the gang walked up to us.

"We're going to Miles' come on."

Jode looked uncertain, but after a while nodded quickly. "Alright let's go."

He tried to walk away fast but stopped in his tracks as Hudson noticed me. "Oh Reef, what are you doing here, standing all alone? Planning to stay here the whole break?" He grinned cockily. "Well, you obviously have nothing better to do."

I opened my mouth to say something but was cut off.

"Hey, are you blind? If you ask me, he's not standing alone."

All eyes simultaneously turned to Jay who was still standing by his car.

I saw Jode cringe. Hudson's cocky expression changed dramatically. For a second, he just stared, then an odd smile crept across his face. "It's *you*"

Jay didn't move.

When the silence grew overwhelming Miles carefully nudged Hudson. "Let's go man, the holidays are waiting!"

Hudson still had that creepy smile on his face as he turned to leave. "I'm sure we'll be meeting *soon* anyways."

Jay shrugged indifferently as if that comment had no significance in his life, but his eyes told a different story.

Hudson took a few steps then turned around again. "Oh yeah, Spades says he sends his blessings." The expression on his face as he said that was strange, undecipherable.

Jay half smiled, anger flashing through his eyes. "Tell Spades I can't wait."

Hudson's face reddened with rage, he held his mouth in a tight line as if debating whether to retaliate or not. After a few moments he turned around and walked away.

Saved by Jay yet again.

We watched the group of four walk away silently. A few minutes after their car drove off, a loud shriek pierced through the air. Startled, I turned my head left and right, frantically trying to locate the source of the unearthly sound. I was nearly spinning in circles when I saw Jay grin and pull out his cell phone. The shrieking stopped.
"That was your ring tone?" I asked in disbelief.
He grinned wider and put the phone to his ear, then in an annoyed tone addressed the caller. "What?"
There was a pause, and then Jay frowned. "You made me wait for forty minutes."
Another pause then Jay sighed. "Yeah, okay fine"
He pocketed his phone and walked over to his car door. He looked up at me. "Looks like I came here for no reason, you need a ride home?"
"That'd be great"
Jay smiled. "Alright then get inside."
I sat inside and fastened my seat belt. "How about you just drop me off by the *Chocochurn*?"
Jay nodded. "Sure."
I took advantage of the brief silence to contemplate what I had just heard. *Spades,* something was obviously going to happen soon, and as Hudson had stated a while back, it was going to happen a little more than a month later. I did some calculating and estimated there were around ten days left. That was about the time that it would take for me to come back from California. Maybe I could try prying something out of Jay with the little information I had.
I looked at Jay. "So…ten days"

Jay hit the brakes hard and the car which was gratefully still in the near empty parking lot swerved to a halt.

He stared at me wild eyed. "What *about* ten days?"
I blinked and stared back at him, maybe that hadn't been the wisest thing to say. "Uh, ten days of holiday?"
Jay stared at me for a while then relaxed. "Sorry don't know what got into me." Then he grinned, "That stupid Hercules guy always gives me migraines."
He restarted the car and drove out of the lot carefully.
I glanced at him, that reaction had been more than enough to tell me that something big was happening between him, Hudson and possibly this Spades character in ten days and he was worried enough about it to be counting down.
I glanced at him; he was biting his bottom lip as if in deep thought.
He stopped at a red light then turned to me. "Hey, can I ask you something?"
I shrugged. "Sure."
"Okay it's like a scenario thing, so listen to it and answer the question, okay?"
He didn't wait for my reply. "What would you do if I told you that someone had gotten himself into something really stupid when he was really small, and now he really regretted it."
As the silence extended, I realized he was waiting for me to reply. "Wait weren't you going to give me a scenario?"
Jay sighed. "Just answer"
"Well, I guess I would need to know more about the situation before I pass my comment."
Jay continued biting his bottom lip "Okay, let's say this kid was a great person until he met some bad people, and then he got himself into serious stuff and now he believes he's too far in, to do anything about it"

I raised my eyebrows. "Serious stuff as in?"

Jay sighed. "Man, you're slow, aren't you supposed to be smart?" he looked down for a while, and then looked back up, "drugs…gangs…."

I thought about it for a second. "I'd say that this kid should quit now, no matter what the cost."

Jay shook his head. "No, if he tries to stop, really bad things will happen."

"I still say better late than never, I mean how bad can the situation be?"

Jay took a right turn. "Bad enough to end his life."

Now it was me who was chewing my bottom lip, this was tough. "Well, maybe the kid needs to consider whether the life he's living is worth it."

Jay looked over at me, I had never seen him so serious. "What do you mean?"

I looked back into his tired eyes. "I mean that the kid needs to consider whether the existence of his life is more valuable than the way he lives it. If he quits, he may still survive, but if he continues, is his life really one he wants to live?"

Jay was concentrating on the road, but a strange expression had overtaken his features. "Every life is worth living."

I'm not saying it isn't, but a life should have productivity in it, I say the kid should take the risk and no matter how deep in he is, he should just quit."

Jay parked in front of the *Chocochurn* but neither of us moved, then slowly he turned to me. "What if…what if the kid was scared of death?"

I tried not to smile; he had obviously been contemplating our conversation at the *Chocochurn*.

"Everyone's scared of death"

"Yeah, but this kid is scared of what will happen to him *after*

he dies."
I stared at him for a while, trying to decipher whether he was joking or serious. His expression seemed beyond serious.
"So, you believe there's a life after
death?" Jay bit his bottom lip harder.
"Just answer."

I had given a lot of time thinking about what happened after we pass away. I had looked at all the perspectives, Atheist, Agnostic, Christian, Islamic, Jewish, and Hindu.
"Well, it depends on what the kid
believes"
Jay shrugged. "The kid doesn't believe."
I unbuckled my seat belt. "Well, there are so many points of view on what happens to a person after he dies. Unless I know what, the kid believes, I can't really comment."
Jay looked down at his hands. "This kid is scared of going to hell."
I smiled. "Well, most belief systems state that God is all forgiving, if the kid repents then obviously God will forgive."
After a long silence Jay looked up. "But how do you know Who God is…. People worship so many things, some people even worship satan himself."
Chills ran down my spine. I had a feeling Jay knew a lot more about this then he was letting on. "The answer is very straightforward; you know Who God is if He fulfills two simple criteria."
"And what's that?"
"He was not created by anyone, and He never perishes. Satan was created, and he will perish one day, anything that breathes was created—whether you believe it was by God or the Big Bang and natural selection. God, however, is eternal, and the original source of energy and light, He always existed and always will."

Jay stared at me, eyes wide open and then grinned, "okay thanks"

I smiled. "Those were some tough questions." I reached over to open the door, but Jay held me back. "Wait one last question"

I turned around. "Yeah?"

"Do you think both good *and* bad people will go to heaven?"

I didn't even have to think about it. "Here I'll have to agree with the Islamic perspective, that after everyone dies there will come a day when every single person in the world will be judged for their actions, God will read the intentions of the people and if he sees that they were true hearted and they repented for their sins, he will allow them heaven...true Justice"

Jay laughed a little. "So only good people?"

I shook my head. "No, not really, in the perspective I just mentioned, it is believed that even a murderer of a hundred men can attain paradise *if he repents.*"

"Seriously? He just has to repent?"

I shrugged. "That's what I've read, but that obviously isn't an excuse for doing wrong… because to repent means to ask for mercy and most importantly never repeat the crime."

Jay raised his eyebrows. "Doesn't that kind of give people a justification for doing wrong?"

I smiled. "No, it doesn't, in fact it does the opposite. By showing how much love God has for His creation it'll give hope to anyone, show anyone it's not too late. Most people sin because they think God doesn't care about them, they think they've gone too far to be forgiven but if they realize how merciful God is, it could change their life."

Jay ran his hands through his hair and continued staring at

me. "I've never thought about it that way."

I smiled and resettled myself on the car seat. "Now it's my turn to ask you a question."

He looked at me seriously. "Alright, shoot"

"What was the kid scenario about?"

Jay half smiled, "Assignment"

I raised my eyebrows skeptically but decided to pretend that I believed him. Before I closed the door to leave Jay called me one last time. "Hey, so I'm not gonna see you these holidays?"

I shook my head.

He looked like he was nervous. No, not nervous; he looked sad. He shifted in his seat awkwardly as if he were thinking of saying something then he looked up. "Okay, take care and remember… don't do anything stupid."

I smiled. "I think that's something I should have said to you"

He started the car. "Yeah, but it's a bit too late for me to take that advice, make sure you don't make the same mistake."

I smiled. "Better late than never..."

He stared at me for a while then drove off.

I watched his car leave and then entered the *Chocochurn deep* in thought. Could the kid he was referring to be himself? Yes, it must have been. It would only make sense that way. I frowned and after greeting Mr. Gret exited the *Chocochurn* with a medium sized hot chocolate in my hands. I would have loved to stay back and just sit and think but I knew Mom wanted me home right after school.

Ever since the night I had snuck out to the *Natural World* I had practically been shunned to me room. As soon as I came home my mom would question me until nightfall and then I would be banished upstairs. My dad on the other hand had taken to ignoring me almost completely.

I sighed. Honestly, I knew I deserved it. I mean, what else did I expect after openly disobeying my parents like that? I could see why they were worried, and I knew I wasn't offering them a proper explanation, maybe I would try today. I walked quickly and as soon as I reached home, braced myself and entered.

As expected, I could hear the sound of the TV blaring in the family room, the rest of the house seemed silent.

I pulled off my shoes. "I'm home."

When nobody replied I walked over to the family room and peered inside.

My parents were both sitting down on the sofa with their eyes on the large screen TV across the room. Siara wasn't home yet. I cleared my throat and they simultaneously glanced up. Dad turned his gaze back to the TV and mom gave a tight smile.

"Hello dear, how was school?"

I stared at her and attempted to smile back. "Uh, it was good. I got my chemistry test back."

Dad glanced up again. "How did you do?"

This time I didn't have to feign a smile. "Ninety-seven-point five percent, it was the highest."

My mom seemed to relax a little. "Well, that's good news." Dad nodded but didn't say anything.

I stared at them awkwardly and just when I was about to leave dad spoke.

"Tylor, have a seat."

I turned around to see him lowering the volume. Had I done something wrong?

I edged over to the chair closest to the door and sat down. "Do you need me for something?"

Dad waited for a while and then let out a sigh. "What's

going on with you?"

I tried not to groan. "What do you mean?"

He raised his eyebrows. "Don't play innocent; I know how it was when I was your age, with all the influence and peer pressure. You don't have to pretend."

The look of concern on his face was so genuine I grew desperate.

"No, seriously Dad, nothing is going on I don't know why you're so worried."

Mom bit her bottom lip. "It's time to stop pretending Tylor, tell us the truth."

If the situation wasn't so serious, I probably would have laughed. "I'm being one hundred percent honest. The only things that are going on in my life right now are: Grade twelve, nature and poetry."

Dad shook his head. "Alright then why don't you ever spend time with us?"

"I told you, I like observing nature in the forest."

Mom stared at me accusingly. "Then why don't you ever come with us when we're going out?"

I sighed. If I wanted this to end, I would just have to tell them the truth.

"Because all you guys do is watch movies or TV, if you went somewhere else, I would come for sure."

"What's wrong with movies?"

I tried to keep my voice steady. "I don't see the point of them."

They both stared at me for a while and then mom glanced at dad. "I guess I see your point. Maybe we can make an agreement?"

Dad thought it over then nodded. "Alright, you spend more time at home, and we'll watch less TV. Deal?"

I stared at them in disbelief. Had it really been that easy? "Alright, sure." And then grinning from ear to ear: "Actually that sounds great!"

Both my parents looked extremely shocked at my bout of enthusiasm. They hadn't seen me this excited in a long time and in reality, I hadn't felt this way for quite a while. Could you blame me? The thought of spending actual quality time with my family was more than enough to make me want to jump for joy; it was practically a dream come true.

Thirteen

The ride to California was short. Before we all knew it, we were at Grandfather's, unpacking our suitcases and preparing for a week of extreme vacationing.

Even though he lived completely alone he had nine bedrooms in his house. Out of the nine I always took the room on the top floor. The main reason I loved that room in particular was because it had a window that nearly covered one wall leading to a stunning view of his large backyard. You didn't really find many houses like these around this part of America, many people told Grandpa he should move into a more modern home, but Grandpa refused, he believed this house; despite its old creaking floors and old-fashioned furniture, was his real home and no amount of persuasion would pull him out.

I climbed down the old staircase and recalled the agreement I had made with my parents. It was only 9:00am so they were still sleeping, but my excitement began to mount. Maybe now we could actually do things to get to know each other, like families were supposed to.

I walked into the kitchen and poured myself a glass of orange juice.

"Morning Tylor."

I turned around to see Grandfather standing by the doorway; apparently, I wasn't the only one awake.

"Good morning."

Grandfather pulled up a stool and sat down. "So got any plans for today?"

I shook my head. "No not really."

"Well, you should go out explore a little; you'll only be here for a while."

I nodded my head. "Yeah, I'm planning to go walk a little later this evening."

With a nod, Grandfather pulled open a newspaper and began reading. I seated myself on the table and took some time to examine him. Like any other sixty-year-old man he had white hair and wrinkles covering his face and like most other grandparents he always dressed in large sweaters and wool pants. I took a sip of my juice and continued watching him read.

He was a quiet man, and that's what I loved about him. We came from a family of talkers, where if you didn't talk much then you were automatically dubbed abnormal. But Grandfather was different. He barely ever spoke, barely ever opened his mouth unless of course he was giving advice or in a rare occasion, speaking of his life in the Military.

His silence drew everyone's respect. I smiled bitterly; *my* silence just drew anger from everyone. I sighed thinking about all the family gatherings we had in which I just sat there staring at everyone's faces, I had laughed at all the jokes and exchanged greetings, but I never spoke much. Maybe it was because we didn't have much in common, or maybe it was just that I had nothing to say. My family had gotten fed up with my 'bad attitude', at the beginning I got yelled at but then those angry words turned into looks of pity.

Every time I was sitting down contemplating something, I would always notice one person or the other staring at me with a sad look on their face as if they were watching someone with a disease, and silently praying to God to 'help my pitiable soul'. I put my glass of juice down and shook my head. I just didn't have anything to say, was that a crime? *Couldn't silence just be enough?*

"Something wrong?"

I looked up at Grandfather who had apparently been watching me for the past few minutes. "Uh no, nothing at all."

Grandfather continued watching me for a while then a slow smile began to play on his face. "Keeping your problems to yourself isn't always a good thing."

I drained my glass of juice and stood up. "You know what, I'm going to try and tackle some of my holiday homework."

Grandfather shrugged. "Go ahead but choosing to ignore my statement doesn't change the fact that it's true."

At that moment Siara came running into the kitchen. "It's almost ten? Tylor! Why didn't you wake us up?"

I stared at her questioningly. "I thought I'd let you guys sleep in since it's only our second day here and all."

She glared at me. "The *Bliss* back-to-back special is starting today at 9:40am sharp! I have to wake up mom!"

I gaped at her as she ran back up the stairs. Grandpa caught

my look and smiled. "You don't like that show?"
I frowned. "No, I don't like any show actually. Unless it's a documentary on the miracle of life or something."
Grandfather raised his eyebrows. "Interesting, there are very few people who think like that, you know?"
I smiled bitterly. "Trust me, I know."
A few minutes later I heard my mom coming down the stairs. "Morning. How are you guys doing?"
Grandfather nodded. "Perfectly. How about you?"
She yawned and then smiled. "Couldn't be better, Tylor did you have something to eat?"

"I'll have an apple."
She walked over and quickly made herself a cup of coffee. "You really think that'll fill you up?"
"It should for now."
She shrugged and while taking a sip of her coffee made to exit the room. "Alright. If you'll excuse me, I have a show to catch."
I stared at her in dismay. "Uh, but I was thinking we could go hiking or something."
She lowered her cup and raised her eyebrows.
"Hiking? In this weather? You have got to be kidding me."
I faced the window. "What's wrong with that? Just because it's cold doesn't mean the beauty's gone."
Grandfather chuckled. "The boy's got a point."
Siara ran into the room. "Mom, hurry! There's only four minutes left."

Mom stared at me apologetically. "Sorry honey, maybe later?" And then she was gone.

So much for the agreement.

I exited the kitchen and went upstairs to my room. I picked my laptop off my bed and placed it on the only other piece of furniture in the room, the table which was located by the wall to the left of the large window. I seated myself and flipped it on.

I hadn't been on *Souls-ink* for a while.

I opened my profile page and scrolled down, there were three new comments all of which once again falsely guessed my age. That *Ihatefreaks* person had commented again.

I clicked 'poems and her list opened. It was a long list, the titles once again made me smile. Out of the forty-two poems she had on her profile, I randomly selected one. It was entitled *my soul*. That didn't sound so bad.

My SOUL


```
 What is my soul, what could it be?
 It's anything to make me a celebrity

My soul is nothing but what you want
it to be
'cause I'll do anything to be a celebrity

   I'll sell my life and my dignity
     cause I wanna be a celebrity
```

```
I don't care about anything but fame
   To me life is nothing but a game

So let me be popular and well known
 To you my heart and mind I'll loan

 Let me be famous, let me be free
   'Cause I wanna be a celebrity
```

I blinked; the rhymes weren't that bad, but the content was horrifying and extremely blunt. I hoped this girl didn't really mean what she said.
I exited her page and continued to stare blankly at the screen. That had been scary, I don't know what had happened but while I was reading, I had felt extremely odd.
I contemplated for a while then realized that that odd feeling had been fear.

Why? Probably because her poem had been so true, so, on the mark.
I don't know what she had been thinking when she wrote it, or even if it came from the bottom of her heart but it had made perfect sense.
My soul is nothing but what you want it to be
I couldn't help but shudder. When was the last time people thought for themselves? When was the last time people bothered to consider why they were doing what they were doing? Nearly all of humankind were doing something that they would regret dearly if they ever realized.
They were selling their souls, selling their souls to something that was indifferent to their wellbeing or even their existence.
These people had sold something as valuable as *their soul, their wisdom of thought* to something that couldn't care less.

They had sold their souls to something that didn't even know it owned them.

The weather in California was much warmer than in Canada. In Canada I had to wear a jacket plus all my winter gear to keep myself warm but here, a light sweater was enough to keep the cold out and there wasn't even any snow on the ground.
Before I left the house, mom saw me and quickly pulled her shoes on.
I looked at her hopefully.
She smiled. "Sorry about yesterday. I guess we did have an agreement."
Was this really happening?
As we walked outside mom kept complaining about how cold it was, but her face lit up when I would point out the different plants and trees and explain their phytology to her.
The absence of snow caused a slight tug at my heart. I couldn't help but miss the *Natural World*. Sure, it was only my second day here, but I hadn't even taken one last trip before my flight.
"I miss the snow"
Mom looked at me in shock. "Why would you miss the snow? If you ask me, it's still too cold here."
"Snow is beautiful."
She gave me a skeptical yet thoughtful look.
"So you really just like going on long nature walks, don't you?"
"That's what I've been trying to tell you."
I saw the relief wash over her face. She actually believed me.
We continued walking down the road; it felt so strange to be

outside with her, no distractions or anything else between us. I felt ecstatic to say the least. I couldn't say the same for mom. She really looked like she was forcing herself to do this. I was grateful.

I realized that we had been walking aimlessly for a good half hour. Maybe now would be a good time to actually explore something.
I quickly scanned the rows of stores in front of me. They were all small stores, roughly the same size. Mom pointed at a store "did you know your dad was an expert painter back in the day? Let's check that out."
It was entitled '*Painter plaza*'
We walked over to it and glanced through the large window. Through the window I could see rows and rows of paintings hanging on walls and placed on shelves, as well as a section for painting supplies. I wiped the invisible snow off my shoes out of habit and then walked in.
The woman at the front counter glanced up at us from behind a computer screen. She smiled, clearly in the mood for conversation. Mom gravitated to her and started asking her about the paintings in the store.

As usual, I wasn't in the mood to talk right now.

I allowed myself to walk down the rows of paintings and after a few minutes realized that the paintings were arranged according to genre. The current row I stood in now was filled with different paintings of the sky and the one I had just passed had been based on tombstones. I continued my way down the aisles. I was keeping my eyes on the top shelves; I had already caught sight of a few beautiful pictures that I was considering buying.

My thoughts were interrupted as I felt myself hit someone hard. I had been so distracted I hadn't realized where I was going. "Sorry." I murmured.

I looked up to see who it was; it was a girl around my age. Blonde short hair that looked fake, layers of makeup and regular clothing, a cigarette hung loosely from her painted lips. For some reason, her presence bothered me.

I moved to the side to let her pass, but she was staring at me in a strange way. She raised one eyebrow. "Uh, sorry, that must've been my fault."

For a second something happened to me, that voice. It sounded so... *familiar*.

The girl blinked twice and pulled the cigarette from her mouth. "Okay, I like don't mean to be weird but *Tylor*, is that you?"

I backed away trying to calm my beating heart. My mouth flew open, and I felt shock grip my body. There was one way to clarify whether my guess was correct or not. I looked at her eyes; they were the color of honey.

I tried to keep myself standing, but I felt myself sway visibly. There was no doubt about it; this was Mina Trew. She spoke again now sounding more enthusiastic. "Tylor it *is* you!"

I managed to nod my head.

I looked at her again trying to clarify whether what I was seeing was real. Her clothes were exactly like what Cathy and them wore, her makeup, her hair…was this really Mina? The Mina I remembered had long red hair. Most of all, her aura had been beautiful. A far cry from what I felt now.

"Oh wow. It's been so long since I saw you! How's everything? You still live in Toronto?"

I pushed back the shock, at least for the moment and looked down. "Yes, we still live in Toronto… you live here now?"
She nodded her head. "Yup, moved here four years ago."
The year we lost contact
There was an awkward silence as we both stared at each other. She swayed back and forth restlessly. "Wow you don't even look that different, obviously you're like taller but otherwise you still look the same!" she giggled, "You even dress the same!"
I scratched the back of my head awkwardly. "I wish I could say the same to you."
She looked confused for a while then she smiled. "Oh! You mean the hair? I'm trying something different."
The silence persisted on for a long time. Both of us were starting to feel extremely awkward, but we couldn't walk away, we hadn't seen each other for so long.
"So…" she said. "Is Carlton public school still open?"
I nodded; the name of my old school caused the years of memories to come flooding back to my head.
Her eyes lit up at my nod. "Ohmygosh, remember how stupid we used to be when we were little? We always said the dumbest things, we were so weird!"
I couldn't help but smile. "Those were good times"

She popped her eyes out. "No way! Don't even remind me how boring we were. I was such an embarrassment, I hope no one remembers!"
I stepped to the right. That was enough I didn't need to hear more from her, didn't need to stare at her longer. This wasn't Mina. It couldn't be. I cleared my throat which had become incredibly dry. And decided to clarify, maybe, *just* maybe I was guessing wrong. "Mina? It is you right?"
She looked at me as if I were stupid and then she laughed. "Oh

you're still the same! Of course, it's me! Who else did you think you were like talking to?"

Her words hit me hard, I tried to control my emotions, but it was too hard. All the times I had imagined how she was faring, whether she was battling the world the way I was, whether she had invented newer, wiser philosophies of life that maybe one day we would share together. I turned my head away from her and left.

I didn't bother saying bye; I just turned and walked away. I could feel her staring at me, but she didn't say anything, she let me walk away. I walked down four aisles and then leaned against the nearest wall.

How I wished I had just walked by the store, why did I have to come inside?

Fate.

That much was obvious. Fate had led me here, to see something I should have seen a long time ago.

I heard the shop door open and then close. She had left. I stayed against the wall for a while trying to keep my thoughts straight, I felt like I was at the verge of passing out. What felt like an eternity later, mom nudged me and woke me out of my trance. She had bought a few paintings.

"I found the perfect gifts for our neighbors, and some painting supplies for your dad. Maybe he'll start painting again when he sees these. Come on, let's head home now!"

She was so distracted she didn't realize my mood. Or maybe she thought nothing of it because I was almost always sulking.

I nodded and disheartened headed with her for the door, right before I exited the aisle, I passed by a picture that caught my eye.

It was a beautifully painted picture set in a golden frame. The moment I realized the content of the scenery, I froze in my tracks.

It was a picture of a lone cherry blossom tree standing strong against a moonlit night.

The irony was enough to make me cry.

I stared at the package.

I had bought the painting three days ago, yet I was still staring at the unopened package blankly as if I hadn't the faintest idea what it was. The owner had taken about fifteen minutes to wrap it in brown paper and I had taken a taxi home so I wouldn't have to lug it across the street. It had been expensive but that hadn't been a problem since I hadn't been spending my allowance on anything but snacks for nearly half a year.

Every time I stared at the brown wrapping; I couldn't help but ponder on the coincidence of it all. Meeting Mina was one thing but then seeing this painting right after? It was so beautiful how fate worked its way to bring out the most of everything. But along with that bewilderment staring at the brown paper also brought fear. Sure, I would be fine with it as long as the paper never had to be removed, I had some irrational feeling that if I were to ever remove the paper and set eyes on the painting then something horrible would happen.

I pried my eyes away from the package and the feeling of depression settled itself into my heart once more. The incident with Mina was driving me crazy. At least when I was in Canada, I could have visited the *Natural World* for some peace, but now I had nothing.

I closed my eyes and attempted to remember the scene to the best of my ability, but it wasn't the same.
Suddenly I sat up and walked over to my suitcase that was still resting on my side table. I *had* to have packed it. I opened the side zipper and dug inside. I smiled as I felt my hands clutch a small paper, the size of an average photograph. It was the picture of the *Natural World.*
For a few moments I just held it, and then slowly I pulled it out. As soon as my eyes settled onto the picture and the tree, lake and sky came into view, peace encompassed my being, and I felt a sense of relief. The effect was not nearly as strong as when I visited the actual place, but it was still enough.
I viewed the scene and automatically Mina flew into my head. So many times, I had wondered what she would feel about the *Natural World,* now I don't think I wanted to know. She had changed so dramatically, she used to think just like me, and now... I felt my sadness overflow. I closed my eyes and allowed my feeling to come out in the form of words.

"This wisdom of the soldier's sight, how rare it is to see;
What once was, no longer is, life's true philosophy."

She *had* had the soldier's sight, but now I didn't know what to think.
I pulled myself up and walked down the stairs. Halfway down I halted and considered going back up. For the past few days, I hadn't felt like conversing at all. Grandfather had been the only one to notice my change of mood, nobody else had noticed that I was barely eating or talking.
Well, I hardly ever talked even before, but now I hadn't talked *at all.* At the very moment my family was out to a movie. Me

and Grandfather were the only one's home.

The thought that nobody was home, but Grandpa urged me down the stairs again. He was probably reading a book anyways so no talk would be required.

Sure enough I found him in the main sitting room on a one person sofa reading away. I walked over to the chair nearest to the door and sat down. I allowed myself to get lost in my own thoughts but was interrupted a few minutes later as Grandpa realized my presence.

"Oh, Tylor, when'd you come down?" I looked at him. "Few minutes ago."

He stared at me for a while. "What's on your mind?"

I tried not to frown; I should have realized that I would be questioned.

I Shrugged. "Nothing really."

Grandfather raised his eyebrows. "I've been watching you these past days. The first day you were fine but after that, it all went downhill, you didn't even eat dinner yesterday."

I shrugged again. "I wasn't hungry"

Grandpa shook his head. "You think I believe that? Haven't you thought about what I said last time? It's not always wise to keep your problems to yourself."

I didn't reply.

"I can help you..."

I got up and walked upstairs. I knew I was being rude but for some reason I couldn't get myself to tell him what was on my mind. Maybe it was fear that he'd think I was crazy for thinking something that was apparently so small was so huge. I laid back in bed, a position I had gotten used to these last few days and allowed myself to space out.

A few hours later I had popped open a book and was reading distractedly when my door opened. Grandfather stood there with a glass of orange juice in his hand. "Here, drink this, it's fresh"

I sat up and accepted it. "Thanks."

He turned to leave and then caught sight of the big brown package. He turned back to me. "Hey, what's that?"

I looked away. "Just a painting I bought."

Grandfather walked towards it. "Is that where you went that day?"

I nodded my head even though he couldn't see me. He picked up the package. "Are you saving this for someone?"

"No."

He looked at me with a smile. "Mind if I open it for you?" I smiled slightly. "Be my guest."

My heart rate increased as he began to rip open the brown paper, I don't know why but I felt once again like I would pass out. I watched him carefully as he peeled the brown paper off. As soon as he finished, he heaved the painting up onto the table so that he could see it properly.

I couldn't see his expression because he was facing the other way, but I could tell he was transfixed. He stared at it for a long time then turned around slowly.

He had a twinkle in his eye. "What made you pick this one?" I shrugged. "Let's just say… it brought back memories." "Good or bad?"

I frowned. "I guess I would say good memories with a bad aftertaste."

Grandfather smiled and turned back to the painting.

"Thirty-three years ago, when I was still in the military my friend and I were given a two week leave. Both of us decided we would stay in the same area until the time was over."

I listened carefully; Grandfather was talking about his life in the military; this was rare.

"We were on leave, but we had been given one assignment by our commander. This commander of ours told us that we should both do something before we fight again, leave something behind for the world so that all humanity could benefit."

He stopped talking as he walked over to sit down on the chair by the table and then cleared his throat. "This something was plant a tree."

I looked at him curiously; he had said the painting brought back memories. "So, you planted a cherry blossom tree?"

Grandfather smiled with a faraway look in his eyes. "You got that right."

"You were in Japan?"

Grandfather laughed lightly. "No boy, cherry blossom trees can grow other places too."

"Then where did you plant it?"

He squinted his eyes as if trying to remember. "I believe it was somewhere in Toronto, where you live."

I smiled, that was something I'd like to see. But I still had questions unanswered.

"Why did you pick that particular one?"

Grandfather glanced back at the portrait. "That friend who was with me had been my companion from childhood. We did nearly everything together, and one thing we had always marveled over was the pink blossoms on that tree."

I nodded, that made sense, but Grandfather wasn't done.

"My other friend who had passed away three years prior to that had spent his last months with me in Japan, and he had breathed his last in a cherry blossom orchard."

He paused for breath.

"So yes, there were many reasons why I picked that tree, I'm telling you there's something special about it."

I couldn't help but notice the wrinkles that had overtaken his skin, the crowsfeet crowding his eyes every time he smiled, the haunting wisdom in his eyes. He was old, very old, why was it that all of us detested to be called old when it looked so beautiful on grandfather?

After he finished examining the painting, he looked at me "You know Tylor, everything happens by God's will. You can't change the way things turn out, but you can learn from them and give yourself the gift of wisdom. That's what I've learned through all my years of living."

I looked back at him a slow smile spreading across my face. Those words had lifted something from my heart.

Sure, Mina had changed and she probably wasn't ever going to turn back but instead of sulking about it I could learn something from it.

Mina had changed so much even though she used to think just like me. The reason for her changing was unknown to me but I knew that it had to do something with her dissociating herself from her truth. These thoughts brought me to one verdict:

Stay true to my ideologies no matter what anyone says.

This was the gift of wisdom I was willing to give myself.

Grandfather stood up to leave. "Anyhow, it's a beautiful painting."

I looked at him. "You can have it."

He turned to me again, this time shocked. "No. I couldn't."

I urged him on. "I don't even have space for it in my room in

Canada, plus I wouldn't want to deal with it at the airport."
Grandfather smiled gratefully. "Thank you, this means a lot."
I smiled back "No Grandpa, thank *you*."

Fourteen
JODE

The phone rang and I braced myself. The first two rings were normal, and then it started:

> *"Oh potatoes why do thy taste so chippy?*
> *Is it 'cause Jodettes a hippy?*
> *A soccer ball he thinketh he can kicky But truly*
> *my boots he does licky"*

I tried to stop myself from slamming my head against my computer table. I had been listening to that all week; Only God knows what Jay had done to get his annoying voice reciting that dumb poem as our phone ring-tone, but the point was that he had done it and it was driving me up the wall. The song wasn't so bad itself, but the fact that everyone in the house burst out laughing, especially Jay, whenever it happened was what really made me mad.
The poem kept repeating itself over and over as no one was bothering to pick up. After the fifth ring I got up and went

to the family room where the phone was located. I walked over and without thinking pulled the cord right out of the wall, cutting the poem at mid *thinketh*.

It was then that I realized the only reason no one had picked up was because no one was home.

My anger subsided slightly, and I returned to my room. Honestly the Holidays were dead boring. Nothing was happening, TV was getting repetitive, and the *Natural World* wasn't the same without Tylor. I had only attempted to visit it once after he left; even though it did bring the peace that it always did it just didn't feel the same. I guess it made me miss having some sane company around.

I sat down on my bed and stared at the ceiling. The worst part of the holidays though was my *friends*.

Ever since the day Hudson had broken the news to us everyone was acting different. They weren't normal seventeen-year-old guys anymore; they weren't even teens trying to have fun. Or maybe it was fun for them to pretend they weren't childish in any sense.

As Miles had put it, 'they were rolling with the big boys now'. Well, technically Hudson was rolling with the big boys, but everyone wanted in on the action, so I guess they liked including themselves.

My heart felt like it was constricting as I remembered what Hudson had said. I had only understood half of it, but that one half that I knew was enough to make me sick. Especially considering Tylor's findings and the paper in my locker.

I stood up and threw on my jacket, maybe I could try talking to Hudson about it one last time, it was possible that he would listen. Wasn't it?

Twenty minutes later I found myself sitting in Hudson's car as he drove us to the *ChocoChurn*.

He was in an extremely grim mood. Maybe today wouldn't be the bes and images of how I had seen that face change over nearly a decade was enough to convince me that I had to persuade him not to do it, no matter what the cost. Suddenly I had an idea.
"Hey Hudson, how about you drive down a little past the *ChocoChurn*."
He glanced at me. "Why would I do
that?" I smiled. "Come on, I'll show
you"
Hudson frowned but when the *ChocoChurn* came he continued driving. "Now what?"
I grinned. "Keep driving." I let him drive for more than 'a little past the *ChocoChurn*.'
In fact I let him drive for a good fifteen minutes, all the while he kept glancing at me questioningly. I grinned as we reached our destination. "Yeah, now stop here."
Hudson raised his eyebrows and looked around. We were in a barren place at the end of town. "What is this?" he asked suspiciously.
I pushed open the car door. "Get out I'll show
you" He remained seated still eying me
suspiciously.
I laughed out loud. "Stop acting like a kid, I'm not gonna kill you."
Those words did enough to his pride to get him out of the car in less than a second. I walked down the sidewalk and after a few moments he followed me. We walked in silence until the sidewalk curved in, and we found ourselves

standing before an oddly familiar scene.

An old broken park.

I turned to Hudson and caught him grinning from ear to ear. It was then that I realized that I hadn't seen him smile for a really long time.

"This is! This…"

"Our childhood hangout." I said grinning back.

Still smiling, he took a few steps forward, taking in the scenery of the broken slide, the worn-out swings and the

monkey bars with missing handles. "I totally forgot this place existed!" he turned to me. "What made you remember?"

I shrugged and walked over to a swing, running my hand over the worn-out ropes that we had held so many times. "I just thought it'd be cool to visit after so long."

Hudson nodded and walked around as if he were in another world. Stepping carefully.

I observed the scene and smiled. Me and Hudson back in this old park after eight years. Talk about time flying. I glanced at Hudson and the compelling feeling of talking to him about the event came back. Now we were in the perfect place, I just needed the perfect words.

I opened my mouth to speak but he cut me off. "Hey, you remember that guy…?" His voice trailed off as he chewed his bottom lip in thought.

I looked at him cocking an eyebrow. "Wanna be more specific?"

Hudson was still biting his lip. "You know, that one… the guy."

I grinned mockingly. "Oh *him*, you mean the one with the arms and legs?"

Hudson looked confused. "What? Every guy has arms and legs"

I bit back a smile. "Yeah, that's what I meant."

It took Hudson a while to realize the joke and when he did, he didn't smile. "You seriously don't know who I'm talking about?"

I shook my head.

Hudson kicked the frozen dirt on the floor. "I think his name was… ah never mind."

Absentmindedly I walked over to the swing and sat down. The ropes at the side stretched but they didn't give out. I grinned and looked up at Hudson. "Hey, you wanna?"

Hudson sneered. "Yeah right, I wouldn't be caught dead on that thing."

He was attempting to look disgusted, but I could see that his words didn't match his thoughts. I widened my grin trying to ebb him further. "Come on man, for old time's sake?"

He looked around to make sure no one was looking and then his mask of disgust weakened. "I remember how much we used to go on that thing."

He walked over to the swing on my left and seated himself cautiously, his swing creaked and groaned but once again, it held. For a few brief moments we just stared at each other not knowing what to do, as if we had forgotten how to swing. Then I began kicking my legs. I moved very little, swinging incredibly low, Hudson started a few seconds after me, but he was swinging slightly slower. I glanced at him. He looked like he was trying to maintain a bored expression but once again he was biting back a smile.

I on the other hand was grinning freely. I had to admit that it was embarrassing to be sitting on these elementary school swings when we were in Grade twelve, but the memories it was triggering were priceless. I dared myself to pump harder, but I wouldn't do it unless Hudson would too. "Hey,

remember that game we used to play?"
Hudson looked at me and once again, failed to keep his bored expression on. "Yeah, what about it?"
"Let's play it, come on." I begged, feeling like a little kid again.
Hudson shook his head in denial. "No way, you should be happy I'm sitting on the swing, don't expect me to start going crazy on it."
I started pumping faster. "The one who kicks harder is the one who kicks Beef Harder and therefore is the person who wins" Repeating the long-forgotten ruling out loud felt strange. Hudson stared at me with an odd expression on his face and that's when I realized that the guy with the arms and legs, he had been talking about earlier must have been Beef. No wonder he didn't want to say his name, even when I said it,

   It had felt like I was bringing him back to life or something. I felt   a gust of strong wind rush past my face, Hudson had begun the game.
Just a few seconds later both of us were swinging so far up that it felt like we would go over the top any moment. I remembered how long it used to take to get this high when we were little, we would work at it for fifteen minutes at least and then finally get somewhere near this high. I resisted the temptation to hoot and yelp like a little kid when going down but gave in when I heard Hudson scream hysterically. "Man, I forgot how fun this was!"
Hearing him say such a childish thing in such a childish way was more than enough to break the barrier.
I joined him in laughing and exclaiming with immature glee as we swung higher and higher. The strong bursts of winter air pushed against my face, the creaking and groaning of the

swings filled my ears, and the sound of Hudson swinging beside me filled me with joy; It was just like when we were little, there was absolutely no difference. I glimpsed Hudson's face. And what I saw wasn't Hudson now; it was the Hudson I knew eight years ago.

"I'm winning!" I screamed.

Hudson laughed out loud. "Keep dreaming, I always won when we were little; don't think that's about to change anytime soon!" With that he pumped so hard that I was sure he would go over the top. Just as he reached the highest point, I heard the swings groan in a strange way, different from the rhythm I had been observing for the past few minutes and a feeling of dread filled me. My mouth flew open as the rope holding his swing snapped with the pressure and sent him flying halfway across the playground. A fraction of a second later I found myself soaring across the sky too as my rope snapped, and before I knew it I was laying a few feet away from Hudson face first in the melting snow.

I took a few moments to recover then pulled myself to a sitting position. I glanced in Hudson's direction; thankfully he was sitting up too. We stared at each other blankly for a while trying to comprehend what just happened. Hudson scratched the back of his head. "That was..."

I blinked twice and rubbed my nose stupidly. "Ouch."

That was too much for Hudson, he immediately burst out laughing. I joined him and before we knew it we were rolling on the floor with hysterical laughter.

"That... was... so... funny" Hudson managed to pant between his laughter.

I held a stitch at my side and tried to say something, but my laughter wouldn't let me. Sure, it had been scary, but the fact that we had been at the pinnacle of our excitement when it happened was more than enough to keep me laughing. And to think, I was embarrassed because I sat on the swing, imagine if someone had seen *that*.

As if Hudson read my thoughts, he stopped laughing and quickly looked around. When he saw that the coast was clear he allowed himself to smile and helped me up. "That was literally crazy."

I stood up and shook the snow off my jacket. "Yeah, that thing chose the perfect time to give out on us."

Simultaneously we turned our heads to face the swing set and seeing its condition set about another round of laughter. It looked like it had been hit by a tornado. Not only had the ropes snapped, but the beams supporting the ropes had somehow broken apart and fallen to pieces. That's what you call a really old swing.

We walked to the car still laughing and talking about the crazy things we did when we were little. When we were settled inside, I remembered the real reason why I had led him here. Now that his grim mood was gone it was the best time to attempt it.

I cleared my throat. "School is gonna start again soon."

Hudson frowned. "Yeah, the last thing I need right now is to be forced to think."

I hid my smile and nodded as if what he had said was perfectly sensible, I needed to steer him into that direction, but how? At this rate I was going to run out of time. I bit my bottom lip; maybe I should just come out and say it. I braced myself and then spoke. "So, is that plan still on?"

Hudson seemed taken aback for a moment then his frown deepened. "Of course, it is."

"Are you serious?"

Hudson nodded. I watched him for a while and felt my anger

slowly begin to rise. "You can't be serious! You know it's just a few days away?"

Hudson looked at me angrily. "Obviously I know! I've been counting down every last hour; you think I wouldn't know when it is?"

I shook my head. "That's insane; I'm telling you don't go."

Hudson shrugged indifferently. "Nothing's gonna make me back out, okay?"

I felt myself lose it. "Are you retarded? Don't you realize what you're getting yourself into?!"

Hudson shook his head trying to remain cool. "Not again, we had this conversation a billion times. Just drop it, it's gonna happen whether you like it or not."

I stared hard at him. He kept his eyes on the road, but I could tell there was hesitation in them.

"You don't want to do it, do you? You're just scared because you know Spades'll call you a baby if you back out."

Hudson almost stopped the car in the middle of the road but then caught himself in time. "Spades calling me a baby is the least of my worries. I'm in far deeper than you think."

Those words came as a shock. I had been positive Hudson was only sticking to the plan because he had been afraid that his cousin Spades would mock him eternally if he backed out, but now Hudson was saying something else was up. Was Tylor right? Only one way to find out. "Outbreak isn't just a normal gang, is it?"

Hudson's head snapped towards me, and the car swerved slightly. "What d'you mean?"

I pulled the paper I had found in my locker out of my pocket. "This is what I mean… you seriously believe in this stuff? What even is this?"

His face darkened as he set his eyes on the paper and I felt chills run down my spine. His next words brought bile to my throat.

 "Jode… I didn't want to have to tell you this… but I can read minds; I can control them… Spades showed me a whole new world."

My mouth flew open, and I leaned in closer to him "Are you listening to yourself right now? You didn't answer me, what's this paper?"

Hudson stopped at a red light and turned to face me fully. "Revenge."

"Revenge?"

"You humiliated me at the coffee shop, I had to teach you a lesson." His eyes were dead, dull, serious.

"So, you scribbled on a paper, stained it with ketchup and put it in my locker?"

"No, you idiot, I cursed you — and that's not ketchup, it's blood."

 I desperately searched his face for hints of humor but found none.

"This is just a piece of paper. Tell me this is some sort of sick joke?"

He laughed. An ugly empty sound. "It's just temporary though, the effects will wear off."

"Effects? Effects?! I'm —" he didn't let me finish.

"They made me a part of Outbreak"

I let the words sink in. They had recruited Hudson as a member of their gang?

"No way…But that means that you did the… the deed."

Hudson looked slightly pale. "No, not yet. But they said they knew I would do it, so they swore me in."

I tried to comprehend what he was saying. "Oh…my…GOD! So they want *YOU* to do it!?" I could feel my face color with anger, my mind felt like it was being possessed by something unreal.

"I thought you were just going to watch! Do you know what that mea—?"

My words were cut off as Hudson hit the brakes, this time for real, and the car skidded to a stop.

He was trembling. "DON'T YOU THINK I KNOW? What do you want me to do about it now? If I back out now, *I'll* be the one getting killed! It's too late to do anything, I'm too far in…and now I have to deal with it."

He took a deep breath and then allowed his face to rest in his trembling hands. "I have to deal with it, even if it means someone else's life." Hudson remained in that position.

The cars behind us were honking like crazy. When he didn't move, I decided I'd have to do some shotgun-driving; I kicked his foot to the side and pushed the acceleration with my own foot. I leaned over to steer the car until it was on the side of the road, fairly good for someone who couldn't drive. After the path was cleared, the cars eventually stopped honking, and we were the only ones left on the street. Hudson still had his face in his hands. I unbuckled my seatbelt. "At least tell me where, and who. Who's the person?"

Hudson started trembling more visibly. I looked down and then forced myself to look back up again. "Tell me."

I waited for moments which felt like hours, and then Hudson slowly lifted his head. I was taken aback to see that tears were flowing down his cheeks, he was crying.

He shook his head. "N-no, I can't tell anyone."

I blinked. "Fine."

I pushed open the door and climbed out of the car. "Talk to me when you've got some sense knocked into you."

I slammed the door hard and walked away.
I couldn't believe it had only been an hour ago that I had been sitting on the swings with him like I was a kid again. I closed my eyes and tears involuntarily fought their way out. How I wished I could just go back eight years in time, back to fourth grade, where my biggest worry had just been fear that I would get picked on by some guy with arms and legs.

Fifteen

The screen opened and I typed in my username and

password. I hadn't been on *Souls-ink* for a really long time. A little message box popped up on the bottom right of the screen, someone was sending me a message. I clicked the box and a smile spread across my face as I read the name.

NBW: Hey.

My mind flashed back to the time I had seen Tylor in the lab signing on to *Souls-ink*. He was NBW, but he didn't know *I* was JH. So why was he messaging me? To him I was just supposed to be a random guy. I decided to find out.
I replied with a 'hi', and a few minutes later he asked me something I would have never expected.

NBW: Guess my age.

I stared blankly at the screen. What in the world? Why was he asking me to guess his age? Clearly, he had no way of knowing that I was Jode…


```
JH: What?
Why? NBW:
Because. JH:
Well?
NBW:     I just want to know how
Old you think I am.
JH: But you don't even know who I am.
NBW: Yeah so?     Just guess.
```

I grinned; he was so weird. Maybe he wanted me to guess his age because his profile made it seem like he was a little kid. There was no way a seventeen-year-old would think along those lines. I decided to give him a little scare.

```
JH: You are Seventeen.
```

There was a brief pause.

```
NBW: You mean seven
right? JH: No, I mean
seventeen. NBW: What!?
How?
```

I tried not to laugh; maybe I could take advantage of the situation.

```
JH: Now let me ask you a question.
NBW: Okay, what?
```

JH: Why did you want me to
guess your age?
NBW: It's just something
I like doing. I ask everyone to guess.
JH: That's weird.
NBW: No, what's weird is that
you guessed accurately,
how is that possible?
What made you say I was seventeen?
JH: ☺

NBW: Well?
JH: One more question.
NBW: What?
JH: what does NBW stand for?
NBW: Answer my question first, how did
you know?
JH: That's not the only thing I know, I
also know that you go to Raymond High and
you're the star basketball player of your
team.

There was another pause as the words sunk in.

NBW: Jode?
JH: Tylor?
NBW: Haha very funny, how did you know
it was me?
JH: I saw you in the Lab
NBW: Oh… and no need to be so sarcastic
about the basketball thing, you know I
AM pretty good.
JH: yeah sure, I'll believe it when you
actually get your hands on the ball. So,

```
what does it stand for?
NBW: Needy be wedgie
JH: WHAT?!
NBW: lol
JH: w/e how's California?
NBW: just great, and your holidays?
JH: ...........
NBW: did you do anything exciting?
JH: ......
NBW: anything at all?
JH: You were right about Hudson, Outbreak,
the Sigma
```

NBW: Of course, I was. Did you finish reading Holmes?

JH: On the last three chapters. It's my favorite so far.

Tylor: I'm done, mine too. I g2g eat, tell me details when I see you in a week
JH: k
NBW: Oh yeah, I was kidding, it means a natural and beautiful world

A few seconds later he signed off. Well at least *he* seemed to be having a good time. I looked back at the screen and went to Tylor's profile page. He hadn't put up any new poems. I scanned through his list and noticed for the first time a poem entitled 'Thief.'
Curious I clicked it, for some odd reason I had never seen it before.
The page opened and I began to read:

Thief

The one thing I possessed and loved;
from me you solely stole.
It was my love, my art, my life,
embedded in my soul.

Those silent letters spinning true from
early morn till night.
Those sounds that spun like golden webs
of radiant delight.

Your prying hands have stole from me
that for which I live.
You've stripped and burnt my hope to love,
my will to forgive.

This will keep on dreaming has flown
with the birds.
Your evil thieving hands have stolen
my language, my words.

There was a small note at the bottom which read: This is
how I react to plagiarism.

I couldn't help but smile; someone had copied his work so
he had written a poem about it? That was hilarious; I was
pretty sure he was referring to the philosophy incident when
Ryan, being as lazy as he was, had plagiarized his poem.
Thinking of his words reminded me of what I had thought

of him only a few months ago. I couldn't believe that I had been too scared to talk to him before, now we had made a habit of meeting after school; he had even come over a few times.

I went to his profile; he had added a favorite quote. I read it and smiled bitterly, right on target yet again.

"What once was my peace, has now become my sorrow, what once brought me ease, has me wishing for tomorrow."

The conversation I had had with Hudson ran involuntary circles around my mind. I remembered how he was before, how he had been at the park. But I knew what he was now, what he had become.

I sighed and stared out the window. My March break had been going bad, but after yesterday it had taken a nosedive for the worst. I had actually done my homework this morning in an attempt to distract myself. He just had to go and do something this insane. The only reason I even knew what was going on was because of Jay. Apart from Hudson, Jay was the only one I knew who was into this stuff. When Hudson first told me, he was planning on joining his cousin's gang. It had started off as a dumb thought, I can't believe he had actually gone and done it.

The scariest part of Hudson joining this gang was that these guys were seriously messed up. You see, if you wanted to join them like any other organization you had to undergo some sort of test, which in this case was taking down their next target. By taking down I don't mean hurting or inflicting pain, but I mean the *real thing*. And now, after hearing Tylor's theory, it was clear why. It wasn't to test their bravery or commitment;

it was literally a sacrifice to the devil. I felt dizzy, how could this be real? How could humans sink so low just for a little power or money? Hudson had known this better than anyone else. I bit my bottom lip in thought wondering who the victim was. The victim could be anyone the gang chose, for any reason they could randomly select someone. I couldn't help but think about the paper I had found in my locker. *No you idiot I cursed you.*
He had been so serious it was hard not to get carried away with my thoughts.
The only thing keeping me going was reading. I had to admit, it had a opened a whole new world in my life, I can't believe I had been missing out on such an amazing experience for so long.
Maybe I should go read over at the *Natural World* right now, that would definitely be calming.
As I walked to the stairs something caught my attention. I cocked my head in an attempt to listen; I had heard the word *Spades* coming from Jay's room. I bit my bottom lip and tried not to jump to conclusions, maybe he was talking about cards? I recalled the little incident that had occurred a few days ago in the school parking lot. The little showdown between Jay and Hudson. Jay knew who Spades was, but what had Hudson said about meeting soon? Suddenly my face paled. There was no other explanation to it. How could I have been so blind?
The enmity and hatred between them, Hudson's words that they would meet soon…
I bit my lip; I should stop jumping to conclusions. But I knew they weren't conclusions, they were fact. I tried to prevent myself from spinning with dizziness,
My best friend against my brother.

I blinked a few times then slowly crept towards Jay's room

trying to step carefully. The last thing I wanted was to be caught eavesdropping on him. There was a silence and then once again Jay's muffled voice could be heard. "No, I've had enough, this is the last time."

There was another silence then Jay sighed. "Fine, I don't care about you but after this I'm out, I don't care what happens." The tone of finality in his voice sounded so foreign.

I didn't get a chance to develop my thoughts as the door opened, and a disheveled Jay stared back at me. For a few moments he didn't register what he was seeing, but when he did his distracted look turned angry. "Were you listening?"

I blinked a few times and attempted to smile. "Uh, no?"

For a second, I was sure he was going to hit me, but then his look of annoyance underwent another transition and he half smiled. "Yeah, sure Jodette, because standing in front of other peoples' closed doors and *not listening* is everyones favorite pastime."

I watched him; my mouth slightly opened; I was too shocked to speak. He hadn't hit me. I looked at him carefully he didn't even look angry.

He pushed past me and started making his way down the stairs, still shocked I turned to go to my room, when he called me from the stairs. I looked back at him. He was standing on the sixth stair with an odd expression on his face. He scratched the back of his head in an attempt to look casual "Uh… I'm going out to eat, you wanna come?"

I blinked dumbly and then managed a nod. Jay never took me anywhere with him even if I begged, and now he was offering? I might have even said no just to spite him, but I could have sworn that I had heard a hidden plea in his words.

He bought me everything I ordered and trust me I ordered a lot. I watched him dumbfounded, as he paid the guy at the counter and came back to sit with me. Even weirder, he was smiling.

He caught me staring at him and frowned. "I think Tylor's rubbing off on you."

I raised my eyebrows in question. "What do you mean?"

He sighed. "Just eat."

I shrugged and dug into the plates of fried food in front of me. He watched me eat for a while then picked up a fry. "So, he's still in California, right?"

"Yeah, he's coming back the day after tomorrow." I managed to mutter through a mouthful of chicken.

Jay's eyes glazed over. "The day after tomorrow."

The way he said it sparked something inside me. Suddenly it was hard to swallow. He was coming back the day after tomorrow, *the day the big event was happening.* Had that much time really passed?

I took a few sips of my drink to calm myself down and then stared down at my plate. Jay's generosity didn't seem so odd now.

I tried to chew on a slice of pizza but barely got through halfway before Jay noticed my switch in attitude. "Hey, what happened? You were eating like a starved hippo three seconds ago."

I looked up at him and tried to smile. "Nothing, I'm fine, I'm just trying to savor the taste."

Jay raised his eyebrows skeptically. "You know I already paid for it."

I looked at the vast variety of fried goods spread before me on the table and began regretting my greed. "Don't worry, I'll eat it."

The faintest hint of a smile began to play on his lips. "That's my fat Jodette, never turning down food."
I chewed silently trying to think of a way to finish all the food without throwing up. He watched me for a while then his

grin intensified. "Hey, you remember how you got that nickname in the first place?"
I smiled despite myself. "How could I forget?"
He grinned. "That was hilarious; I wonder what happened to her anyways, she probably joined the circus or something."
"Why in the world would she do that?"
Jay shrugged. "I dunno, she just looked like someone who'd join the circus."
I grinned, as weird as it may seem, I actually agreed with him. "Yeah, she'll probably be the new attraction… people would come from all over the world to see her."
Jay threw another fry into his mouth. "They could call her the rancid runt, the only kid in the world that drinks toilet water for fun."
I had to smile at that.
Jay noticed my content smile and immediately reverted to his old self. "Ah, how nice it is to see you look so happy after hearing your sensei's name."
I stared at him confused. He leaned forward grinning. "Yes, *Jodette,* you *are* named after her and you *are* her star pupil, she taught you everything you know, heck you probably even drin-"
His random statement was cut off by a piercing shriek. I jumped in shock and was about to dive under the table until I saw him pull out his cell phone and flip it open. He grinned. "Relax Jodette, it's just a ring tone, no need to have a heart attack."

I stared at him indignantly and considered telling him off, he was so crazy. He was always changing his ringtone to something insane, but a shriek?

Embarrassed I quickly looked around the room and saw many disapproving looks being shot in our direction; clearly, I wasn't the only one who had gotten startled. I turned back to him ready to yell but he put the phone to his ear and as usual, rudely addressed the caller. "What?" I stared at him as he listened to whoever was calling. I watched his expression transform from normal to angry. "Of course, what do you think I am, an idiot?"
There was a long pause as Jay listened carefully; his features began to contort with anger. "No, I don't care, no arms, we'll do it the old-fashioned way."
The voice on the other side intensified enough so that I could practically make out what was being said. Jay listened then his face began to color up until the point I was sure he would explode. "Then that's what I want!" With that he closed his phone and jammed it hard into his pocket.
I stared at him. "Who was that?"
He returned my look with a glare. "Why do you care?"
"Just wondering."
Jay frowned. "Yeah, well don't."
I stared at him, and anger began creeping across my chest. "I know what the call was about."
He looked at me skeptically. "Sure you do Jodette."
"It's about the day after tomorrow."
For a second, he looked shocked, but he recovered fast. "What about the day after tomorrow?"
I stared at him. "You and your friends are meeting up with Spades and his gang."
As soon as the words left my mouth his cocky expression

melted, and his eyes widened slightly. "H-How….Hercules told you, didn't he?"

I shrugged awkwardly. "I figured it out myself."

He didn't say anything, just watched me with that same expression.

I took advantage of the brief silence. "So, you're actually gonna go? What're you guys planning to do anyways?"

He leaned back in his chair and stared down at his hands, a humble gesture that you barely ever saw from him. "You make it sound like I'm going to a party or something, *what are you planning to do anyways*?"

I crumpled up my napkin and used it to wipe my mouth. "Well, you make it seem like you're going to a party, you don't seem worried or anything, as if you've done it a million times."

Jay grinned. "Oh Jodette, where'd you get *that* idea? I think you've been reading too many poems, they're bad for the brain you know, too much creativity."

Frowning I looked down. "Don't change the subject. Please. Why in the world are you going?"

Jay continued grinning. "Stop being such a fat little pig. Nothing is gonna happen, don't sweat it."

He glanced at the near empty plates on the table. "Okay never mind, maybe you *should* sweat it, it'll help you lose some weight." With that he started laughing.

Ignoring his lameness, I looked down at the plates and was surprised to see how much I had managed to eat in-between the conversation. I wasn't even hungry, but I guess tension could do that to a person. I looked back up at him, he was still laughing. Wow, what a retard. I couldn't help but smile a little as his laughing face brought back all the times we had when we were kids. Most of them involved us ratting each

other out, or beating each other up, but even those were golden. "Hey, remember how much we used to hate each other when we were kids?"
Jay had stopped laughing and now he was chugging down a can of his soft drink. He put the can on the table and grinned. "Who says I like you any better now?"
I bit my bottom lip to hold back an embarrassed grin. "Hey, you do like me better whether you want to admit it or not."
"How?"
I let my grin break lose. "When we were kids, you used to break every new thing I got; now you leave me alone. That obviously means you don't hate me anymore."

Jay frowned, and a look of dawning revelation possessed his face. "Hey, you're right I haven't broken anything of yours for a while now."
He leaned forward and picked up a chicken bone he had recently gnawed, then grinning he threw it at my head. It hit me above my eye and then landed dully on the floor. I was appalled. "What was that for?!"
Jay frowned trying to reenact a display of utmost disappointment. "Man, I was trying to break one of your bones. Preferably your nose."
I stared at him stupidly. "By throwing a *chicken bone* at me?"
He shrugged. "Hey, I don't have many resources here."
I wiped the place where I had been hit and smiled. "Oh yeah, well I do."
I picked up the garlic dip and jerked it in such a manner that the sauce went flying out and landed on his sweater.
For a second, he stared at the stain open mouthed, then he slowly looked up at me, still shocked. "You… little…"
I stood up quickly. "Hey, you can't beat the master at his own game, if you remember, while you were busy breaking

my things when we were little, I was busy throwing things at you." His shocked expression turned into a huge grin, and he stood up too. "Yeah, how could I forget that? But don't think that gets you off the hook." He leaned over and picked up my untouched soft drink.
I didn't get a chance to see how long it took him to open it because before I knew it, I was out of the store, running as fast as my legs would carry me. I pumped harder as I heard Jay spewing out insults and catching up fast. Despite the fear of being soaked I couldn't help but smile as I caught the words fat and *Jodette* in his vengeful rant. I knew I should have felt scared, but rather I felt happy, He was my brother after all.

Sixteen

He had been quiet all morning, and so had I. Now we were

sitting in the family room, the TV blaring at its maximum.
I glanced at Jay; he wasn't even staring at the screen. He was
staring at the remote in his hands, throwing it from one hand
to the other.
I considered turning the TV off but thought better of it. I had
turned off the TV once already, but he had yelled at me to
turn it back on even though he wasn't watching. Maybe he
needed the distraction.
I turned back to the screen; it was some new movie starring
some new actor. Not much of a summary, but I hadn't
exactly been watching either. I myself was distracted beyond
comprehension. The event was today. When? I didn't know,
but the point was that only hours separated us from that time.

I tried to concentrate on the movie but failed, once again the
storyline was incredibly useless. Something about someone

who wanted to live a more exciting life. Come to think of it *I* seriously had no life, why in the world was I watching this? My thoughts were interrupted by the doorbell. I stood up happy for a distraction from my distraction and walked over to the door. Who could it be? I opened the door and automatically grinned, it was Tylor.

"Hey, you came back already?"

Tylor smiled. "Yeah, I came back yesterday, I'm glad you remembered."

I let him inside and closed the door. "Sorry, I had other things on my mind."

He looked down while taking off his shoes. "Yeah, other things… where's Jay?"

I turned to the family room and pointed. "He's in there, so how your trip was?"

Tylor smiled again, but this time his eyes glazed over as if he was remembering something unpleasant. "Let's just say it was a great learning experience."

I pulled drinks out of the fridge and threw a can at him. "So you mean it sucked."

He caught it just in time and grinned. "No, not really…. let's just say, now I understand what you meant."

I cocked an eyebrow. "Meaning?"

He opened his can and looked down. "You know how one time, in the *Natural World* you asked me, *have you ever seen anyone that you knew change dramatically in front of your eyes*, well that time my answer had been no, but now I say yes."

I watched him carefully, trying to guess if I knew the person he was talking about.

I didn't get to ponder more as Jay entered the kitchen; he distractedly walked to the tap and got himself a glass of water.

As soon as he turned around, he caught sight of Tylor and grinned. "Hey when'd you come back?"

Tylor smiled. "Just this morning."
Jay took a sip of his water and leaned against the counter. "So how was your trip, write any new poems?"
Tylor sat down on the kitchen chair. "No, actually I didn't find much time to write, what about you? Did you do anything stupid?"
Jay stopped smiling and turned around almost guiltily. "No." I frowned. "By *no* he means not yet,"
The words didn't shock Tylor, he looked down. "I think I know what you mean, I had plenty of time to think on the plane."
He looked up at Jay. "So, you're really going to go?"
Jay shrugged, still facing his back to us. "You guys worry too much, I'm gonna go watch a movie and *relax,* like a normal person."
I couldn't help but smile as I saw Tylor cringe at the word movie.
Tylor followed Jay to the door and peered into the hallway. "So, what's he watching?"
I shrugged "I dunno just some new
movie." He cringed again.
"Why do you keep cringing?"
Tylor tried to prevent a shudder and failed. "Why's he wasting his time?"
I took a sip of my drink. "I dunno, maybe he's trying to distract himself?"
"Yeah, he must want a distraction, considering his circumstances. It *is* today, right?"
I was taken aback "Yeah, how did you know?"

He half smiled. "You wouldn't believe how much a person can learn through silence."

"You mean you eavesdropped again?"

Tylor stood up. "Hey, I can't help it if I hear things. I heard you trying to talk Hudson out of it in the lab, did you try again?"

"Yeah, I guess you could say I tried, but he's still going. He actually thinks he can control minds, and that sigma? It was supposedly a curse on me."

Tylor examined me thoughtfully. "Come to think of it, you do look slightly cursed."

"What's that even supposed to mean?"

Tylor was saved the trouble of justifying himself as Jay's electronified voice filled the air, reciting that annoying poem. Tylor looked at me and grinned. "Wow, Jay really loves you doesn't he?"

My face reddened as I quickly walked over to the phone and picked it up. "Hello?"

"Hey man, what's up?" it was Miles.

I resisted the temptation to slam the phone shut. I would have to see his annoying face again starting tomorrow, why was he bothering me now?

"What do you want?" I said, not even trying to hide the annoyance from my voice. Apparently, he didn't notice.

"So are you gonna go?"

I frowned. "Why in the world would I go?"

There was a slight pause as Miles thought. "You know, maybe just to back him up…"

I wanted to punch him. Back who up, my brother? Or my best friend? He didn't realize what he was saying. I turned the

phone off and moodily placed it back on the charger as it had been before. I turned around to see Tylor standing, watching me grimly. I threw on my jacket. "Let's go for a walk."
His grim expression turned into a frown. "What am I now, your dog?"
I smiled slightly. "Maybe"
He walked over and put on his shoes. "Well, this is the first dog I've seen that's taller than its owner."
I stopped smiling. "Hey, you're not even that much taller than me."
Tylor grinned and stepped outside. "No need to get jealous."
I ignored his comment and walked a little down the sidewalk. "Let's stop by the *ChocoChurn*"

Tylor nodded.
We walked for a little while, until I noticed something was different. *I wasn't cold.*
I looked down at the ground and was further shocked to see that the snow had almost melted.

Night had fallen and we were still in the *ChocoChurn*. Surprisingly enough we were the only two, apart from the store owner. Tylor had asked where the customers were, and the owner had said some singer was coming to town, and he was holding a concert from 7:00pm up until the morning so everybody was down there. It was being held at the town square.
I finished my drink and a familiar feeling of uneasiness settled in my stomach. Had Jay left the house yet? Had Hudson?
Tylor was talking to the owner by the counter. He had been

talking with him for the past hour about government stuff.
I had slipped away after the first few minutes to sit at the back. I needed the quiet right now, plus from where I was sitting, I could see the moon from the window. It was only a sickle, but it looked absolutely beautiful.
A little while later, Tylor finished talking to Mr. Gret and walked over to where I was sitting.
"These concerts seriously need to stop; it feels like we're living in a ghost town."
I glanced up at him. "Yeah, not a person in sight. Why doesn't the store guy just go too? It's not like he's getting any business."
Tylor seated himself and smiled slightly. "He wouldn't go, he's too different."
"Maybe that's why you guys get along so well."
Tylor grinned. "Probably but being different isn't a bad thing."

I turned back to the window. "Yeah, sometimes it's better to be different; it's easier to go against the flow."
Tylor took a few minutes to sip his hot chocolate then turned back to me. "Hey, when I was away, you came on *Souls-ink* as *JH*. I didn't know you had an account."
I stared at him, an amused smile playing on my face. "Well, you did know I liked poetry. And while we're on that topic, mind explaining to me why you asked me to guess your age, when you didn't even know it was me?"
Tylor grinned. "I thought it was obvious, my profile makes me seem like a little kid, or according to others an old man so I like asking people to guess."
"That can't be the only thing, what do you get out of it?"
" I'm trying to figure out why being 'old' or a 'kid' is an insult,

you know what I mean?"
That took me by surprise. "Isn't that obvious?"
Tylor almost choked on his hot chocolate, "wait, what? You know the answer?"
"I'm glad you think so highly of my intellect" I replied dryly.
"It's not th—", I cut him off.
"People hate being called a kid because it means you're vulnerable…dependent and people hate being called old because old people remind you of...dying."
It was as if a meteorite had hit Tylor, his face changed completely, lips slightly parted, he was frozen. "That's why..."
"Are you okay?"
His mouth twisted as he tried to calm down. "Yeah, it's more than fine actually... You answered my question perfectly. Perhaps I remind people of reality too often and that reminds them of death, which makes them associate me with being old."
I stared at him. "I don't see you as being old."
He half smiled. "Then I guess you're not exactly socially normal either."

I grinned. "That's the biggest compliment I've ever gotten." Tylor stared at me strangely and then a slow smile spread across his face. "It's amazing how much a person can change." I raised my eyebrows but chose to ignore his statement,
even though I knew it was true.

He pulled something out of his pocket and slid it in front of me, it was a photo. My eyes widened slightly as the beauty of the scene hit me. It was a picture of the *Natural World*. "Wow, this is… beautiful."

"Yeah, I took it on the first day I visited."
I tried to absorb every detail of the scene. It was winter at its perfection.
"I came up with a new verse."
I looked up at him. "Let's hear it."
He cleared his throat and with his eyes fixed on the photo, spoke:

"This wisdom of the soldier's sight, how rare it is to see;
What once was, no longer is, life's true philosophy"

The verse instantly reminded me of what he had said when he had entered my house. "You're referring to that person you said changed, right?"
Tylor smiled. "Yeah, she used to be my best friend, I saw her after four years…"
"And?"
Tylor stopped smiling. "Trust me, you don't want to know."
I nodded my head and the verses he had recited ran around in my mind.
He couldn't have been more correct. How rare was it to see someone who thought like the soldier? Who actually cared about the natural side of the world and wasn't lost in the superficial ways of life? It may have once been common to care about our true nature but now nobody cared, that is, except the silent soldier. The rare few.
Tylor put the photo back in his pocket. "I want to visit again, are you going to come too?"
I grinned. "Of course, I'll come, actually I was just thinking about going."
I got up to leave when my phone rang; annoyed, I pulled it out of my pocket.

"Hello?"

"Uh… hey". The voice shocked me; it was Jay. What was he doing calling me at this time? Was he still at home?

"What happened?" I asked trying not to sound too panicked. There was a brief silence.

"Nothing happened…just…uh." There was another pause, longer this time, then he continued. "Uh... Sorry."

I blinked dumbly. "For what?"

He didn't reply

"Did you leave yet?"

His phone turned off.

I stared absentmindedly into space. What had that been about? Tylor was watching me, growing tension in his eyes. "Who was that?"

I bit my bottom lip. "It was Jay…"

Tylor's panic intensified. "Jay? What was he saying?"

I looked down. "He said sorry and then turned off the phone."

Tylor eyes looked glassy. "He came to me yesterday…and he…"

"He what?"

Tylor unzipped the front of his jacket and Mr.Snake poked his head out. "He told me to take care of Mr.Snake."

We stared at each other for a long time not knowing what to think or say, and then Tylor started walking towards the door. I followed him and before I knew it, we were halfway to the forest.

The air was piercingly silent. The town square was on the opposite side of town, so everything appeared eerily empty. It was hard to believe how thick the silence was. It wasn't a peaceful silence; this silence was filled with tension.

Suddenly voices filled the air. I stopped abruptly in my

tracks and so did Tylor. It was people yelling, all at once. For a second, I thought that the concert racket had somehow carried this far but then I realized that the voices were too few, too quiet to be produced by the audience of a concert. I glanced at Tylor, he was chewing his bottom lip violently as he strained to listen.

I glanced to my left; the sound was coming from there. My heart skipped a beat as I realized the only place that existed in that direction. The old park.

Tylor glanced at me, and I nodded my head silently. Together we walked towards the source of the noise.

As soon as we reached the entrance of the park, I felt myself go pale. A group of people stood by the slide; apparently, they were having a heated discussion. Without thinking I dropped myself to the floor and crawled forward, there was a set of bushes to the left. Tylor looked at me and then followed.

After a few agonizing moments we were both crouching behind the bush staring through a gap in the center. The darkness veiled our position and gave me confidence to move the dry branches enough for me to see. From this new position everything was much clearer, I could see a group of six people, no younger than seventeen. I nearly jumped out of my skin as the guy nearest to the bush spoke in a loud voice. "Naw, they aint showin', I knew it… they're scum."

Another guy who was standing a little more to the right stepped forward. Even in this darkness I could tell he hadn't showered for weeks. "Well, *you* weren't gonna show either."

The guy standing by the bushes glared at him angrily. "Shuttup, nobody was talking to you."

The un-showered guy ran his hands through his greasy hair.

"You're just freaking out; you should learn to be calm like me."

The guy by the bush stepped forward and made a grab for the greasy haired guy's neck but someone pushed him back.

"What are you idiots doing? We didn't come here to fight each other in case you forgot."

My heart skipped a beat as I realized it was Jay. The two guys stepped back reluctantly, and an uneasy silence filled the air. Unfortunately, the silence didn't last long. A few minutes later loud voices filled the park again, this time they were coming from the right. I slowly turned my head to see a group of guys similar in age and number walk into the park; they stopped by the broken monkey bars and simultaneously grew silent.

The guy at the front; the apparent leader stepped forward: His light hair was slicked back and looked completely foreign against his skeleton-like face. His dress shirt was rolled up until his elbows and his pants were so long, they trailed across the floor; he was dressed completely in black. One look at his attire told me that he was Spades. Even in the dim light I could see the tattoos covering his arms and the piercings on his face. The smaller tattoos were indecipherable, but one was clear, an enormous horned beast with a look so dark, so evil, it could only be an image of the devil himself.

I felt Tylor tense up with fear beside me. I tried to hold back a gulp, what were we doing here again?

It didn't take me long to realize that if Spades was here then Hudson must be too. I strained to see but they were too far away, honestly, I think I preferred it that way. Spades took a few steps forward; His eyes glinted in the dim moonlight as he took in the six guys standing across from him.

"Well, looks like you guys decided to attend the rendezvous after all." His quiet voice filled the air.

I didn't know whether to laugh or sink lower into the ground.

Rendezvous? Who did this guy think he was?

Someone from Jay's gang stepped forward; I bit my bottom lip and silently prayed that it wasn't Jay. My prayers were left unanswered.
Jay's equally calm voice filled the park. "Yeah, we're here now let's get this over with."
Spades laughed quietly. "Why the rush? These pre-fight dialogue exchanges are what I live for."

Jay frowned, his voice dripping with sarcasm. "What a great reason to live."
Spades laughed again this time a little louder. "Funny you would choose those words."
The guy who had startled me earlier stepped forward. "Alright enough with the drama, let's get on with the action."
Spades turned to his left and gently prodded someone forward. "Well, I suppose he has a point, come on cousin, it's time to prove yourself."
My eyes blurred for a second then cleared as tear overwhelmed my being. Hudson stood there looking paler than ever, he looked like he had lost an extreme amount of weight since the last time I saw him. Spades had prodded him forward, now everyone was waiting for him to do something. When he didn't move Spades smiled slightly. "Come on already, it's just one movement, I'm sure all those *gentlemen* are too scared to even react. Just pick a random one, the choice is yours...preferably I say the one on the right I believe he is the source of this rancid stench filling my nostrils."

The greasy haired guy tensed up immediately. "H-Hey… you th-think it's gonna be th-that easy? We didn't c-come here to get shot."
Spades raised an eyebrow. "Oh really, then why did you come?"
The greasy haired guy was at a loss for words, he seemed too scared to continue.
Another person, his face shrouded in a hood stepped forward. "We came 'cause we had a rivalry to settle, you know that better than anyone." He took a few more steps forward and pulled something out of his pocket. "I'm ending this now."
He made a motion to aim his gun towards Spades but before he pulled the trigger Jay grabbed his arm, there was no need to ask why; Hudson was already pointing his gun at him.
Both of them stared at each other, the hooded guy swore under his breath. "Just a stupid kid, he wouldn't have the guts."

Hudson didn't speak but Spades seemed almost delighted at the challenge. "Alright Cousin, prove your worth, don't forget your oath, now do it while you still have the chance."

Once again no one stirred.

Spades was getting openly annoyed. "I'm giving you until the count of four and if you don't, then I'm pretty sure you know what will happen."
Spades tilted his head to the sky and closed his eyes. "One… two… three…"
I heard shuffling beside me and turned my head in shock.
My shock turned into dread as I realized that Tylor had stood up. *"Are you insane? Sit down!"* I whispered harshly, but he

wasn't listening, he stepped over the bush and walked forward.

Spades was in the middle of saying four when Tylor's clear voice cut his count. "Stop!"

Everyone jumped. Spades' head snapped towards him, and an expression of confusion took possession of his features. "Who is that?"

Jay stepped forward squinting in the dim light. "What are *you doing here*?"

Tylor stared at the group of people grimly. "If it's a rivalry you want to settle, there are other ways to do it."

I was shocked as to how confident he sounded; it was as if he was talking to a bunch of kids, not gang members armed with guns.

Spades' forehead creased with annoyance, but then he smiled, smelling an opportunity. "It seems Jay knows him… alright Hudson this is your last chance, shoot the kid or die."

Hudson's face paled and he turned his body towards Tylor, I could see him trembling from here. He closed his eyes, and his hand began to shake harder. Tylor stared back at him a determined expression on his face.

"Really, a gun? Too scared to fight me?"

I closed my eyes, too terrified to move, what was he saying? What was he trying to do?

Spades examined Tylor top to bottom and scowled in disgust. "I hate arrogance. Especially when its unsubstantiated. Let's make this more interesting."

He turned to Hudson.

"You get rid of *this one* with a pocketknife. Save the gun for round two."

Hudson looked over at him "...y-you want me to actually?"

"OF COURSE, YOU IDIOT!"
Hudson didn't need more prompting, he pulled out his pocketknife, lunged forward and knocked Tylor to the ground in an instant. It all happened in a matter of seconds. Tylor didn't stand a chance.

It was over for him.

A loud piercing scream of agony filled the air.

 Tears fell down my face and I threw myself out of the bushes, ready to join the brawl when I realized, the scream had not come from Tylor.

It was Hudson.

He continued to scream in pain while laying and convulsing on the floor. I was puzzled until a hint of gold caught my attention.

Mr.Snake.

The deadly viper had his venomous fangs deep in Hudson's arm, and then like a flash of lightening, he was gone.

 "YOU IDIOT! WHAT IS WRONG WITH YOU?"

Spade's voice didn't seem so quiet and polite anymore. No one had a clue what had happened. Tylor was still laying there a few feet away from Hudsons convulsing body. Paler then ever, sweat dripping down his face and a look of pure astonishment on his sharp features.

The guy with the hood took advantage of the moment and shot at Spades, the poor lighting caused him to miss and hit the person standing at the back.

After that I couldn't follow any longer as all hell broke loose. I ducked and covered my head with both my hands as gun shots fired one after the other crashing through the air like thunder, there was an abundance of screaming and swearing, and then a loud blood curdling scream. Tears filled my eyes as I realized that the only people, I cared about were in that chaos.

I summoned my courage and stood up; now the fear of being seen was completely ridiculous.

The scene looked worse than it sounded; everyone was all over the place hitting whatever they could reach. I tried to look through the array of flailing limbs and caught sight of what I was looking for, a flash of maroon hair. I moved to the side so I could see better, I saw Jay punch Spades hard in the stomach, and then I lost him again.

I ran to the other side praying I wouldn't be targeted and after a few long and agonizing moments I caught sight of Jay again, this time he was on his knees, blood coming out of his mouth.

My eyes widened up until the point I was sure they would explode. Without thinking I pushed myself into the crowd trying to reach him, as if I could stop the blood. I made it three steps in before I got my first blow; someone punched me hard in the stomach. Sweat dripped off my face and I felt ready to faint, a few moments later something cold and metal collided with the back of my head. I stumbled to the floor and my vision became impossibly blurred. I felt myself begin to black out.

Out of all the commotion, I heard a piercing siren rip through the evil night. Weapons were immediately pocketed, and everybody broke up. Whether a person was brutally injured or just scratched; they were all running in separate directions, probably to their cars, too scared to face the hands of justice. The speed at which they cleared was amazing. I tried to pull myself up to see if Jay was still there, but the effort caused my vision to alternate between white and color, I tried to hold on, but only moments later I blacked out.

◆◆◆◆◆◆

Bright lights greeted my tired eyes as I forced them open. I sat up and looked around; I was in a hospital bed. I blinked and rubbed my eyes trying to adjust them to the light. As soon as I sat up a nurse entered the room. She was holding a clipboard. "Oh, great, you're awake. Sorry but we need you to clear out, another patient needs the room."
I felt my head, it wasn't hurting as bad as I would have expected. The nurse noticed my slow reaction. "You just passed out, you got hit hard on the head you'll be fine though." I stood up and after a few moments was able to walk steadily.
"Uh, okay thanks, but how did I get here?"
The nurse pursed her lips in annoyance. "You were carried here with a couple other boys around your age."
My heart skipped a beat as I remembered the fight, the scene, the others.
"Where are they?" I asked urgently. She clicked her tongue as her annoyance intensified. "How should I know?"
I felt my vision blur at the thought of Jay. "Please tell me."

She frowned and flipped through her clipboard carelessly. "Ask the secretary, but don't expect your friends to be up yet, some of them didn't look too good."
"Thank you." I managed to mumble.

She gave me a disgusted look and pointed to the door. "You can leave now."

I hurried out of the room and walked down the unfamiliar hall. I didn't have time to feel bad about her annoyance; she probably thought I was some drug addicted gangster, who could blame her? I found my way to the lobby and walked up to the old lady at the counter. "Hi, can I know where my brother's room is?"

The secretary looked up at me with a small smile on her face. "His name?"

"Jay… Jay Haves" I silently prayed she would find him.

She typed the name onto her computer and then waited. "Ah, yes, room 108, floor 3B"

I turned around and hurriedly made my way to the elevator, an eternity later I found myself staring at the large sign hanging from the wall that read floor 3B.

I walked forward, unsure of which way to go first. I eventually decided to continue walking forward. The rooms inched by; 90, 91, 92…

I held my breath as I stood in front of room 108. Slowly I moved the curtain aside and walked in. It was empty.

I stared at the bed confused, I was positive she had said room 108. My hopes lifted as I thought that maybe he had been let out because he had recovered.

My thoughts were interrupted as a nurse walked into the room with a small child. The kid was around six years old and he looked like he hadn't eaten for weeks, I moved to the side as she helped him into the bed, the mother followed shortly afterwards, her eyes were red from crying. The nurse turned to me. "Oh, who are you?"

"Uh sorry I was just looking for… was there a guy in here before?"

The nurse's eyes filled with shock. "Yes, actually there was, do you know him?'

I nodded my head slowly. "Yeah, why?"

She bit her bottom lip. "He was transferred to the surgery room upstairs a few minutes after he came in."

My eyes nearly popped out of my head. I tried to collect myself. "S-surgery?"

The nurse's eyebrows furrowed with worry. "It's just one floor up, there was someone else with him."

I turned around and bolted to the staircase, I didn't have time for the elevator. A few minutes later I found myself in another brightly lit hall. There were a few rooms with closed doors, and many chairs on the left, they were placed in neat rows, probably some sort of waiting area. I tried walking quickly but to me my steps felt slow and heavy.

As I neared the collection of chairs, I realized that one of them was occupied, his head was bandaged, and his arm was supported by a cast. He looked up at me and relief flooded my body, it was Tylor. He blinked a couple of times. "Jode?"

I smiled slightly and sat across from him. "Yeah, it's me. Wow you look pretty bad."

Tylor observed his cast. "Yeah, I don't feel that bad though, the doctors did a good job, got me fixed up in an hour. They said I would only need it for three days then I can switch to something smaller."

He observed me. "Thank God you didn't get badly hurt."

I frowned. "Yeah, didn't even get a scratch."

Tylor continued staring at me. "I wouldn't say that you didn't even get a scratch—"

I didn't let him complete his sentence as the events of the fight caught up with me. "What were you thinking? You almost got yourself killed!"

Tylor allowed himself a small smile. "I wasn't thinking at all, I had to do something. I just wanted to distract them… buy time. I guess I got really lucky Mr.Snake was there. He saved me."

I let his words sink in "It was stupidly risky…. how did we even get here?"

Well, as soon as the fight started getting crazy, I made a break for home to grab Siara's car. By the time I came back everyone was running away, and you and Jay were sprawled on the floor, so I just threw you guys in and here we are."

"How'd you get hurt?"

Tylor frowned. "Everyone was running away, and I sort of got stuck in the stampede."

I blinked. "Was anyone else on the floor? How bad was Jay hurt, some nurse said he was in the surge—?"

I didn't get to finish my sentence as someone walked up behind me; I turned around to see a short balding man in a doctor's coat. Tylor stood up immediately. "Well, are the results in?"

The doctor cleared his throat and spoke in an unusually light voice. "Actually, the real results won't be in until the day after, but for now things don't look very good."

I slowly turned my body to face the doctor. I looked at Tylor questioningly. Tylor looked at the floor. "He was the one working on Jay's surgery."

I felt myself pale. I gulped and faced the doctor. "W-what do you mean things don't look good?"

The Doctor scratched his arm awkwardly. "You are Jay's brother?'

I nodded my head slowly, unable to speak.

The Doctor looked down and then up again. "Your brother suffered a severely fatal blow which damaged his cerebral

cortex…”
Tylor took a step back, I looked at him, his eyes were wide. “Fa-fatal? Meaning enough for the damage to be permanent?”
I couldn't help but notice that it was the first time I ever heard him stutter.
The doctor looked down. “The tests will be in the day after tomorrow. But once again it looks like there's no way out.”
Tylor's mouth hung open, he gaped at the doctor. “Surely there has to be some mistake…”

The doctor frowned. “Sorry, there's nothing I can do, you can come see him if you want, his surgery is complete even if it was unsuccessful.”
With that the doctor turned to leave, I watched him disappear into a room on the far right.
I turned to Tylor, fear straining my voice. “What was he saying?”
Tylor sat down in his chair and his eyes glazed over “I…I can't believe it…”
I stood in front of him. “What? What did he say!?”
Tylor looked at me, his lips curling at the edges. “He… Jay got hit in the head really bad, bad enough for his brain to be permanently damaged.”
He paused for breath then he stared into my eyes
“He's in a coma right now; if the damage is permanent his coma will be permanent too.”
I felt myself sway visibly. “But the doctor said it might not be permanent…the results are coming in the day after tomorrow.”
Tylor looked at the floor chewing the inside of his bottom lip. “All we can do is pray.”
My mind fogged over, I felt myself sit down on the cold chair

as something drained from my body.

Tylor leaned forward and placed his good hand on my shoulder. I guess it was an attempt to comfort me, but I was beyond that now. Tears flooded my eyes as I remembered that it was just this morning, I had seen him carelessly tossing the remote from hand to hand. Would he ever have guessed this would be his fate?

I stood up slowly and walked over to the room I had seen the doctor walk into earlier. Slowly I opened the door and edged inside.

The room was small, with one bed and a wall full of electronic devices. An IV stand stood beside the bed; I didn't need to guess who was laying in it. There were pipes going

into different parts of his body, it looked like they had been surgically inserted.

I walked forward trying not to sink to the ground; his head was caressed in a heavy layer of bandages. His face looked paler than ever, but his eyes were still open. I crept forward and forced myself to look. I had never noticed their color before, somewhere between light green and gray. They looked so different in this setting; one might even say they appeared lifeless. The more I stared at him the more obvious it became that he wouldn't be getting back up.

My eyes traveled to the familiar scars stretched across his face. A helpless feeling possessed me as I realized he had done this to himself. No one had told him to do it. He had called himself the flag of life, like he thought he was going to live forever. I watched his near lifeless body. *The flag of life*?

I couldn't help but wonder how long it would be before I found myself in a similar state.

I closed my eyes as I remembered the conversation he had

been having on the phone. He had said that this would be the last time he would fight. If only he could have known.

I opened my eyes again, this time I caught sight of my reflection on a monitor that had been turned off. My reflection was nearly transparent, but it was clear enough for me to see something on my face. I leaned forward shocked to see a scar stretching from the end of my right eye to the bottom of my nose. It wasn't deep, in fact it didn't even sting, but the unfamiliar sight shocked me. I must have gotten it during the fight somehow.

Unable to stare any longer I turned around and headed back out the door, my feet feeling like weights anchored to the ground. I lifted a trembling hand and traced the long-jagged shape of the scar, at least now I would always have something to remember him by.

Seventeen
TYLOR

The bright morning sun and clear skies seemed very out of

place as we stood around the grave of Hudson Grand. A surprisingly small number of people had come to his funeral considering how popular he had been. His parents, his girlfriend, Miles, Ryan, Jode and Myself.

I wasn't going to come. But it felt like a duty, especially considering my role in his death. I tried to apologize to Jode, but he stopped me.

Mr. Snakes venom had killed Hudson within two hours. He had died on the night of the fight.

A few words were said and then everyone was told to go home. Jode cried throughout the whole thing. I cried too.

It was obvious that things would never be the same again.

A week had passed since that cursed night and yet it still plagued my mind like a newly discovered disease. We had contacted the doctor on Wednesday, and he had reaffirmed that Jay was under a coma. That piece of news had changed my life and it had turned Jode into a whole new person.
His parents had been so shocked by the event they had considered moving somewhere quieter for a while, but Jode had refused.

There was still hope he would be out one day. I still had hope.

Jode stopped hanging out with his gang and started sitting with me in all classes including lunch. To him a social status meant nothing now, funny how things changed.
The gang didn't really object mainly because they had already lost their main source of power, their ringleader.

This weighed heavily on me. In a way I had killed him. Even though it wasn't on purpose. I had no intention of poisoning Hudson to death, even if Hudson had the intention to kill me.

I was eternally grateful to Mr.Snake.

I wouldn't be here otherwise.

I recalled the night I first laid eyes on the golden viper. He was about to die, freezing in the middle of the forest.

He repaid my kindness.

The sad reality was that no one else cared about Hudsons death. Miles had taken the position as the head, and they continued living life as they had before, almost as if nothing had happened. What's more, they accepted me. If one thing was for sure, it was that there would be no more bullying from them.

I glanced over at Jode. We were sitting in computer class and as usual Mr. Damon had given us time to work on our assignment of the day. Jode was sitting beside me dully working away at the assigned work, not even bothering to try and think of an entertaining way to pass time. He had lost a lot of weight; one could even say that he was almost as skinny as me.

My right arm jerked in pain as I moved it too fast to reach the keyboard. The cast had come off yesterday, but the doctor had re-bandaged it with lighter materials, warning me to give it lots of rest.

Every time I looked at the bandaged hand, I couldn't help but praise God. It was a miracle I had survived with just a small bump on the head and a nearly broken hand. Things could have been, and in fact *should* have been much worse. I glanced over at Jode; the thin scar stretching from his eye to his nose was clear against his strangely pale face. Even though I had gotten used to the scar, I couldn't stare at it for too long; it just made him look so much like Jay.

"Is the philosophy test tomorrow?" Jode asked; his eyes still fixed on the screen.

I stared at my own screen equally emotionless. "Yeah, it's tomorrow."

He nodded and continued clicking away. It was obvious that he didn't really care about the test; he had just wanted to fill the silence. I glanced at the instructions on the board and tried to compel myself to follow them, but I knew my attempts were futile. There was absolutely no way I could convince my mind or body to do work at this point in time.

The past few days I had drowned myself in work to forget the events and so had Jode. We hadn't left our houses or even talked freely during lunch. I had thought that devoting myself to my academic life would be a good way to pretend that night had never passed, but now it was becoming obvious that I had to do something.

My soul felt like it was being gnawed on by an invisible parasite that loathed peace. I turned back to Jode and was shocked to find him on *Souls-ink* he was reading a poem. I leaned forward to see his screen better and filled with sorrow as I saw he was reading *Forgotten Songs*.

He looked at me, his eyes dull and sad. "You know the first time I read this? I thought of how I used to be when I was a kid and how I had ruined so many people's lives by going with the flow."

He looked down. "But now when I read it, I think of Jay because I know if there was anyone who had forgotten songs calling them back, it was him."

I nodded slightly. "He did ask me about God before. Do you think he believed in God?"

Jode stared at the verses on the screen. "I don't know."

I looked at his ghost like face and once again couldn't believe that he had changed so much. "Do you?"

Jode looked up at me. "To be honest before I wasn't so sure, but after seeing the *Natural World* it's hard not to."

I smiled. "I get what you mean."

Jode stared at the screen for a while more and then turned to face me directly. "It was *his* fault. He had a chance to change, but he didn't take it."

I could see the pain in his eyes, as if he was silently begging me to tell him he was wrong. I forced myself to stare back but said nothing.

Jode's mouth twisted in a strange way. "He was into drugs."

I stared at the screen. "Maybe it was because he didn't acknowledge the songs that call him."

Jode glanced at the ceiling. "He didn't really give himself much time to think, since he was so busy getting high or going crazy with his friends. He didn't give himself the time to just sit and reflect, so he didn't ever find peace...he didn't ever discover who he was."

I looked down. "Just like any of us he thought he was going to live until he was really old or something. It just goes to show how insignificant we are and how powerful God is. We have no idea whether we will live or die. We can't even guarantee our next hour. Just like everyone else neither Hudson nor Jay had any idea what was coming..."

Jode ran his hands through his hair in an attempt to look casual, but the discontent was clear in his eyes. "Yeah, like you said, all we can do now is pray...I can't believe it's really over for Hudson."

My heart sunk. "I feel so guilty."

Jode glanced over at me. "Don't. I've missed Hudson for years now. The real Hudson died a long time ago."

I stared out the window, the dark night glared back. I squinted and turned my head to the side, I could just make out the outline of the moon hanging placidly in position, almost as if it were alive.

But tonight, even the moon couldn't distract me; I stared

down at my bandaged hand, the anesthetic had worn off and now it was beginning to hurt. My parents had nearly fainted when they saw the injury for the first time, not because they cared but because it confirmed their doubts about my late-night walks.

They had demanded an explanation and I had dully told them that I had slipped on ice outside. Maybe they wouldn't have believed me, but their weariness from the previous night's concert had made them believe me.
They were at another concert again; apparently last time was such a huge success that the singer came back for another go.
They also hated the idea of me owning a pet snake. But they had agreed when I told them I would only keep it half the time, and Jode the other half.

My heart sank. If I needed anything right now it was the *Natural World.* I pulled my eyes from the alluring scene and glanced at the clock; it was 12:10 am. My parents and Siara were still out at that concert.
The agreement I had made with them seemed like a faint memory; in fact, it might have even been nonexistent considering how lightly it was being taken.
I filled my bookbag with the series of children fiction novels Jode had found. It had started off as a humorous challenge to see who could actually get through a single novel geared towards middle schoolers, but we both ended up thoroughly enjoying a lot of the story lines. They were so innocent.

 I pushed the door open and stepped into the fresh night air, bookbag on one arm, and Mr. Snake tucked carefully under my sweater. It was strange, how comforting, and normal it felt to have him wrapped around me.

Jay had trained him well.

I walked for a few minutes before realizing that it wasn't that cold out. Confused I looked at the ground. I immediately underwent a transition of emotion as my confusion turned to shock. I was walking on pavement; melting patches of ice lay a few feet to my sides. Had this much time really passed? I walked slowly back in the opposite direction to a nearby row of trees. It was dark out, but I could make out the shapes of buds growing on their edges, the leaves were coming back.
Dazed I walked forward. I had been in California for a week, and the past week had been so distracting I hadn't noticed anything. Who would have guessed that those few weeks were all Canada needed to switch seasons? I listened to my feet hitting the pavement hard, no more crunching snow.
At this time of night there were no spring-like sounds to be heard, but I was sure I would be able to hear the birds chirping in the morning.
My attempts at trying to listen to the soft sounds of spring were eradicated as screaming suddenly filled the air. For a

moment I was sure the events of earlier last week were coming back to haunt me, but after a few moments I realized that I was by the town square.
I had been so distracted by the realization of spring's arrival that I had walked all the way here. Once again my feet had lead me just as they had lead me to the *Natural World* for the first time.
I made to turn back, but curiosity forced me to continue towards the sound. I turned into the thin alley that I knew

would lead me to the square and stopped when the noise intensified to the point that I was sure I would go deaf. People were screaming at the top of their lungs, and a heavy song was being played at an abnormally fast pace.

Dazed by the commotion I stepped forward and was blinded by the artificial lighting that was always installed at the arrival of a star.

I allowed my eyes to focus and when they did, I saw an amazing sight.

A vast sea of people stood before me, they stretched out as far as I could see, every last inch of ground was occupied by fanatically screaming people jumping and dancing to the rhythmless music. I lost my ability to observe as the sound became near deafening. What was I doing here?

I turned to leave when someone caught my eye. It was Miles, standing in the back row jumping and screaming with the rest of them, an expression of extreme craving masking his face making him look like someone from another world.

I lingered for a while, watching him and immediately regretted it as I was sucked into the crowd. Within a few minutes I was fighting my way through trying to reach the alley again. My attempts, however, were in vain as the crowd was too strong. In my frenzy I caught sight of the stage, I was much closer now and I could see that there were four people, three playing instruments and one singing. I couldn't make head or tail of the lyrics as the crowds screaming pierced through my ears.

I felt dizzy as the noise got to me.

I braced myself and turned around ready for one final fight when I caught sight of Siara jumping and screaming with the crowd, I doubled back as I saw the expression on her face, she looked like she was crying, her mouth wide open as she screamed and screamed along with the music.

Not even a few feet away stood my two parents equally as captivated, they were jumping up and down their hands reaching for the star on stage. My eyes lingered on their arms. I looked around and slowly realized that nearly everyone around me was doing the same. Idolizing the man on stage by trying to reach their arms out to him, as if trying to catch some of his fame.

The screaming voices, the desperate faces, the pointless gestures all combined and hit me like a hammer.

A wave of nausea washed over me as childhood memories flooded my mind. That time I had been left at home for the concert. I had only been four, and now?

The exact same scene played before me. I was an outcast, a reminder of reality, death.

I closed my eyes trying to stop the memories.

I couldn't let them do this to themselves anymore. I walked forward, determined and held on to mom's arm. She turned around and screamed in delight. "You guys! Look who decided to join us!"

Siara and dad turned around. Dad threw his arms around my shoulders. "That's my boy. Finally developing some taste for music?"

The screaming around me was intense and the instruments were piercingly loud. My heart felt like it had moved from its place. It was a display of pure barbarianism.

"No actually dad, you guys are coming with me."

Still holding mom's arm and pulling her behind me I somehow made my way to the alley again. Once I was away from the crowd, I looked back to see dad and Siara had followed, concern on their faces.

Siara was extremely annoyed "Tylor, this better be good."

I grinned knowing she would never back down from a challenge. "Keep up if you can!"

I ran past the trees and patches of ice towards the forest. I paused for breath and checked to make sure Mr. Snake was still under my jacket. Gratefully, his familiar face greeted me.

I wouldn't let my memory haunt me anymore. I couldn't help but wonder at how my question had remained unchanged and unanswered even now. Why in the world were they reaching their hands out so desperately to someone who wasn't God?

Dad caught up to me completed winded. "Hold on Tylor, you don't actually want us to go in there, do you? Do you realize the hour of night?"

He didn't trust me. Before I could say anything, mom interjected. "I think we should give it a try."

I smiled and then led everyone through the familiar forest path. A light breeze pushed through my disheveled hair as I passed the fork, and the path began to narrow. I reached the log and climbed it without care. My family followed suit, complaining the whole time.

I was thrilled when I landed on my feet. Siara, mom and dad weren't so lucky. "You guys are really clumsy. Clearly, you need to work on your survival skills."

As soon as Siara regained her footing, she pushed me and I landed face first in the snow once again. "That's for pulling me out of the concert for no reason! *This* is what you wanted to show us?"

I was in no mood to struggle against anything but my own emotions, I got back up and gave her a small smile

"Follow me."

Nothing stood before us and the gap.
I pushed my way through and as I reached the other side an unbelievable amount of peace engulfed me and carried me away. This feeling, I hadn't felt for so long. The feeling of my problems draining the feeling of true peace.
I turned around to see if mom, dad and Siara had made it through, and my heart melted as I saw the look of wonder and amazement on their faces.
"I've never seen something so beautiful." Mom said.
Siara walked up to the lake "Hey you think we could skate on this when it's fully frozen over? Have you ever tried?"
I shook my head. "I haven't tried, but maybe."
Dad inspected the area and then slowly walked up to me. His eyes carried great relief and an unspoken apology.
 "The last time I felt this much serenity was ages ago. Do you think I could bring my painting easel here? It looks like a great place for art."
I nodded and grinned. All three of them started talking excitedly with each other and exploring the area.

I looked around myself and was astonished as I realized that the normally winter scenery had been replaced with a new one. The floor was no longer a sea of white but rather a prairie of green. I walked over to the lake my eyes wide with wonder, the ice had almost melted. I reached out my hand and gently touched the surface of the cold water.

The ice may have melted but the lake didn't fail to glisten in the dull light of the moon. I turned around, the peace had now nestled into my heart, and I wanted to do nothing more than just stare. The tree standing strong in the middle caught my eyes. I walked towards it slowly, now that spring was here its bare branches would soon support more than bark, it would fill with life and love.

I walked forward until I was standing only a few inches from its great branches. I reached out to touch a delicate bud and was shocked to see that it wasn't green, even in this light I could see that the bud was lighter in color. I blinked in shock as I realized the bud was *pink*.

My heart filled with wonder as I examined the soft blossom. Something so fragile and beautiful could only be the result of a Divine Creator. The mere delicacy of the petal caused everything to come crashing back into my mind.

Everything that had happened in the past few weeks: first Mina, then Jay and Hudson and now my family with the crazed town.

What was going on? What caused people to behave this way? Mina had been so different before but now she had become like everybody else, deserted her true self. Jay who had been so full of life… now he lay in a state of near death unable to amend for his mistakes. And then there was Hudson, who would never breathe another day of life again.

Why was everyone so far away from the truth? My mind was driven to one word.

Desire.

The desire to fulfill our desires regardless of consequence was what brought the downfall of every soul on earth. I stood straight trying to view the tips of the branches; now it was clear that the cherry blossoms were growing everywhere.
I closed my eyes and the unbelievable emotion that had collected poured out in one final verse:

"The evil whim of man's desire, the evil of its goal. It wills for him to sell his heart, to give away his soul."

I took a few steps back and observed the entire scene again; before I could lose myself in thought I heard someone clear their throat. I turned around to see Jode beside my family. They had all been listening to the verse.

 I watched him wordlessly as I noticed the tears pouring down his determined face. He stared at me for a while then in loud clear words he spoke:

"Shimmering, glowing, moonlit beauty; forgotten is the nature of men.
Sparkling, illuminated winter beauty; revived through paper and pen

Glowing calm, overwhelming peace, man's nature calls him back.
Illuminated stars, garlanded trees, our old forgotten track.

The silent soldier stands alone, contesting natural with fake.
He finds true joy to be a standing tree, true peace a
shimmering lake.

He sees the moon as a smaller sun, perfecting an icy night.
He neither speaks, nor does he say, but his vision is his
light.

This wisdom of the soldier's sight, how rare it is to see,
what once was, no longer is, life's true philosophy.

The evil whim of man's desire, the evil of its goal, it
wills for him to sell his heart, to give away his soul.

He paused for a second to wipe the tears from his face then
in a shaky voice he added.

"Yet despite the vice that haunts the air, the trees and lakes
are still.
The paper and pen have done their work, fulfilled the
soldier's will."

My mouth opened slightly as I heard the words come out,
like musical notes spinning daintily in the late-night air. The
silence grew as he continued wiping his tears and mine
began to fall.
"That was absolutely beautiful."
Jode smiled slightly, making his sad eyes appear out of
place. "You wrote it, they're your words"
I watched him, a feeling of gratitude overpowering me. "The
last verse, *you* made it"

To my surprise he grinned and shook his head. "No, I didn't make it." He spread his arms, "This place made it."

My soul felt like it was soaring.

I walked over to the tree and Mr.Snake slithered out of my sweater and onto the closest branch. His beautiful glistening scales looked more regal than ever, and every moment I had spent with Jay came flashing through my mind.

 He curled himself around a branch of the miraculous tree.

The astonishing contrast of the deadly viper sitting so close to a bunch of delicate cherry blossom buds was the most bewilderingly beautiful sight I had ever seen. I observed the scene, knowing I would keep coming here until the branches filled up and the grass grew tall.

I didn't even have to ask my family or Jode to know that they would do the same. After all, a soldier did not need words to convey his thoughts; sometimes silence was more than enough.

281

ACKNOWLEDGMENTS:

First and foremost, I would like to say all praise belongs to God for
allowing me to complete this project.
A special thanks goes to my daughters for inspiring the character of Mr.Snake.
Also, to my parents for putting up with my endless
hours on the computer to write this novel.
My friends Mubina, Ghaziya, and Fatima
gave great advice to help shape my writing.
My sister's Noor and Safa, and my Brothers Noman and Burhan also encouraged
me tremendously throughout the writing process.

Last, but not least, I would like to thank Asfiya for editing the original first edition and
reminding me to focus on the ideal.

Note to the reader:

I hope you enjoyed the novel! As this story finishes, I would like to
wish you good luck in finding your next reading adventure to dive into.

Best wishes,

I.M.Nameless

9 781778 271007